"I'VE MISSED YOU."

"The feeling is mutual, my dear."

He tilted her chin up. Her lips parted. Her eyes widened with expectation. He had no intention of disappointing her. "Angela," he whispered and lowered his head. Their lips brushed. Twice. The third time, he pressed his lips against hers until she opened for him. She sighed and gave herself to him as his tongue met hers. Then she took him, her mouth working his, her tongue exploring, taking as much as he gave and returning the wild heat of her need. She pressed closer, molding herself against him. Her hips shifted as she nestled into the circle of his arms.

She said something. It could have been his name, an endearment, or the height of the trees around them. He didn't give a tinker's cuss. Nothing mattered but Angela's warmth in his arms and the passion in her lips.

Also by Rosemary Laurey

Love Me Forever
Be Mine Forever
Keep Me Forever
Midnight Lover

Rosemary is also featured in these anthologies

Immortal Bad Boys
Texas Bad Boys
The Morgue the Merrier

BE MINE FOREVER

ROSEMARY LAUREY

ZEBRA BOOKS
KENSINGTON PUBLISHING CORP.
http://www.kensingtonbooks.com

ZEBRA BOOKS are published by

Kensington Publishing Corp.
119 West 40th Street
New York, NY 10018

All Kensington titles, imprints, and distributed lines are available at special quantity discounts for bulk purchases for sales promotion, premiums, fund-raising, educational, or institutional use.

Special book excerpts or customized printings can also be created to fit specific needs. For details, write or phone the office of the Kensington Special Sales Manager: Attn.: Special Sales Department. Kensington Publishing Corp., 119 West 40th Street, New York, NY 10018. Phone: 1-800-221-2647.

Zebra and the Z logo Reg. U.S. Pat. & TM Off.

ISBN-13: 978-1-4201-1497-3
ISBN-10: 1-4201-1497-2

First Printing: July 2005

10 9 8 7 6 5 4 3 2

Printed in the United States of America

Chapter 1

September. Devil's Elbow, Oregon.

"Miss Connor, your father will see you now."

Alan Grant was the newest in a long line of personal assistants. "Thanks! He's in the library?"

Alan nodded. Elizabeth crossed the slate-floored hall and turned the crystal knob.

An interior designer had worked long and expensively to create a British nobleman's library on the Oregon coast. The room had fascinated her as a child, but now she'd actually seen a couple of stately home libraries and knew a fake when she saw it.

Her father was standing by the window, beside Laran Radcliffe. Darn! She'd purposely come to the house rather than the office to avoid Laran. What was the man doing here? Had he moved in? They seemed so joined at the hip, it made her wonder if her father slept with him. She held back a smile at *that* thought.

"Lizzie, my dear!" Her father greeted her with open arms. "This is a surprise." She hugged him and they air-kissed, just missing touching. He stood back, his hands on her shoulders. "Now, what's so important it brought you all this way?"

"Good afternoon, Miss Connor."

"Good afternoon, Laran." The man made her flesh creep. It was those eyes, and the belly-of-a-snake white skin that looked as if he never sweated. "Could I talk to you alone, Father?" She was not discussing this in front of Laran Radcliffe, like as not he was in cahoots with the Marshes.

Her father hesitated. Was he going to insist the man stayed? No, thank the Goddess! At a nod from her father, Laran walked noiselessly across the Aubusson carpet and closed the door behind him.

"Well, Lizzie? Shall we sit down?" Her father indicated the leather-covered wing chairs by the now-empty grate. "What is it brought you all this way, that you can't tell me on the phone, and you won't say in front of Laran?" He leaned back in his chair, elbows resting on the arms and fingers steepled. His air of amusement irked her. He wouldn't smile when he heard what she had to say.

"There's something major wrong at Mariposa. Fraud perhaps."

He looked her up and down. She resisted the childhood urge to make sure her hair was smooth and her socks pulled up. "What makes you think that?"

"They have two sets of financial records."

That got his attention. His eyebrows rose as he

lowered his fingers and meshed them as if praying. "I never realized you were an auditor."

"I'm not, but I do know how to add up. They've got something funny going on: a separate record of transactions only identified by numbers. Some quite big amounts. I think they're skimming off into their own pockets. Corresponding amounts don't appear in the ledgers."

"That's quite an accusation. Can you be sure?"

"Sure enough to come all this way to tell you." At the time, it seemed important to discuss this face to face, but now . . .

"How did you explain that to the Marshes?"

"I told them I needed a week off to let you know they were cooking the books!"

"Lizzie! Please!"

"Dad, I'm not stupid. I told them I was coming home for Heather's birthday."

"Heather?" He frowned as if not recognizing the name. "Oh, Adela's girl."

"My sister." The only one she had, despite her father's four failed marriages. "I'm going to see her before I return."

"I hope you'll spend some time here."

She'd planned to. "A couple of nights."

"Good. Now, what exactly do you think you found over there?"

She explained, as best she could, and to her surprise her father listened to every word. "You're sure about this?"

"Dad, I'm not a CPA. Let the experts check. If I'm wrong, fine, but if I'm right, something downright sleazy is going on."

"So it would seem." He frowned. "Have you mentioned this to anyone else?"

"Dad, I'm not stupid! From things the Marshes said, Laran approached them to buy when the company was foundering. They don't exactly cross themselves when they say his name, but they'd do anything he asked." As would most of the small workforce who regarded Connor Inc. as their savior.

He pursed his lips as if considering the possibility. "You think Laran would set up something underhand?"

She'd have no trouble believing anything of her father's right-hand man, but she kept that to herself. "I didn't say that, Dad. I just think having someone other than him check this out would be a good idea."

He smiled. "Lizzie, you're right; this won't go beyond these walls. I'll have it looked into. Get yourself unpacked, and this evening I'll take you into Florence for dinner. Maybe we can spend a little time together."

"That would be great."

Assistant Alan was hovering in the foyer as she closed the library door behind her. "Miss Connor, I took your bags up to your room. If there's anything else you need . . ."

Everything else she needed right now was beyond the talents of eager Alan. "I'm fine, thanks."

Once in her old room, she kicked off her shoes, pulled a chair over to the window and, propping her bare feet up on the window ledge, gazed at the white caps and the gray ocean, and wondered why she'd come all this way to get brushed off, and how soon she could decently leave.

*   *   *

"You heard?" Piet Connor knew the answer. Laran looked angry enough to spit nails or bite the nearest neck without foreplay. "I'm not sure how to handle this . . ."

"I'll take care of it. If all she has is an unlucky guess, we have no problem. If she persists in delving where she shouldn't . . ." He paused. "It's a shame we involved her."

Piet frowned. It was Laran who'd suggested they draw Lizzie into the operation by degrees. "It was your idea."

"My idea was to have it known she'd set up the system. She wasn't supposed to unearth the alternative records and maybe jeopardize the entire setup!" He scowled. "She talked to no one else about this?"

"She said no, but . . ." Piet's stomach knotted. "Maybe she already has. To the FBI."

"If she had, I doubt you'd be here to discuss the matter."

Piet's knees wobbled, and he was already sitting. "This is terrible! What are we going to do?" Panic rose, as if to swallow him from the inside out and engulf him and the organization he'd spent years establishing. What if word spread to his confederates? "This could be a disaster!"

"It could," Laran agreed, "but it won't be. I'll see to that." He stepped over to the antique walnut desk and took Piet's hand in his. "You're worrying too much." He held the hand to his face and listened as Piet Connor's blood raced through his body. "Calm down, Piet." He gently licked the skin covering the pale blue veins. "Relax. Elizabeth mustn't sense your concern." He lapped back and forth until the veins protruded through the skin. As Piet's heart-beat calmed and his shoulders untensed, Laran bit.

Piet let out a slow sigh of satisfaction, and smiled—a smile softer and more genuine than anything his four wives had ever seen. His little murmurs of pleasure were cut short as Laran stopped sucking and licked the wound to seal it.

"You stopped too soon!" Piet protested, his body ready for, and needing, more.

Laran shook his head, a hard light in his dark eyes. "No, Piet. We'll consummate this after dinner. Patience."

Ocean watching wasn't enough to erase the sense of menace and disorder that got worse each time Elizabeth came home. As a child she'd felt chaos and tension around her, and it had been Adela, Heather's mother, and the second of Elizabeth's three stepmothers who'd taught her how to protect herself from unsettling influences.

She needed those skills now. The turmoil around her was overwhelming. If she was to stay calm and focused the next couple of days, she needed a safe refuge.

She took two bay leaves from a small box in her suitcase and crumpled them in the four corners of the room. That done, she lit a pale gray candle, set it on the floor by the sliding-glass doors, and sat cross-legged in front of it. Breathing slowly, she concentrated on the light dancing on the narrow wick and the cleansing influence of the slow-burning flame. She shut her eyes as her mind embraced the calm.

Some minutes later, relaxed and at peace, she blew out the candle and crossed over to the adjoining bathroom. After showering, she pulled on a fresh pair of slacks and a clean T-shirt. She picked a purple one to go with the new silver and amethyst chain she'd bought in England. A touch of mascara, and the new lipstick she'd treated herself to at the duty-free, and she was ready. She picked up her black leather coat and her pocketbook and, closing the door behind her, went slowly down the wide, curved stairway.

Out the front door, she crossed the gravel drive to stand on the cliff edge, and watch the breakers below. She loved this spot; as a child she'd all but lived out of doors. Maybe in the morning, she'd climb down to the beach, as she had as a child, or do it the grown-up way and take the path.

Right now, she needed to convince her father to do something about the setup in Devon. Tonight at dinner, she'd talk to him again and convince him, to at least send someone to check. Things there were so rotten, even she had found the stink. An auditor would no doubt crack the shenanigans wide open.

She walked back toward the house. Darn! Laran was waiting, hip propped against the car, obviously all set to join them. Before she had the chance to suggest he stay behind and let her spend an evening alone with her father, Dad arrived and hustled them all into the car.

As the sound of the engine faded down the drive, Alan took the stairs two at a time and made straight for Elizabeth's room. His skeleton key was unnecessary; the door was unlocked. His instructions were to search the room, make copies of any floppy disks or CDs he found, and photocopy any papers. There were no papers, other than a letter from a woman named Heather. A thorough search revealed no disks or CDs, and her wallet held fewer credit cards than his own, plus a driving license and a library card.

The letter, IDs, and cards copied and returned, he checked her rental car. He found two CDs: *Aida* and John Michael Montgomery. He didn't think much of her choice of music. Just to be certain, he slid both disks into the CD player. He was right, Miss Connor's taste in music sucked. He put one back in the player and the other in the glove compartment where he'd found it. Job done, he double-checked the house and settled down to watch a Terminator video.

So much for a father–daughter dinner, with Laran brooding over the meal. Elizabeth wasn't sure who she was most frustrated with—herself for failing to convince her father he really did have a potential problem, her father for brushing her concerns aside, or Laran for pretty much telling her she had no idea what she was talking about.

The serenity she'd created by meditation, and her time on the cliff, had been zapped. If she was as stupid as they both made out, it was a wonder her father had ever trusted her to work for him.

Serve him right if the Marshes were robbing him blind. She'd done her best. If he chose to ignore her, tough cookies! And with that last thought, she undressed, and got into bed.

She woke rested, and much calmer. She'd let herself get steamed up last night. She'd have another go at talking reason to Dad at breakfast—except Laran would be there. Apparently he did live in the house, so as to be always on hand. The man needed to get a life! No, Connor Inc. was his life. Just as it was her father's.

She drew back the curtains on sky as gray as her mood last night. As she watched, the first drops of rain hit the glass. So much for climbing cliffs today. Perhaps she'd drive inland to Eugene, or browse the bookstore she loved in Florence, or just stay in and finish the novel she'd started on the airplane.

She glanced at the book with a blue and yellow design on the cover and realized it had been moved. Looking around, she noticed details she'd been too weary and wound up last night to catch: one of the hangers in the closet was a little askew; even the underwear in her drawer was more neatly folded than she ever left it. That was the giddy limit! She'd come all this way to warn her father someone was trying to rip him off, and what did he do? Brush her off while someone searched her room! Who? She couldn't picture Laran poking through her panties. She shuddered and laughed simultaneously at that image! Had to have been eager, helpful Alan. The damn sneak! She was tempted to complain to Dad. Let him know Laran's stooge did a piss-poor job.

Why waste her breath? Dad wasn't interested in what she thought, and she wasn't staying here so Alan could count her Tampax in his spare time. She'd planned on visiting Heather. She'd arrive a couple of days early.

That decided, Elizabeth showered fast, wondering if they'd checked out her body wash and loofah, and dressed, before repacking. Leaving her case upstairs, she went downstairs for caffeine and toast.

Alan, the presumed sneak, arrived as she was spreading the local marionberry jam on toast. Was it her imagination, or did he look shifty as he said good morning and helped himself to coffee? Maybe he was trying to decide if she had the black or the pink bra on this morning. She was tempted to tell him and wrap the other one around his neck. "I wasn't sure what Dad does about breakfast these days."

"He has it in his suite, as does Mr. Radcliffe. I take them up coffee and cereal and fruit about eight."

It was only just after seven. "I'm glad I didn't wait." She took the second slice and buttered it.

While Alan left to do whatever a good little spy did in his master's office, Elizabeth reached for the phone. Might as well let Heather know she was coming. Given the time zones between Oregon and Chicago, Heather would already be at school, but she'd leave a voice mail.

". . . a damn nuisance!" She almost hung the phone back up at her father's voice, but her own name caught her attention. "I sent Lizzie to get her involved. I wanted it on the record that she'd been there. How the hell was I to know she knew that much about computers?" If he'd been to her graduation, he would have.

"What are you doing about it?" an unidentified male voice asked.

"I can't have her broadcasting this. It would kybosh the entire operation. Laran is taking care of her."

It seemed a leaden fist clenched her heart, lungs, and mind. Her pulse raced, her chest heaved, and her sweaty palms almost dropped the receiver. Whatever was going on in Devon was deliberate, and downright crooked. She had made the right decision to get out of here, and she intended to do it before Laran could "take care of her."

She set the phone back, as gently as her shaking hand permitted, left her half-eaten toast and coffee on the table, and fled to her room. Bag over her shoulder, suitcase in hand, she crept down the back stairs. They were dusty and unswept. Obviously unused these days. Good. That diminished her chances of running into Alan. The stairs came out to a small hallway between the kitchen and the garden door. With no sight or sound of anyone, she grabbed her chance, opened the door, and raced the few yards to her rental car. Throwing her suitcase in the back, she started the car and was down the drive in seconds. She headed for Florence, passed through the waking town, and sped on. As she approached Eugene, she took the interstate and headed north for Portland. It was another three hours, but if Laran was after her, he'd expect her to head for Eugene. Plus, Portland offered many more chances of finding a flight. A half hour later she stopped for gas and coffee and called Heather. She caught her home, playing hooky.

"I needed a day off, Lizzie. Only way I could get my paperwork done. So I called in sick."

Heather would never change. "Get well fast. I'm on my way. I'll let you know the flight number when I get a ticket."

"Something's wrong, isn't it?"

"Yes. Very. I'll tell you when I get there."

"How long has she been gone?"

Alan Grant took a slow breath. Deep doo-doo was putting it mildly for where he stood right now. "I don't know exactly, Mr. Connor." He didn't even want to look Mr. Radcliffe in the eye—he gave him the creeps. "It can't be more than thirty minutes. I left her drinking coffee and reading the newspaper. I came in here to send the faxes you left and download e-mail. When I went back to get another cup of coffee, her car was gone." By the look on both their faces, he'd be lucky to only get sacked.

The two men exchanged glances.

"The airport?" Mr. Connor asked.

Mr. Radcliffe nodded and looked at Alan. "Take the Taurus to the airport. Find her but don't let her see you. You understand?"

Alan nodded. "Yes, sir."

"Discover where she's going, what airline, and what flight. I'll expect that information within the next two hours."

"What if she's already left, sir?"

"I hope for your sake she hasn't." Laran replied.

"Yes, sir."

"Her incoming flight and car rental information are on the desk," Mr. Connor added. "That may help you."

Alan Grant grabbed them and ran. It was a good hour's drive into Eugene.

Piet Connor sat down behind his desk. "Think he'll find her?"

"Let's hope he does. If she decides to share her little discovery with the FBI, you'll be facing a long prison term."

Piet's head jerked up. "I didn't set this racket up!"

"Agreed, it was my brainchild, but do you think any mortal law enforcement agency will be able to put me in jail?"

"You expect me to take the rap for the whole operation?"

"No, I expect you to deliver me Elizabeth. I'll make sure she remembers nothing to tell."

"You were supposed to do that last night!"

"Unfortunately, she was wearing silver. Even I have my limitations."

"What the hell do you mean?" Piet took the call from Alan but switched to the speakerphone to share the bad news with Laran. "Christ almighty! This is Eugene airport we're talking about, not LA! You have to find her!"

A slight lift of his eyebrows was Laran's only reaction. Piet knew better than to think he wasn't worried.

"Mr. Connor, she isn't here. She hasn't turned the car in. I've gone through the entire airport three times—even bought a ticket for the San Francisco shuttle to get myself through security. I'll watch the check-in counters to see if she turns up, but . . ."

"Do that, Alan." Where the hell was she?

Laran moved closer to the desk. "Stay there until we recall you. She may have stopped to eat, or gone in another direction entirely. Where's the information you found last night?"

"All the photocopies are on the file marked *Elizabeth Connor* in the in-box on Mr. Connor's desk. There's not much, but it was all I could find."

"Stay where you are until I call." He punched the button to cut the connection. "Fool! At least we know where he is until I can take care of him. Now we need Elizabeth."

Piet reached for the folder and flipped it open. As he turned the photocopied sheets, Laran read over his shoulder. Alan was right, it was regrettably thin: Lizzie's airline tickets to and from Eugene; copies of her passport, driver's license, and credit cards—seemed she had her own as well as the one he'd given her—a used rail ticket to London and a return; a few credit card receipts; and a bill for an overnight stay in a hotel. Not much. Until the last two sheets. Talk about bad handwriting.

"Who's Heather?" Laran asked, reading over Piet's shoulder. "She calls Elizabeth 'sister,' but . . ."

"Stepsister! Adela's daughter. She and Lizzie got close when we were married."

"Maybe that's where she's gone," Laran said, tapping the just-legible address with his finger.

"Chicago. This Heather talks about looking for-ward to seeing her."

Piet nodded. "Could be. They were thick as thieves as girls."

"That has to be it! If I take the company jet I can beat her there."

"A long way to go on a hunch."

"Would you rather she ran off telling everyone she meets that she suspects creative accounting in Connor Inc.?"

"God! No!" Piet shivered at that prospect. "She couldn't!"

"She won't!"

The cold purpose in Laran's voice shook Piet. "Now this is Lizzie, not some nosy bookkeeper. My daughter!"

Laran smiled. "Would I hurt your daughter? I'll just convince her to keep her suspicions to herself. Remember, I hold her in the same regard I hold you." He ran two fingers down from Piet's ear until Piet let out a little moan and leaned over to expose the white length of his neck. "Not now, Piet. Wait a couple of days. Much as it flatters me to be offered your blood, I need you strong enough to run your business. I drank deeply last night. Let your body replenish itself. When I get back, then you may bare your veins for me in gratitude."

Chapter 2

"Heather! Wonderful to see you!" Elizabeth clasped her sister as if she were her last hope.

Heather hugged back. "Me too. You had me worried with your phone calls."

"I had me worried." Terrified some of the time, but now that she was a safe distance from her father and Laran, she could relax. "It's okay now." She exhaled as if she'd been holding her breath for hours.

"You're here now, that's what matters. Got any luggage?"

"No. I didn't check anything. This is it. Let's get out of here." She couldn't rid herself of the dread that Laran Radcliffe might appear any minute to "take care" of her.

Heather looked her elder sister up and down. "You don't look at all good. When did you last eat?"

She had to think a minute. "Breakfast. But I didn't finish it."

Heather rolled her blue eyes. "The first thing you do is eat. We'll stop on the way home." She linked arms with Elizabeth. "It's so wonderful to see you. Now, tell me everything about England."

"I'm not sure you want to know!"

"Of course I do. Everything! Including what got you so upset. But first, food. You pick: pizza, Chinese, Indian, or the greasiest, best-tasting kebabs in Chicago."

They stopped for kebabs in a narrow little shop that smelled of cooking and warm spices. After ordering, Heather insisted they share a bottle of wine. "I can't wait to show you my house," she said, "It's old and needs a lot of work, but . . ." Heather shook her head. "I never thought, in a million years, I'd settle down like this, but when I started teaching, Mom offered me a loan of the down payment. And to be honest, I love having my own space."

"You like teaching?"

"Love teaching. Loathe the paperwork, but the pay is regular, I have time to pot, and I have money to buy clay and pay the enormous utility bills. I do dream of one day making enough with my pots to live on, but until then it's seventh- and eighth-grade special ed."

"How's the pottery doing?"

"Can't complain. I've a couple of shops that take my stuff on consignment. I go to craft fairs when I have the time and the money, and Mom's even found me some outlets. I make sacred bowls, chalices, and censers, some decorated with enamels, and sell them at Wiccan gatherings."

"That doesn't go against your principles?" She couldn't resist the dig at her sister's skepticism.

Heather grinned. "It's money, dear sister. Good money too. I make quality articles and sell them at a fair price. If the purchasers choose to use them for superstition, that's up to them."

"I assume you're not so outspoken to your customers."

"Lizzie, when was I ever stupid!"

"Only when you scorn your mother's calling."

Heather chuckled. "She forgives me. Besides, she has you as a daughter in spirit."

"I've nowhere near her skill."

"Mom insists you have."

So Adela had told her repeatedly, and Elizabeth knew better than to doubt a witch of her stepmother's skill.

Their food arrived, and as the waiter left, Heather asked, "Okay, tell me what had you so running scared."

"Can we eat first?" Her stomach was growling, and she rather felt a good meal might help her get her mind around the past twenty-four hours—and the two weeks before that.

Heather nodded. After a good ten minutes of chewing, and another glass of Australian Shiraz, Elizabeth's anxieties eased.

"So tell," Heather said with a wry smile as she refilled their glasses. "What devious plot is my wicked stepfather hatching?"

That jest was too near the truth to be anything but unnerving. "Sure you want to know?"

Heather closed her hand over the bottle. "You want the last of the bottle? Tell!"

Elizabeth told.

Their food went cold, and wine sat forgotten in the glasses.

Heather listened, jaw dropping and eyes widening as Elizabeth repeated everything. "My God!" Heather gasped as her sister finished. "If anyone else had told me that, I'd say they were making it up."

"You don't think I am?"

"No way! I've never known you tell a lie, and I heard how scared you were on the phone. I believe you. What do we do now? You think they'll be after you?"

That thought had never entered Elizabeth's head. It should have. "I hope the hell not. I don't want to drag you into this."

"Why not? I'm your sister, and my mom's your mom too. How's that for contacts?"

"You believe in her skills now?"

Heather gave a little snort. "That's neither here nor there. She's my mother. She has to help us. It's in the mother–daughter rule book."

"Maybe we should talk to her."

Heather grinned. "Thought you might want to. We will. I'm taking tomorrow off as well." She grinned. "I have this terrible bout of intestinal flu. We're off to Oak Park for lunch with Mom." The prospect sounded wonderful. Adela's advice had never failed. Surely it wouldn't now.

"That's settled!" Heather retrieved the bottle and drained it into Elizabeth's glass. "You finish it. I have to drive. We'll be home in ten minutes, have an early night, and in the morning go seek advice from one of the most powerful witches in the Midwest."

The house was empty and dark. Damn! But it was hers all right. The name Heather Whyte was neatly stenciled on the mailbox—clearly visible, even in the dark, to his vampire sight. Were they both gone? If so, where in damnation? And if Elizabeth hadn't come here, where else could she be? He'd give it until dawn and then think again. Laran perched on the porch roof and waited. It was a cold night, all to the good: the neighbors would keep their windows shut tight.

Less than an hour later, a little red Honda, with Elizabeth in the passenger seat, pulled into the narrow drive. Bingo! One at a time was preferable, but two mortals was no challenge for one vampire. Laran closed his fingers around the gun he'd acquired from a pawnshop on his way in and jumped down as Heather locked the car. She gave a little scream but cut it off mid-breath when he pointed the gun at Elizabeth's head and promised to shoot her if there was another sound.

Elizabeth fought back, kicking and trying to twist her leg around his. He let her waste her strength, but when she bit down over the hand that held her mouth, he hit her on the side of her head with the gun and dragged her to the side door.

"Open it!" he hissed at Heather, but it wasn't enough. "Ask me in!"

"Getting formal are we? What's your name? Emilio Post?" Sarcastic bitch! He released the safety to let her know he meant business. She glared at him but acquiesced. "Come in!"

She couldn't have been less welcoming if she tried, but it was all he needed. He stepped over the threshold and dropped Elizabeth on the kitchen floor.

He let Heather lean over her and cluck and fuss like an old hen for a couple of minutes.

"That's enough! She's not dead!" Yet. As if on cue, Elizabeth sat up and shook her head. "Hello, Elizabeth!" he said. She went pale enough to faint. He kicked her. "Get up!"

She managed, with Heather's help.

"Who the hell are you?" Heather asked, her hands around Elizabeth's shoulders.

"Ask her. She knows."

"He's Laran Radcliffe. He works for my father."

"The creep you mentioned?"

"The very same."

"Ladies." He made a point of smiling as unpleasantly as he could. "We need to talk. Or rather Elizabeth and I do."

"I'm not telling you anything!" Her voice was a little shaky, but her eyes glared defiance.

"Yes you are, because if you don't, I'll shoot your little friend's kneecaps."

"He's bluffing!" Heather said. "He doesn't have

a silencer on it, and a gunshot and my screams would be heard all over the neighborhood."

Time to start scaring them. He grabbed the shrew around the neck with one hand and squeezed until she passed out. Dropping her on the floor, he turned to Elizabeth. She was halfway to the door. He beat her to it, yanked her back, kicked the door closed, and threw her on her back on the kitchen table. When she recovered from the shock, she started to fight and yell.

He took care of that by snarling and treating her to the sight of his half-descended fangs.

She froze, mouth open and eyes wide with horror. He loved it when mortals did that. She was bleeding where he'd hit her forehead. At the rich aroma, his fangs descended completely. She opened her mouth to scream again, but his hand blocked her mouth as his arm pressed down on her chest and pinned her to the table. "Make one sound I don't ask for, and your little friend dies. She's only unconscious now, but I can fix that. Understand?" When she nodded, he moved his hand off her mouth. "Good. Now tell me all you know about auxiliary accounts in the Devon operation."

"Ask my father if you want to know."

He splayed his fingers. Nice breasts. Perhaps another time . . . . She squirmed. He dug his fingers deeper. "I know everything you told him. I heard your conversation." Her heart raced in shock. Nice. "I want to know the rest of it."

Her chest heaved against his fingers. "I told my father all I know. There's a second set of financial records and they seem to be in code. Just numbers." She threw him a glare. "If you heard me, you know that already."

"You know what the numbers refer to?"

"If I did, I'd have told Dad."

"Any idea what they are doing?"

"Something underhand, illegal, and illicit!"

"Smart-ass answers put your little friend in real peril." She glared. He chuckled. Mortals were so pathetic. "I'm giving you—and her—a second chance. Do you know exactly what the Marshes are doing?"

Her breasts rose and fell under his fingers as she took another deep breath. Beads of sweat broke out on her upper lip. Mortals were fascinating when terrified. "There was no way of guessing. It looked fishy, so I decided Dad needed to know." She paused. "He already did, didn't he? You've got a racket going on."

All this trouble for a woman's guess. "Your father and I have an arrangement. In the future, we won't need your help in the business."

"I wouldn't dirty my hands with it!"

Silly girl! Mouthing back at him, refusing to acknowledge the evidence of her own eyes. He snarled, and a little mewl came out in her efforts to hold back the scream. She looked up with defiant dark eyes, the fair hair drawn back from her forehead as sweet-scented blood trickled down the side of her face.

No point in waiting. His spread hand pinning her down, he leaned over her, licked the line of blood from her face, and relished her shudder. He lifted his head, looked her in the face again, and, holding her eyes with his, lowered his mouth on her neck.

She never stopped struggling. All the better. The rise in her blood pressure sped the flow of luscious blood, and her fear only added piquancy. He drank deep. Finished, he paused long enough to lick the punctures to seal them. He'd leave no evidence.

She was weaker now and lay quiescent, looking at him with pure, undiluted, scrumptious fear.

Usually he left this memory with his victims, to return in nightmares during dark, lonely nights, but not this time. Casting a glamour over her, he reached into her memory, stripping it. "You remember nothing of this, Elizabeth. Nothing at all." He cupped his hands on her head, forcing his will on hers. "Do what I tell you. Forget!" Her mind gave way, accepting his compulsion.

Her eyes went blank. Had he taken too much? Screw it! His survival, and the success of his plans, was what mattered. He rolled her off the table to the floor and reached for Heather. He hadn't intend to feed off her as well, but what the heck? He had a long flight back to Oregon and her neck was available. He drank hard and fast, sealed the wound with a lick, and dug into her mind, erasing her memories. "Heather, you'll remember nothing. Absolutely nothing. Understand?" He compelled her as he had Elizabeth, and her mind, too, collapsed under his superior will.

Heather gave him the same glazed look. He dropped her to the floor and stood up. He had the grandfather of all erections from the power and thrill of imposing his will on two puny females. He walked out, leaving the door open to give the impression of a robbery. Taking the keys Heather had dropped on the floor, Laran drove away in her car, abandoning it, unlocked, with the keys in the ignition. With a bit of luck some delinquent teenager would find it and leave an abundance of incriminating fingerprints.

He jogged the block or so to his rental car and, with the satisfaction of a job well done, drove back to the airport.

The cold brought Elizabeth to her senses. Her head ached. She had no idea of her name, what had happened, or where she was. She crawled over to the other woman muttering on the floor.

She sat up and stared at Elizabeth. "Who are you?"

"I don't know. Do you?"

She shook her head slowly, as if it hurt to move. "I thought you might." She looked around. "Where are we?"

Heather tried, but thinking caused a dull ache inside her skull. This place was familiar . . . it was just . . . Through the aching fog of her fragmented reason, she grasped a stray memory. "It's a house. Someone lives here."

Elizabeth looked around. "Who?"

"Hell if I know."

"What if they come back?"

An exchange of sheer terror crossed between them.

"We mustn't be here!" Elizabeth said, pulling herself to her feet. "If they come back, maybe they'll do it again."

"Do what?"

"I don't know, but it was hideous. Wasn't it?"

Heather nodded. Caught in the horror, neither of them could remember. "We've got to get away!"

They clasped hands, and, seeing the still-open door, headed outside. In the empty carport they exchanged another frightened glance. "Where?" Elizabeth asked.

Heather didn't try to answer. She pulled Elizabeth's hand and ran.

They fled the miasma of horror that enveloped the house. Past streets and shops Heather had once known, they ran on, down dark alleys, skirting yards and leaping walls. As the miles passed, they fatigued and slowed but never stopped, driven by the need to put distance between themselves and the forgotten terror behind. Hours later, they collapsed in a corner of a park. They had no idea where it was, or why they were there, but the sense of menace was gone, and they slept huddled together.

Hours, days, passed. They had no idea how long. A homeless man approached them but retreated fast when they snarled. No one else ever came near. Until . . .

A middle-aged man, strolling through the park, paused and then walked past them a couple of times. They were drawn to the quiet power emanating from him. He looked around the park and back at them. "Where is your controller?" he asked.

"Tell him this is my territory." They stared, not under-standing. "Who controls you?" he repeated.

"We don't know," Heather said.

"Who are we?" Elizabeth asked.

As the man looked at them, they both longed for the safety his presence offered. "Wait here. I will come back for you."

They waited, unable to judge time. When he re-turned, he offered his hand. Elizabeth stared, but Heather remembered what the gesture meant and offered hers. Elizabeth copied.

"I'm Mr. Roman," he said. They sensed he was as different from the mortals around as the secu-rity he offered was from their remembered horror. "Call me Vlad. I have a taxi waiting. You will be safe now. I give you my word."

Chapter 3

Havering, Yorkshire. The following February.

"Are you sure?" Stella Corvus, née Schwartz, looked up from dropping teaspoons of cookie batter on a baking sheet.

Angela smiled. Stella had to be the only vampire in the country, maybe on the planet, who baked cookies on a regular basis. Come to that, she was probably the only one with a kid. "No, I'm not sure, but I've got to do something. Tom won't share anything he's discovered—if there is anything to share. I feel I'm at the same point as when Vlad found us in the park."

"You're a good bit beyond that."

"I know. I'll be eternally grateful to you and the rest of the colony. You given me a home, clothes, sanity, a job when I needed one. But I can't stand this anonymity much longer. I want to be more than a name I picked out of the phone book. I look in the mirror and have no idea who I'm staring at."

"At least you can look in the mirror! Ghouls have that over vampires. I live in dread, I'm going around with my hair on end and smudged lipstick."

Angela chuckled. Stella seldom wore lipstick, and her new, cropped hairstyle always looked sleek. "Please understand, Stella. I need to know who I am. I'm falling in love with Tom. What if I'm married? Have a lover somewhere looking for me?" She sighed. "I used to worry I'd abandoned children or babies, but Justin reassured me there."

"Yup, it's handy having a doctor in the house."

"You've got a good man there, or rather a good vampire. I keep thinking, perhaps Tom and I . . ." She sighed.

"That's why you left him?"

"I left him because I got sick of Tom Kyd telling me *he'd* take care of everything. *He* followed up leads. *He* decided if they were red herrings. *He* studied the old lore books in the library. *He* declared what was fact and what was fable. *He* drove me bonkers!"

"I can see why." Stella pulled up a stool beside Angela. "They have a way of taking over. I'm not sure if it's testosterone, the 'me vampire' act, or both."

"At least you can 'me vampire' back!"

"You could try 'me ghoul.'"

"Doesn't quite carry the same weight. Not yet."

Stella raised her eyebrows. "Not yet?"

"If I can look Tom straight in the eye, and tell

him who I am, he'll have to do something about his 'poor, little ghoul' attitude."

"Any idea how you're going about it?"

"Stomping the sidewalks. Tom's looking for the answer in old tomes. I'm going to search the here and now."

"He's used the computer too, just as Kit has."

"Yes, and every so-called lead is a dead end. I have one clue: my leather coat. I want to go down to Totnes and search for the shop—Mariposa, according to the label. Maybe they keep records of customers." She sighed. "I doubt it's that easy. But it's a chance and I'm grabbing it. If it's a dead end, at least I've done something."

"Maybe it isn't a dead end, but you could be in for a shock. You don't know what you will discover."

"I really doubt I'm a long-lost heiress. More like something very ordinary like a teacher or secretary. But at least I'd know. It might be fun to look Tom in the eye and say, 'I'm Tallulah Bloggs and I'm a cocktail waitress.' "

"If that ends up as the name your mother gave you, you'd better stick with the one you picked out of the phone book."

Angela's smile faded. "That's what's so hard. Hell, I don't even know if I had a mother!"

"You must have, once upon a time." They were both silent a few moments, until the buzz of the timer distracted Stella for a few seconds. She pulled out one cookie tray, and slid in the next batch. "Don't forget the reason behind everyone's caution. Somewhere out there still lurks the vampire who made you."

Not a thing she was likely to forget in a hurry. "The odds are he's the other side of the Atlantic."

"He could get on a plane as easily as we did."

Angela nodded. "Trust me, Stella. I'll never forget the horror and terror we fled from. If that monster were anywhere near, and I mean within miles, I'd know." Just thinking about it made her shudder.

"Maybe. But we can hide ourselves when we want to. Be careful." Stella started easing the cooling cookies off the sheet. "It might be wise to leave before Justin gets back from this conference. He's bound to give you every bit as much flack as Tom."

Good point.

Stella picked up the mixing bowl, but as she turned on the water, Angela grabbed it. "No point in letting good cookie dough go to waste." She scraped it half clean before she realized Stella was eying her. "Miss it, do you? I'm so wrapped up in myself, I forgot that you, too . . ."

"Had a life-altering change?" Stella smiled. "I soon got over the shock. Given the alternative to being vampire, it didn't take long to accept the inconveniences. But I do miss cookie dough. And ice cream. And chocolate." She sighed. "No point in going there." She snapped the lid on the flour canister and put it away.

Angela held out a spoon. "Sure you won't have a taste?"

Stella shook her head "Thanks, but no way. I

tried it once. It tasted of nothing, and for days afterward, I had the awful sensation of a lump stuck in my throat."

Angela reached for a still-warm cookie. Life as a ghoul did have its compensations, and Stella made great cookies.

"Bye, Sam." Stella watched her son as he crossed the crowded playground and joined a group of other nine- and ten-year-olds. Satisfied he was safe inside the school gates, she smiled at Angela. "Here we go." She turned down the village street and headed for the Moors and York. "How long are you planning on going?"

"Maybe a couple of days. I'll either find out something or I won't. I don't plan on hanging around." With a bit of luck, she might be back before Justin. He was liable to be just as unreasonable as Tom. Male vampires tended to act as if they ran the planet. "I don't want you catching flack over this. Do you think Justin will cut up rough?"

Stella shrugged. "If he does, it won't be the first time, or the last. Quit worrying! And for Abel's sake, take care of yourself. I don't want you ending up in the same condition as when Vlad found you."

"I'll be careful," Angela promised, half smiling to herself at hearing her friend invoke Abel's name. Stella fitted so easily into a vampire existence. She couldn't help but envy her. Vampires had the colony for support and company; being a ghoul was an empty pain in the patootie. Not much point in complaining. Better up stakes and do something about it. Good thing she hadn't said the last bit aloud. Vampires could get touchy.

"Sure you'll be okay?" Stella asked as the train drew into the platform.

"I'll be fine, honest. You know where I'm staying?"

Stella nodded. "The Royal Oak. Call me. Promise?"

"I'll tell you everything I find out. Drive carefully, and let's hope the rain keeps up." Angela worried that Stella would get stranded in sunlight. Not that there was a lot of chance of that in February, but . . .

"The car protects me."

"You should have just dropped me and driven home. I'll be fine."

Stella shook her head. "I wanted to be able to assure Tom, if he asks, that I saw you safely on the train." But he'd still throw a hissy fit. Another reason to get back quickly.

A signal failure outside Birmingham added fifty-seven minutes to the six-hour journey. By the time Angela stepped down onto the platform at Totnes, she was ravenously hungry. Train food wasn't the sort to sustain a ghoul. She had to find meat, probably should look for her hotel, and wanted above all else to scour the leather shops. The town looked small. How hard would it be to find one shop?

Harder than she anticipated.

The clerk at the Royal Oak, a woman called

Sarah, hadn't heard of Mariposa but admitted she didn't live in Totnes. She drove in every day from Kingsbridge. She suggested Angela walk up Fore Street and look for herself, and gave her a small street map. Seemed there were only three main streets— Fore, High, and Castle. Mariposa had to be on one of those. With a bit of luck she'd find it this afternoon, return in the morning, be back before Justin, and never be missed.

Food was her next most pressing need. Cattycorner from the hotel, near the river, was a butcher shop, not a full-scale grocery store but a narrow shop front with a window display of sausages, chops, roasts, and steaks set out on a marble slab. Couldn't be handier.

Angela indulged in local venison steak, lamb chops, and organic corn-fed chicken. Famished as she was, she hauled her booty back to her hotel room. Chewing on a raw steak in public was not the way to pass as mortal. Putting aside the chicken and half the chops for later, she ate, her energy returning as she chewed and swallowed. Rounding off with a cup of coffee, courtesy of the kettle and supplies in her room, she wrapped up the leftover bones—no point in leaving them in the room for a curious maid to find—and set off. Armed with her map and resolution, she started up Fore Street in a soft Devon drizzle.

It was later than she realized. The afternoon was already fading, and some of the shops were closing. Interesting old shops lined the steep street, but none was called Mariposa. A clock arch spanned the street halfway up. Different enough. Surely she should remember it? She didn't. It was a fascinating curiosity—something England seemed to be full of—but as a trigger for her fragmented memory, it was useless. She walked on up the hill, promising herself she'd stop at the used bookstores after she found the all-important Mariposa.

At the top of the hill, Castle Street veered off to the right. Twice she walked up and down the steep, twisting street with its mix of old cottages and shops, but there was no sign of a leather shop. She darn well was not giving up. Tomorrow, when the shops opened, she'd ask in every single one. Even if, as she was beginning to suspect, Mariposa had closed, someone would remember it.

It was close to full dark, and the drizzle showed no signs of stopping. She might as well save her efforts for the morning and get out of the dark and the rain.

She was halfway back up the street, and more than ready to be back in the warmth of her hotel room, when she passed a little shop she'd half-noticed earlier: Crystals and Dreams. Angela paused briefly to look in the bow window hung with crystals, candles, and hand-painted scarves. No leather jackets, but there were two pairs of soft leather slippers in a corner.

A bell jangled as Angela pushed the door open and stepped into a cluttered shop that smelled of joss sticks and pot. She looked around, not sure how she recognized the two smells but certain the hand-rolled cigarette in the woman's hand wasn't made of best Virginia Bright. Not that she had any idea what Virginia Bright was; like so many snatches of memory, it just poked her mind. But Angela felt pretty certain Virginia Bright was a whole lot more legal that the sweetly smouldering contents of the gray-haired woman's toke.

"Can I help you?" She smiled at Angela but didn't move from the bentwood rocker.

Angela postponed her mission to find a leather shop as she glanced around the little store. "I'd like to browse, if you're not closing."

"Not to worry, my love." The rocker creaked in the quiet. "You have a good look around. Anything special you want?"

Other than her true identity? "I'm not sure." Something about this cramped shop that made her feel—comfortable, as if she belonged. Odd thought! She'd been comfortable at Stella and Justin's. They and Sam treated her like another member of their family. Tom's London house had impressed her. She'd wandered from room to room, marveling at the size and luxury, but not overwhelmed. She'd felt at ease among the Adam fire surrounds and the antique furniture. But in this overstocked shop full of the scents of incense and cannabis, she felt surrounded by familiar things. Obviously, she was affected by secondhand inhalation of illegal substances.

Angela moved from a display of crystals to boxes of candles in all colors, jars of dried flower petals, and sachets of herbs. The smells of lavender and rosemary, pine and anise, tugged at her blocked memories. Or perhaps her senses were heightened in the close atmosphere of the overheated shop. Outside, a gust of wind blew rain against the small windowpanes. Better in here than getting drenched outside, if the owner didn't mind her using the shop as a place to stay dry.

Moving away from the shelves of herbs and jars, a display of tarot cards twanged Angela's fogged memory. As she reached for a deck, recognition came in a rush. She read cards! Not these pictorial ones, but true cards. She could because . . . The floor seemed to shift under her feet. She grasped the table as she fought to stay upright and retain the fading shreds of memories.

"Hang on!" a voice called from a distance. "Came over funny did you? Here, have a seat." With more strength than her gray-streaked hair suggested, the woman had Angela by the waist, steadying her until she plonked down in the rocking chair. "Keep your head down a mo . . ." She pushed Angela's head between her knees.

Ungainly and undignified, but effective. Her head cleared fast, and as the pressure on her shoulders eased, Angela raised her head to meet a pair of worried, dark eyes. It was the first time she'd actually looked closely at the woman. Her complexion was almost Hispanic in tone, and her long, dark hair was abundantly streaked with gray, but her face was alert, intelligent, and wise.

"Take it easy, my love. You came over faint."

"I'm okay." It was a lie but . . .

"You sit tight there and I'll bring you a cup of tea."

"Please don't bother." Surely she could stand up and go. It wasn't that far back to the hotel.

"No bother!" The woman shook her head. "I

have a pot brewing in the back room. I made it just a minute before you walked in. I always have a cup this time of day. You stay put." The last came out as an order. Angela stayed put. Maybe a nice, warm drink would help. She'd learned one new thing this afternoon—ghouls could faint.

Angela sat back, the chair creaking in a reassuring way as she rocked. She looked down at her lap and noticed the deck of cards in her hand. Not these. She wanted simple telling cards. Ones like she'd always used . . .

"Here we are." The woman returned with a small tray. "Milk and sugar?"

"Please." Angela let go of the cards, and took the mug, closing her hands around its warmth. The woman pulled in a straight-backed chair from the room behind and sat beside her.

"Cheers," she said and drank. "Since we're sharing a cuppa, I'm Meg Merchant." She set her mug down and held out her hand. It was strong and her handshake was steady.

"I'm Angela Ryan."

"Welcome to this part of the world, Angela. Come far, have you?"

"From Yorkshire."

Meg nodded and sipped her tea.

Tasting the warm, sweet tea had her remembering how Tom had convinced her to try sugar and milk in tea. Tom! Angela fingered the jet heart she wore around her neck. It would protect her, Tom had insisted when he gave it to her, by linking her to the earth. She felt a pang of guilt at absconding,

but not for long. This was her life and her past,
and it was her job to delve, and with a bit of luck,
uncover.

Had she been frowning? Talking to herself?
Meg was watching her with speculative light in her
dark-rimmed eyes. "In some sort of trouble?" she
asked after a long silence.

"Not really." Even if she wanted to tell this old
woman, where could she begin?

"Something happened to you." Meg sounded
concerned, almost anxious. "Your aura," she said
after a pause, and shook her head.

Heaven help her! A New Age grannie! A nosy,
New Age grannie! But kind and thoughtful. "I had
an accident and lost my memory."

Meg shook her head. "Lost your memory! More
like someone tried to steal your mind and soul!"

A chill settled in Angela's bones. How could this
old woman possibly suspect? "Just amnesia." Meg's
eyebrows shot up. She said nothing, just waited,
her body language expressing skepticism. That
irked. "What's wrong with my aura?"

"You don't have one. Not to speak of. Never seen
anything like it in my life." She paused. "You've
nothing, not even gray or black. Just nothing. When
you fingered your locket, I saw pink flashes near
your heart. A little while back as you touched those
cards, you had some faint flashes, but other than
that . . ." Intent eyes met Angela's. "You didn't lose
your memory; more like someone took it."

Meg was so darn close to the truth, Angela's
heart went tight. Who was this old woman? "It was
an accident. That's all." Meg was as hard to con-

vince as a judge. "Seeing the cards brought back a memory. My stepmother taught me to read them." How did she know? Did she even have a step- mother? Yes, and she'd taught her to read cards, and other skills. Angela glanced at the deck still in her lap. "She used a plain deck."

Sounded like blathering to Angela, but it made sense to Meg. Putting down her cup with a soft clink, she stood up and went over to the shelf. "Here," she said, "this what you're talking about?"

It was. Angela broke the seal and tapped the deck out of the box. The shiny, new cards fanned out easily. Just as she remembered, the numbers were only printed on one end. "Yes." She snapped the fan shut. "I had a deck just like this"—she wasn't sure how she knew but she was certain. "How much are they?"

Meg shook her head. "You see what they tell you. If you can do nothing with them, just bring them back. If they let you read, then we'll talk pay- ment."

"You're very trusting."

Meg shook her head. "You won't cheat me. May- be the cards can help you find what you've lost."

Angela wanted to race back the Royal Oak and lay out a spread and . . . and what? She had no idea but felt a burning need to find out. Her fingers tingled where she held the deck. There was power in them, and she needed to . . .

"Finish your tea," Meg said. "The rain's eased off. Make sense for you to get back before it starts again."

Good advice. "I'll be back in the morning."

"Take your time. I'll be here when you need me."

Angela was so occupied with the promise of the cards in her hand, she was on her way out the door before she remembered why she'd entered the shop in the first place.

"Meg," she said, turning back. "Perhaps you can help. A friend told me there was a wonderful place in Totnes to buy leather things. I noticed the slippers in your window."

Meg smiled. "They come from Bangladesh, not local at all."

"What about a leather shop called Mariposa?"

Meg frowned, as if thinking. "Can't say I know one, not here. Ask old Mr. Lee up the High Street. He does shoe and leather repairs. Been here forever. He might know."

It was grasping at straws, but a straw was more than thin air.

"Where is his shop?"

"Up to the top of the road, turn right at the corner and you'll find him on the right, along a little ways. But he'll be closed by now."

Darn. Morning seemed a long time away. But Mr. Lee would still be there. If he'd been in business for as long as Meg claimed, he was unlikely to disappear overnight. "I'll ask him. Thanks for the tea, and the cards."

"My pleasure. I enjoyed the company. Take care of yourself. Wear that locket of yours."

Angela caught the shiny black stone between her thumb and finger. "I will."

Meg smiled. "Someone gave you that for protection. Jet, right?"

"Yes." And that was all she was saying. "It was a gift from a vampire" might be a bit much, even here among the crystals and the element bowls.

"Take care!" Meg said as Angela closed the door.

Angela was halfway down Fore Street before she wondered what element bowls were for and how she recognized them.

"You let her leave! Just like that!" Justin couldn't credit it. Thank Abel, he'd come back a day early! Three days in Reykijavik for a medical conference and Angela absconds, with Stella's blessing and connivance. Did they have no understanding?

Apparently not. Stella looked unconcerned. "Did you have a good conference?"

"Hang the conference! Angela's gone off, Abel only knows where, and . . ."

"I know exactly where she is. She's at the Royal Oak in Totnes, checking on that coat of hers."

Devon! Abel help them all! The pair of them had no idea!

"I have her hotel and phone number. She'll be back in a couple of days."

He wished he shared Stella's optimism. But the West Country! "I can't believe you abetted her! Didn't you think?"

"Hey!" Sam ran in from the kitchen and pushed between them. "Don't you dare yell at my mom!" He was nose to Justin's enameled tiepin, but ready to take him on. Even his little fists were clenched and raised.

"It's okay, Sam." Stella rested a hand on her son's tense shoulder. "Justin and I are discussing something. That's all."

"He was yelling at you." Sam frowned up at Justin with all the machismo of his nine years. "He'd better not try it again."

Justin fought back the smile that Sam would take as an insult. "Sam, your mother's right. We're just discussing. I'm not going to hurt her."

Sam gave no quarter. "You were yelling at her."

"I wasn't, Sam. Not really."

"You were." Stella folded her arms across her breasts and gave him a half smile. "That was yelling."

He'd take her word for it. "Apologies, my love." He bent down so Sam was eye, rather than tie, level. "Sorry, Sam. How about I promise not to yell at your mother, and you go back and finish your homework? Stella and I need to talk."

"About Angela going away?"

"Angela—has—not—gone—away." Stella enunciated each word deliberately. "She went on a trip for a few days. She'll be back. Soon."

Justin restrained the urge to shake her. She had no idea of the dangers that lurked once they left their own territory. "Stella, we have to talk."

"Just a minute." She watched as Sam walked back into the kitchen, glancing over his shoulder as he went, obviously keeping an eye on both of them.

Once Sam was out of sight, Justin looked at Stella. He loved her to the point of insanity and she'd have him right there if she pulled many stunts like this. And when Tom heard about this, the universe would crackle. "Let's go in my study. This is serious, and I don't want Sam to overhear and worry."

Chapter 4

"Justin," Stella began as she closed the door, "you're overreacting."

"I'm not, love. There's far more to this than you and Angela realize."

She folded her arms under her breasts. "That so? Any plans to share it with us?"

"We didn't plan to. Not yet. But in the circumstances . . ." How to start? A two-minute guide to two millennia of distrust and confrontation? "It's complicated."

"I don't see why. You're mad because I helped Angela do what she needed to do. Tom's going to be pissed at you and that will make a rift in your centuries of male bonding."

Abel give him strength! "Have a seat, Stella."

She must have sensed his reined-in frustration. She sat down on one of the chairs by the fireplace. He took the other, and pulled it up so they were knee to knee.

Her wry smile hit him hard in the heart. How he loved her! But how could she have let Angela leave? And to Devon of all places? Because he and Tom had failed to share the dangers with them. There was a lesson there. "Stella, it's a lot more serious than Tom getting put out with me." A trace of worry creased her dark eyes. "The problem isn't Angela going off on her own, it's where she's gone."

"To Totnes to find the shop where her coat came from."

"Totnes is in Devon. We don't go there."

She frowned as she thought that over. "By 'we' you mean vampires?"

"Yes."

"And I'm assuming there's a very good reason why we should avoid Devon?"

The hint of sarcasm irritated him. But more than that, he anticipated her shock when she heard. He reached forward and took her hands in his. "It goes back to before I came here. Even before the arrival of the first Romans. We avoid the West Country, Cornwall, Devon, Somerset and parts of Dorset, and almost all of Wales." She nodded, listening. A little furrow appeared between her eyebrows. "Those parts of Britain are steeped in magic and abound with witches."

"And that's why vampires don't go there?" He nodded. "But Angela's not a vampire."

"No. And perhaps may pass unnoticed, but if one of them recognizes her as vampire get . . ."

"What?" Her eyes widened. "She's in danger?"

"I don't know for sure. Possibly. Possibly not.

Stella, we have nothing to do with them and they have nothing to do with us. That's how it is."

"Why?"

He should have expected that; why hadn't he told her all this earlier? Because there had been other, more pressing things for her to learn. "It goes back to even before Gwyltha's time, and she was made in the first century BC."

"I thought she started this."

"She started our colony, as the Druid society was declining." Stella nodded and leaned forward to listen. "Before then, long before my people—the Romans—came, the Druids held sway by magic and old knowledge. My understanding is that when the first offspring of the resurrected Abel reached these islands, no one noticed. As our numbers increased slowly, the high priests realized our powers. Vampires were admitted to the inner circle of priesthood, like Gwyltha was. Some vampires were even worshipped as gods, but in time, the two arms split through mistrust, jealousy, fear, who knows what.

"Later, as the Druids fled with their magic to the far west and the hills of Wales, we stayed behind, concealing our nature. When Gwyltha made me, we were already an invisible people. Survival dictates we stay that way. We remained hidden and kept to our part of the country. They stay in theirs."

"Are there no witches in the rest of the country?"

"A few, but they are mostly amateurs, players of games. The old lore witches fled with their magic, and we've stayed apart ever since."

"What happens if you don't?"

"The last time witches tangled with us, a coven tried to extinguish Kit."

"Kit Marlowe, Dixie's Kit?" Too blunt! Shock and worry widened Stella's eyes as she jumped up. "We have to warn Angela!"

He stood up and pulled her to him. "I doubt she's in immediate danger. The attempt on Kit was planned in advance and timed for when he was weakest." He smoothed Stella's short, dark hair to calm her. "We just need to get her back. I'd call, but you might have more success. She might dismiss me as playing the heavy vampire."

"She just might." Stella paused. "I don't want to scare her, either. I'll tell her we've discovered something that needs her to get back here ASAP."

She would have, if she'd gotten through. The hotel rang Angela's room for several minutes, but no reply. The clerk assured Stella she would give Angela the message, and other than leaving her number, there wasn't much else Stella could do. "I hope she gets it," she said as she hung up.

"She will." Justin pulled Stella close. "I didn't mean to worry you, but she's taking a risk going there."

"It would have been nice to let us in on all this."

She was right. "I did suggest Tom tell her, but he wanted to wait until he discovered something certain."

"You mean in all these centuries, he hasn't yet discovered few things are certain?"

"I know of one." He grasped her hips and pulled

her close. There was no mistaking how he felt about her. "I love you and I've missed you like hell."

"Maybe we should take care of that!"

Her mouth came to his as she raised up on tiptoe. Her lips were sweet and moist and soft, and he'd missed her more than he'd ever imagined possible. He wanted this woman. His vampire. Stella. Her arms wrapped around his shoulders, pulling him against the glorious fullness of her breasts. As he pressed her lips apart, her tongue caressed his, and wild vampire need coursed through his ancient blood.

The phone on his desk rang.

She pulled away, but before she moved the two paces to lift the receiver, it stopped. She paused, a hand's length from the now-silent phone. "Must be Pete or Jimmy calling Sam about homework or the new movie playing in Whitby. I wish Angela would call."

He pulled her back against him, not to kiss her this time but to hold her hand against his chest and cup her head in his hand. "She'll call back. Don't worry."

"What if she calls while he's nattering away to his buddies?"

"She'll call again. She hasn't been there long enough to alert anyone to her presence. Things will be fine."

She looked up. The trust in her eyes almost broke him. What had he accepted, taking on a wife and child? Joy and worry beyond belief. He bent to kiss her again.

"Pardon me!" They both looked up. "Sorry." Sam gave an almost wicked grin. "I can see you're busy, but Uncle Tom's on the phone." He held out the portable phone from the kitchen.

"Thanks, son." Justin reached for the phone.

Stella took it first. Might as well get this over. At least Tom was at the other end of the receiver. Two irate, elder vampires were a bit much for anyone to face. "Bless you honey. How's the homework?"

"Almost done. Can I watch *Robot Wars* when I'm through? It starts in ten minutes."

Sam had wasted no time acclimatizing himself to Brit TV. "Yes, and when it's all finished, you can treat yourself to a Penguin, but make sure those teeth are scrubbed before you go to bed."

"Thanks, Mom!" He hadn't taken long discovering the best of British snacks either. But she had to take his word for how good those rich, chocolate sandwich cookies tasted.

"Hello?" Tom's voice yanked her right back into the hole she'd dug herself.

"Hi, Tom." She ignored Justin's outstretched hand. This was her doing, she'd handle it.

"Hello, Stella. You've a very sharp young man there. He was telling me all about Newcastle's chances against Sunderland."

"He's their staunchest supporter, I think." Soccer had been a godsend. Right from day one, he'd made friends in the playground on the basis of heading and dribbling. "How's London?"

"Wet! Is Angela handy?"

Her palms might not go sweaty anymore, but her throat still tightened. She was about to upset a four-hundred-year-old vampire. "Tom, Angela's not here right now. She decided to go to Totnes to see what she could find out." Silence greeted her announcement.

Tom didn't ask her to repeat it. He'd obviously understood fine. His irritation seethed through the wires. "Have you no sense?"

Plenty, but now wasn't the time to point that out. "Tom, until Justin came home an hour or so ago, I was unaware of the problems with the West Country. So was Angela. No one thought to mention the matter to us."

It was the first time she'd heard a vampire splutter. The line went silent for several seconds. "Where is she? And how long has she been gone?"

"At the Royal Oak in Totnes. She went on the ten o'clock train this morning and called me when she arrived. She's fine."

"You don't know that, Stella, and you shouldn't be meddling!"

"Tom, she was going to leave whether I helped her or not. This way, I know where she is, and she's calling me every day. Would you rather I'd refused to help her and she'd gone off without telling me? Do you want the phone number of her hotel?"

"Yes . . . please. And let me speak to Justin." She gave him the phone number, and as soon as she finished, Justin picked up the other phone.

As he said, "Hello, Tom," she realized the door was still ajar. She stepped out to check on Sam. He was engrossed in the action on the flickering screen and blissfully unaware of the worries that welled up in her heart. What if something had happened

to Angela? Justin hadn't been sure if it was dangerous for her, but if witches had tried to extinguish
Kit, an elder vampire, what would they do to a
new-made ghoul?

Stella walked back into the library just in time to
hear, "I agree, but it's done now. And to be honest,
Tom, these women do a darn good job of taking
care of themselves." Justin listened in silence for
several seconds, looking up at her as she closed
the door behind her. "You're leaving right away?"
he asked Tom.

"Let me speak to him again," Stella said.

"If we hear back from Angela, I'll call you at once."

"Justin," she hissed. His ignoring irked. His imperious wave of the hand got her dander up. "Justin,
let me speak to him!" Remembering the Brit insistence on the courtesy, she added, "Please."

"Keep me posted, and good luck."

Justin set the phone on the table after clicking it
off, and he met her frown with a soft smile.

"I wanted to speak to him, to tell him not to go
barging in playing the masterful vampire."

"I was aware of that, my love, but I'm afraid Tom's
self-restraint was in short supply. If he'd caved in
and cursed you from here to Hades, I would have
been in the position of having to call out an old
friend for insulting my wife."

"Oh, give me a break! You . . ." She stopped. It
would be just like them to still duel over her honor.
"Justin, that would not have been necessary."

"Maybe not, if he'd apologized sufficiently, but I
sensed Tom was not in an abject frame of mind."

"He's worried?"

"Frantic might better describe it."

"You should have let me speak to him."

Justin reached out and caught her hand. "Stella, nothing will allay his worries but seeing for himself."

Since she was getting to that point herself right now . . . "He's going to bring her back?"

"Right away, my love, and I did urge him to employ tact and sound reason over emotion."

Once Angela called back, she'd fill her in so she'd be prepared when Tom arrived. It had to take several hours to get there from London. Unless . . . "He is driving?"

"I imagine so. He has no change of clothes down there, and I doubt Angela will have anything he can wear."

She'd already learned from Justin that bat or bird form was the fastest way to get anywhere, but transmogrifying back and standing naked could be a bit awkward. Justin had spare wardrobes all over the place.

"Stop worrying." His arm snaked behind her and drew her close. "I've missed you. Think Sam would settle for me reading to him in bed while you try out the bath oil I picked up in the duty-free?"

His wide lips were just inches from hers. "Trying to seduce me with gifts and sweet words?"

"Why not? It works every time."

That earned him a dig in the ribs and the slow promise of a kiss.

* * *

Angela set off at a brisk pace. The rain had eased but the early nightfall, and just about every shop closing, turned Fore Street from bustling to well-nigh deserted. She'd stayed longer than she realized in Meg Merchant's welcoming shop.

Angela closed her fingers around the deck of cards in her pocket. Even if she never found Mariposa, she had a clue to her past. As soon as she got back to her room, she'd lay out a spread and see what the cards had to say. She couldn't keep them in this paper bag; they needed to be wrapped in silk to retain their power. How the hell did she know that? No idea! She sped up. The sooner she got back to the Royal Oak, the sooner she could grab at another fragment of her past.

"What's the hurry, then, sexy lady?"

Angela stopped midstride as a tall teenager stepped out from a doorway, blocking her path as the sidewalk narrowed. One look at the menace in his eyes, the dangling piercing beside his left eye, and the death's head tattoo on his bare arm, and Angela stepped into the street.

And almost collided with a battered car that just happened to pull up alongside.

"Wanna ride, sweetheart?" someone called from a rolled-down window. The tattooed menace stepped closer.

Fear lasted seconds. Fury came fast. She and Jane had survived homeless on the streets of Chicago. She was not getting mugged, or worse, in a sleepy little market town.

"Get away from me!" she snapped at anyone within earshot.

A hand closed over her left arm. "Unfriendly are you? We can't have that, can we?" Tattoo lad raised a hand and stroked the side of her face, pressing his ring into her cheek.

He smiled at her shudder.

Behind her, a car door opened.

Her anger incandesced. A wild buzzing echoed in her ears, her eyes seemed to tighten, and she snarled, leaning into tattoo boy and fixing his eyes with hers.

He paled, let go of her, and stumbled backward. Recovering his balance, courtesy of the shop window, he darted in front of the car and begged then to open the door.

A voice behind her asked, "Did the nasty bitch frighten you then, didums?"

Angela spun around and glared. The thug dropped the knife in his hand and backed away. "Christ!" he muttered.

He looked around as if searching for help. "Oh God!" He wailed, as he lurched backward. Seemed Providence declined him succor. Thug number two almost leaped into the car headfirst.

"Get the hell out of here!" a voice shrieked from inside the car. The driver followed this advice, accelerating down the hill, one rear door swinging open as the car wove across the road.

"Thank heavens!" Angela pressed her hand to her chest. She gulped air in an attempt to steady her racing heart and almost yelped as she caught her reflection in the shop window.

Red, blazing eyes glared back at her, but they were the least of her shock. Her mouth was drawn back in a feral snarl, and her skin held a livid cast that in the evening light looked fearsome and in daylight would no doubt cause heart attacks. As she watched, her distorted reflection adjusted to the one she was accustomed to seeing and the tightness in her skin eased. In seconds, the monster disappeared, and plain old Angela Ryan, or as "plain" as she could be given she was ghoul, looked back at her.

After some very slow, deep breaths, she walked on down the hill. So! She could scare off those of evil intent. It wasn't quite transmogrifying or exerting mind control the way elder vampires could, or even the physical strength Stella possessed, but it was a start. What else could she do? Fly? Walk on water? Outrun deer? She'd skip experimenting with the first two but maybe try the last one. If she went up on the Moors, she could have a go, see how far she could run and how long.

It would be nice to have a laundry list of ghoul attributes. If Tom could have found that in the old lore books, it would have been useful, but heck, she'd compile her own. Had Jane made any discoveries? She'd give her a call just as soon as she laid out her cards and checked with Stella that all was well back in Yorkshire.

But by the time she reached the bottom of the hill, Angela was dizzy and weak. Seemed the Igor act sapped strength. She hungered for raw meat. Plenty waited up in her room. She almost dropped her key in her eagerness to get gnawing, but made it into her room, slammed the door shut, and grabbed the first package, which happened to be the chicken.

She chewed down the raw meat until only bones remained. The edge of her hunger off, she looked at the small paper bag a few inches from her fingers. She couldn't touch telling cards with greasy fingers. She scrubbed her hands, uncertain what, if anything, she was going to learn.

The new cards slid easily out of the flimsy box. Her fingertips brushed the pristine surface. She shuffled them slowly, letting the cards slip through her fingers as she set her mind seeking the messages in the cards. She was doing this on instinct, harnessing lost memories. Without asking herself why, she cut the deck and dealt out seven cards facedown in a circle on the bedspread.

The sight was terribly familiar and completely strange at the same time. Ridiculous! But she knew what she was doing, or would when she turned them faceup. Her fingers shook a little as she turned up the six of spades. Threats! She'd just had that. In spades. She couldn't stop the giggle. Had to be delayed shock and relief. One never laughed over cards. They were too sacred. The next turned was the king of hearts: a kind, fair man. Tom was more brown-haired than fair, but his skin was certainly very pale. Did a vampire count as a man? Jack of spades: a bad-mannered man. No, it was reversed. A false friend, a traitor. Ha! Another card and she found Tom for sure: the jack of clubs, a good lover and a clever, dark, young man. Okay, young was used advisedly, but he had been young when he

died. Next, the eight of hearts: love and romance.
She wished. Maybe after she found out who she
was. More clubs. The six reversed. She needed to
be careful. Over what?

She hesitated over the final card: the ace of
spades. She had love ahead of her. No point in asking how she knew all this. Confidence seeped into
her mind. She'd read the cards once and would
again.

If Tom were here, she'd have him shuffle them.
As it was, she shuffled for him, keeping in mind
his slow, sexy smile and the memory of his cool
body, skin to skin with hers.

She missed him!

Why did he have to be so unreasonable and difficult?

She cut the cards and remembered the press of
his lips against hers and the sweet taste of his skin
on her tongue.

Once she sorted things out here, she'd call him.
Maybe go back to Havering via London. But only
after she learned something about herself. She was
not returning to his "be a good ghoul and let me
handle all this" line.

It was as if the cards were coming alive for her.
Her fingers warmed as she placed each card facedown. This time she turned them all at once and
scanned the spread. From hers she'd received
fragments. Maybe together she'd learn more.

Maybe.

The same reversed king of spades. Was it the
same evil man? Did they both face the same threat?
Hardly likely, as they were on opposite sides of the

country. He had three hearts. Looked as if he was headed for luck in the love direction. Was she there with him? Was she the queen that smiled up at her from the chintz bedspread? And as if Tom wasn't sexy enough for a dozen men, the ten and the four side by side promised him marriage and success in love. Two of diamonds: an argument. They'd had that already. Seemed they couldn't spend twenty minutes together without one. What did the four and nine of clubs foretell? An unfamiliar place? Heck, she was the one in unknown territory. This was Tom's country and had been for centuries. And the nine? Money coming, or friends getting together. He had no shortage of money. Interest accumulated over the years, and his friends did seem to stick together. They'd pretty much invaded Ohio back in November.

Love and evil foretold for Tom. An evil and clever man for her, and satisfaction in love and the need to go carefully—not surprising if an evil man lurked ahead. Plus she had to face the uneasiness of five black cards in her seven.

She certainly owed Meg for the cards. She'd pay first thing in the morning. Angela gathered them all up and sat, staring at the deck, now warmed by her hands.

How did she know this? Hell if she knew! But she *had* read the meaning in the cards. What else waited to be discovered?

The power of the cards skimmed over her skin. She had a whole lot more to find out—about herself and her past and how she ended up on the streets.

Angela looked around at the soft bed. She was dog-tired. The journey, the encounter with the thugs, and now the power in the cards together drained her abundant energy.

She set the cards on the nightstand, pulled off her clothes, and stretched out on the bed.

She was asleep in moments.

And completely oblivious to the dark shape that peered in her window a few hours later.

Chapter 5

Angela squinted at the sunbeams lighting up the room. She'd been so tired, she hadn't drawn the curtains before falling asleep and had slept late. She was light-headed and weak, and the phone ringing inches from her ear made her brain hurt. Darn it! She'd intended to call Stella last night. It had to be her, frantic with worry.

"Angela!" Heaven help her, it was Tom! She tried hard to concentrate on what he was saying, but the general impression that he was complaining was lost between the fuzziness in her brain and the aroma of glorious, raw meat. The last of the loot from the butcher's practically sang to her to consume it. Fast.

"Okay, Tom," she said and hung up, with no idea what she could possibility have agreed to. She leaped out of bed and across the room, chewing through the wrapping in her need to devour. She ended up on her knees on the carpet, tearing at the chops with her teeth and swallowing as if famished. When she sat up, her brain had cleared, and she made a mental note never to let herself go that long without feeding. Heck, at Tom's she'd grazed almost all day, nibbling and tasting the fresh meat he kept in the spare refrigerator, the one with the blood bags for emergencies.

Darn it, she'd left drops of blood on the carpet. She shocked herself by sucking them up. She really had to make sure she never starved herself again, or be darn certain the door was locked before she started licking the carpet. The Royal Oak was a relaxed, easy-going, comfortable sort of hotel, but guests gnawing on the broadloom might be more than they could handle.

Showered and with hair washed, she was ready to face the day. She'd first find this Mr. Lee, then go back to Meg Merchant's shop. Her comments about holes and blackness in Angela's aura seemed worrying on a satisfied stomach. Eating breakfast like a mortal guest might be a good move for a ghoul determined to blend in. Especially after the disappointed comments yesterday when she'd declined booking for dinner.

Besides, even cooked meat satisfied her need for flesh.

The smells of bacon and fresh coffee wafted from the dining room. Times like this, ghouls had the edge over vampires. How Stella and the rest of them didn't get bored to bellyache with their liquid diet she'd never know.

"You're looking remarkably chipper this morning!"

Tom! Angela stared across the lobby. He looked anything but chipper. Scowling, surly, downright pissed off would all describe the vampire leaning against the oak paneling. Sexy and bedworthy were pretty good, too, but now wasn't the time to think in that direction. Not after their argument in London. "It's a lovely morning, and I feel great!" Perhaps not the most tactful thing to say, but drat it!

The creases between his eyebrows as good as matched the linenfold paneling. "Where are you going?"

"To have breakfast." She nodded toward the open dining-room doors.

"Fair enough." He stepped forward. "I'll come with you, and then as soon as you finish, you'll get packed. I'm taking you back to town."

Good luck, Tom! "What makes you think I want to go to London with you?"

"Look here, Angela!"

"Good morning, Miss Ryan!" It was Sarah, the clerk who'd spent ages yesterday trying to find Mariposa in shopping guides and tourist pamphlets. "This gentleman was asking for you." Her tone suggested Tom might look and dress like a gentleman, but she wasn't too sure.

"Thanks, Sarah. Tom's joining me for breakfast." He could hardly cut up rough in a public place, and what she was about to tell him wouldn't improve his attitude. She was tempted to ask for a sunny table by the leaded-light windows, but outright provocation was not the best way to open negotiations, and Tom was going to have to shift from his you're-coming-back-to-London-right-now position.

He was charming to the waitress, refusing break-fast but asking for black coffee. Seemed he saved the snipping and snapping for her. But if he was prepared to act civilized, they might possibly have a conversation without arguing. She reached for the cream. "Did you have a good trip down? Did you fly?"

"Knowing you lack the ability to transmogrify, I drove down, so I could drive you back."

He *was* single-minded this morning. "Before you, or I, go anywhere, I need to tell you what I dis-covered yesterday."

"That you came here on a wild goose chase?"

For that she was half-tempted not to tell him anything. But he was strong enough to carry her off physically, and if he tried his vampire mind-control stuff. . . . She smiled as sweetly as she knew how. "Not in the least. I got a lead on someone who might know where Mariposa is, and I made a cou-ple of interesting discoveries."

"You did?"

He didn't need to sound so blandly disbeliev-ing. "Yes, I did. I'll tell you about them after break-fast."

And damn the man! He didn't even ask! Just drank two cups of coffee while she wolfed down bacon and sausage.

Angela was just about bursting by the time she did tell Tom, which was most likely his intention. Vampires could drive you crazy with their blasted self-control.

They left the Royal Oak behind and were walking along the river. The water ran high from the winter rains, and the island opposite was half-inundated. The overcast sky only added to the mood. They were going the opposite direction from Mr. Lee's shop on High Street, but Angela wasn't sure she wanted to go there with Tom anyway. If he was so dismissive of her efforts, she'd manage on her own.

"What did you find out?" Tom asked, looking across the river. The winter bare trees were obviously a lot more interesting than anything she'd discovered.

"There's an old man, a shoe repairer, who's been in business for years and knows all the leather places around," she paused. "Plus, I can read cards." That got a flicker of an eyebrow. "And when I get angry, my face changes."

That got his full attention. "How?"

She told him.

He was more annoyed than impressed. "You were reckless to do that to a group of mortals."

"Not as reckless as standing there and letting them have a go at me!"

"If you'd stayed with me, you'd never have run this risk."

"You're trying to tell me that a big city like London is safer than a small town like this?" She had her hands on her hips, and they were getting dangerously close to nose to nose.

"You'd be safer because I'd see you were!"

"Right, by locking me up!"

"I never locked you up."

Okay, he hadn't but . . . "Tom, you wanted to keep me in your house twenty-four hours a day, unless you went out with me."

"Angela, you have no idea what dangers lurk."

"I have a pretty darn good idea of danger after three nights on the streets of Chicago . . ." She broke off, her mind snapping in shock as it always did with these sudden memory flashes, but this time she shuddered with a cold wave of dread. "Tom!" Her voice came thin with fear. "How do I know it was three nights? And why is it so bad?" Remembered terror sent her shuddering, as his arms closed around her. Her tremors intensified before easing. It was the same fear that fueled the nightmares and woke her screaming.

Tom tightened his hold, pulling her against him as he fought to brush her mind with reassurance. The horrors were stronger than last time. He tried to read what evoked such fears, but all he found was blind emotion.

He wanted to kill by slow torture the creature who'd done this to her. He held her closer, willing calm into her fright-fuddled mind. Her sobs eased, and he handed her his handkerchief. She wiped her eyes, sniffed a few times, and looked up at him with red-rimmed eyes. "Sorry, Tom."

He kissed her forehead, savoring the sweetness off her skin, but now was no time to indulge those appetites, not when she was halfway to falling apart. "Sorry for what? Ruining my shirt? Not to worry, the laundry can take care of that." He tried for lightness, but missed.

"Tom!" Her voice threatened to break.

"Come on, love." He moved so they stood side by side. "You need to sit down."

A few yards along the riverbank he found an empty bench. The day was far too cold for any but the hardiest mortals, but neither he nor Angela noticed.

"Can you get any handle on the fear?" he asked after he tucked a wet and crumpled hanky back in his pocket.

She shook her head. "I wish the hell I could. Just now it came stronger than ever."

His arm tightened around her shoulders. He wanted to wipe away her nightmare and sweep her up in his arms and carry her away where no one would ever harm her again.

He remembered Justin's words the previous evening. "What can I do to help, Angela?"

That dried up her tears. "What do you mean?"

He laced his fingers with hers. It wasn't quite as reassuring as hauling her over his shoulder and taking her home, but under the circumstances it was probably more politic. "You're hell-bent and determined on digging to the bottom of your past, no matter what. So why not do it together?" As she stared at him with reddened eyes, he added, "Having a vampire alongside might help. We have a few handy tricks up our sleeves."

A weak little chuckle curved the corners of her mouth. "Why the sudden change of heart?"

"The realization you are going to do this and if I want to see you safe, I'd better tag along."

The smile widened. "You mean no more 'me big, strong vampire; you puny, little ghoul' act?"

"I can't promise never, but I'll do my darndest."

She nestled close, her shoulders relaxing as pent-up tension seeped away. "Oh Tom!" She kissed his cheek. "I've missed you."

"The feeling is mutual, my dear."

She seemed, for the moment, to have forgotten her mission. Might as well encourage that.

He tilted her chin up. Her lips parted. Her eyes widened with expectation. He had no intention of disappointing her. "Angela," he whispered and lowered his head. Their lips brushed. Twice. The third time, he pressed his lips against hers until she opened for him. She sighed and gave herself to him as his tongue met hers. Then she took him, her mouth working his, her tongue exploring, taking as much as he gave and returning the wild heat of her need. She pressed closer, molding herself against him. Her hips shifted as she nestled into the circle of his arms.

She said something. It could have been his name, an endearment, or the height of the trees around them. He didn't give a tinker's cuss. Nothing mattered but Angela's warmth in his arms and the passion in her lips. He tried to retake the lead, pressing harder and closing his hand over her breast. He felt pleasure ripple through her, as she pulled his head closer and deepened their kiss. Their need coalesced into a wild frenzy of mutual desire. Her legs parted, one thigh easing over his and . . .

Tom's vampire senses alerted to a mortal nearby. No point in shocking the populace!

"Angela," he whispered, "we'd better find somewhere less public."

A few yards away, a old woman was walking her spaniel along the river and from the opposite direction came a pair of young mothers complete with baby buggies and toddlers.

Angela turned as pink as a Bourbon rose. "Tom!" She stood up, smoothing her sweater down. "Let's walk a bit." She held out her hand.

He wasn't turning down the invitation.

"I missed you," Angela said after a few yards. "I'm glad you came down."

"That's a bit of a change from your greeting at breakfast time."

"At breakfast I was braced for your big, bossy vampire act."

Good thing he'd abandoned that angle. It hadn't worked anyway. "Was I really a big, bossy vampire when we were together in town?"

"What else do you call, 'Don't look at those books, they're mine!' 'Don't leave the house without me!' 'You don't need to do that, it's not safe.' 'Why do you want to ferret out all that stuff?'"

Had it really seemed that bad to her? "I wanted to keep you safe. We don't know anything about the vampire or vampires who made you and Jane."

"Ignorance isn't synonymous with safety." She had a point there. "I need to know who I am."

Fair enough but . . . "Aside from the renegade vamp, I have this hideous fear when you do uncover your identity, you'll discover you have a husband and five children somewhere."

She laughed and shook her head. "I can't speak to the husband, but I don't feel as if I've been married. And I can vouch for no offspring."

"How do you know?"

"Justin told me."

"How the hades did he know?" Justin's centuries of existence meant certain powers but . . .

"He gave me a complete physical. I've never given birth."

The full import of that hit him like a blow in the chest. "You mean you let Justin . . . !"

She tugged his hand. His fingers clenched hers. "Lighten up, Tom! Justin is a physician. Remember?"

He was doing his best, but it wasn't easy. No one was touching Angela but him. "Of course I do! I just don't see why you had to . . . Was it his idea?"

"Of course not!" Her glare suggested their newfound amity might be very short lived. "I asked him. I wanted to know as much about my ghoul's body as possible. I could hardly knock on the door of the local National Health doctor, now could I?" He conceded the point with a grudging nod. "Justin was the only choice, and as I happened to be under the same roof, I took advantage of it. I was relieved to find I hadn't abandoned a baby somewhere back during the lost time in my life."

They should have shared worries. "What else did he find out?"

"That I have blood pressure so low I'd be unconscious if I were mortal. That my digestive system and metabolism operate at five or six times mortal rate. I'm physically much stronger than most women, and my heart rate barely alters on a treadmill. Oh, and I have an extraordinarily high red blood cell count."

"That's it?"

"Pretty much. He's going to do some memory and IQ tests later on. He's got to borrow the protocols from a psychologist friend."

"Tell him not to bother. You're sharp enough to beat anything he can try."

She gave him an odd look. "You really mean that?"

"Love, you outwitted two vampires, three if you count Stella, but she abetted, didn't she?"

"After she tried like the dickens to talk me out of it." He owed Stella an apology.

"What have you discovered so far? You can read fortunes in cards, you might have someone who can tell you where the leather shop moved to, and you can terrify thugs."

"And Jane and I wandered for three days before Vlad rescued us."

"You're sure about that?"

"Yes. I don't know what help it is, but I'm sure."

"Right, then. Let's follow up that leather shop lead." If it turned out to be a dead end, so much the better. He could convince her to leave. Just knowing he was deep into the West Country gave him the willies. Who knew where a witch might lurk? Angela would no doubt smile if he spoke of his worries. She hadn't seen what witches did to Kit Marlowe and had no idea how risky it was just being here. But now he was here. And staying as long as she was. "Where's this shop then?"

"You really want to come with me?"

His hand closed over hers. "Why not? You never know when a vampire might come in handy."

Angela couldn't be more pleased if she tried.

Tom was seeing reason and agreeing to help. She kissed him. Hard. Darn the passersby. "Thanks, Tom." They were just a few yards from the small butcher's shop she'd found yesterday. "I'd better get something to eat. This is hungry work. I almost ate the carpet this morning."

"Having a party, then?" The aproned assistant asked as he rolled steaks, chops, and three chickens in layers of white paper. "You were in here yesterday, if I remember rightly."

She'd better find another shop or her level of consumption would soon get noticed. "Your meat was so good, I decided to come back and stock up."

Tom insisted on carrying the three packages. She let him. Might as well pick her battles. "Where next?" he asked as they stood on the narrow sidewalk.

"Mr. Lee's. The place Meg Merchant told me about. I found it yesterday but it was closed."

"Lead on." He grinned. "Might as well get this sorted out so we can go home."

He was a whole lot more optimistic than she was. But she kept that to herself. Tom was a welcome ally, and maybe today she would find a clue to whom she was. "Come on." They meshed fingers and crossed the street.

Tom paused only just long enough to shove a pack of chops in his raincoat pocket—who knew when she might need them to keep her strength up—and stash the rest of her raw meat in the trunk of his car and together they walked up Fore Street. Angela wanted to look for leather shops;

he'd humor her. He was convinced this quaint little town was a hotbed of witches, but surely for just one day, they'd remain unnoticed and stay out of trouble.

Chapter 6

Chicago. Two days earlier.

Vlad Tepes, one-time Lord of Wallachia, turned from the view down Chicago's Michigan Avenue and looked at his assistant. "You're seriously suggesting I see her?" The woman was an obvious nutter.

Zeke didn't believe so. "Yes, sir, I do. She's persistent and won't let it drop, but she isn't saying anything to the police. How can she? If she told them she thought her daughter was abducted by a vampire, they'd either lock her up, or brush it off as the ramblings of a mother demented by grief. But the fact remains, her daughter is missing, and the mother is right; there are traces of vampire spoor around the abandoned house—though how she knew it was vampire, Abel alone knows—and her daughter disappeared just days before you found your ghouls."

And they were still his ghouls, his responsibility, even after he'd passed them on. "Has she mentioned ghouls?"

"No, sir, just that she believes a vampire or vampires are responsible for her daughter's disappearance, and she calls on you as the local leader to intervene."

As leader of the colony, he perceived more than one problem here. "I'd like to know how she knew to contact us."

"She claims to be a witch."

Vlad turned back to the late afternoon traffic, not wanting his subordinate to glimpse the horror lingering in his eyes. New Worlders never understood these taboos. "A witch? Indeed."

"I did some research, sir. She is a well-known Wiccan. Lives out in Oak Grove. Runs an antique shop when she's not casting spells."

He turned back to smile. "You really want me to meet with a self-proclaimed witch? We have nothing to do with them."

"She's a woman who lost a daughter—literally—and you found two abandoned young women."

"And what if neither of them is her daughter?" A lot of trouble for nothing.

"What if one if them is?" Zeke was right, but he didn't comprehend the full dangers of such a meeting with a witch. Hell, *he* barely did, but he heard what they'd done to Marlowe. Vlad shook his head. In taking up Jane and Angela, he assumed the onus of them. "I'll meet her. In the place of my choosing."

"Where shall I tell her?"

He was tempted to direct her to Strigoica, his goth bar, and play up to her every misconception, but this was a bereaved mother. "She's to meet me at Joe's Java, tomorrow. At a quarter to midnight. I'll be waiting at one of the tables outside."

Zeke nodded. "I'll tell her." He seemed pleased that he'd convinced his leader to meet this pesky mortal.

"How do you contact her?"

"I'll call her. She gave me her number."

"How did she contact you?" He assumed Zeke wasn't listed in the yellow pages under Vampires and Revenants.

"It was weird. I saw her first on the El, just a couple of times. She's the sort of woman you notice. She was there on the platform where I was, or riding the same train. I thought nothing of it; after all, the same people ride the same trains every day. A week or so ago, she walked into the office and point blank demanded to see whoever was in charge of our 'nest.' Took me a minute to figure out what she meant. When I stalled, she looked me in the eye and said she knew I was a vampire and wasn't leaving until I told her where to find the nest leader.

"I tried denying it but didn't get anywhere. She's one persistent lady. She wasn't too pleased when I told her you were out of the country. She came in every day, asking when you were expected. Not belligerent. Not threatening. Just insistent. And since you're here for a few days . . ."

"I might as well take her off your hands." Vlad smiled. Should be easy enough. A little mind con-

trol and the woman would forget ever seeing him
or Zeke. Heck, he'd obliterate knowledge of vampires while he was at it, and he would do the job
properly, not like the butcher who mangled Jane
and Angela's brains. As for the possibility there
was any connection—unlikely in a city of well over
two million. Her recognizing Zeke as vampire was
a concern, but he'd alert a few colony members to
be within hailing distance of the coffee shop, just
in case. . . .

At eleven thirty, Vlad seated himself at a table in
front of Joe's Java. The night was bitter cold. No
wonder they called it the Windy City. Not that sub-
zero temperatures bothered him. He folded his
coat over the back of the chair. A silk turtleneck
and tropical wool pants were ostentatiously light-
weight given the frosty night, but why not proclaim
his nature? It might rein the woman in.

If not, Vlad Tepes was a match for any mortal
woman.

He leaned back, watched the empty street, and
waited.

The taxi arrived to the minute. Vlad made a
point of resting immobile as she stepped out and
looked his way. She was tall; wore a hooded camel
coat, boots, and leather gloves; and in spite of her
gloves, slipped her hands into her pockets as soon
as she paid the driver. Cold? Or seeking the reassurance of a weapon? This was America after all.
A handgun with silver bullets, perhaps? He permitted himself a chuckle.

Her boots tapped on the sidewalk as she approached, pausing a few feet away. "Are you the

one I came to meet?" Her breath clouded in the night air.

Vlad rose and inclined his head. "I believe so." For a second he was stunned by the fear emanating from her. She was terrified, but met his eyes with a steady gaze. "Good evening, Mrs. Whyte. I am Vlad Roman."

"Mr. Roman, I need to know where my daughter is."

"And I know her whereabouts?"

"You're a vampire, and to my understanding the leader of this nest. When my daughter disappeared, her house stank of vampire. Yes, I think you know what happened."

Fear, anxiety, and worry for her child came off her in waves. He understood the pain of losing a child, just as he perceived the challenge in every muscle of her body. A brave woman, ready to face her worst dread for her daughter's sake. "Perhaps I do." Her heart raced at his words, but a tightening of her mouth was the only outward sign of her turmoil. "You may discount my word, but I tell you no member of my colony has harmed your daughter."

"Someone did. And that someone was a vampire."

"You have a picture of your daughter, Mrs. Whyte?"

She reached into her shoulder bag and handed him a photo. "Have you seen her?" Her voice wavered on the question. Her heart pounded. Her anxious breaths echoed in the quiet night.

Short, dark hair ruffled in the wind as the young

woman laughed at the camera. A vastly different soul from the cringing ghoul. His anger at the unknown assailant peaked. He looked at the woman who stood feet apart, fists clenched and chin high. "What is your daughter's name?"

"Heather."

Like the sweet-smelling plants that covered the Yorkshire Moors in summer. A young woman with a mortal lifetime ahead of her. A life snuffed out by a monster. Vlad handed the photo back with a little bow. "Mrs. Whyte, it is too cold out here for a mortal. Let us go inside. I know where your daughter is."

"Just tell me!" He'd thought her pulse couldn't race faster. He'd erred. Her breath caught. Tiny beads of sweat sprang to her forehead and upper lip. She grabbed his arm, her grasp tight enough to bruise a mortal. "For pity's sake, tell me!"

"I will, madam, as much as I know. Rest assured, your daughter is safe. You have my word." Her heart slowed momentarily but sped up again. Seemed his word meant little to her. "She is safe from harm . . . now. Come in, let us sit in the warm, and I will tell you everything I know."

He pushed the issue by opening the door and motioning her to enter. Desperation for news beat out her mistrust. Inside was warm and almost empty. The table by the fireplace was free, as he'd requested. He earned a cautious glance over her shoulder as he offered her a chair. She watched him seat himself opposite. "All right! Tell me," she said.

Joe appeared at her elbow. She looked from him to Vlad and back again, clearly aware she was caught between two vampires. Incredible perception for a mortal.

"May I get you something, ma'am?" Joe asked.

She shook her head. Judging by her reddened cheeks and the way she still kept her coat buttoned up, she was chilled.

"If you trust me enough to come in here with me, can't you trust Joe to make a warm drink? The night is cold." She shrugged, unwilling it seemed to waste her concentration on warm drinks. "You permit?" At her nod, he looked at Joe. "Steamed milk, with honey and a measure of brandy." As Joe left, Vlad said to her. "It will warm you." And relax her, in the event he needed to probe her mind. "It's a long story."

"Then please get started. What do you know about Heather?"

He told her.

Her steamed milk came and cooled as she listened. She let him continue without interruption until he finished. "Why Ohio?" she asked at last.

"Young women need the company of other young women. My friend was able to give your daughter a job, and I thought it politic to put them somewhere distant while we hunted the attacker."

"I want to see her."

"Of course. I will take you, gladly. First I must call my friends and alert them. And lady, be aware that your daughter may not know you."

A spasm of pain crossed her face. "My mother

didn't know me before she died. She had Alz-heimer's. But Heather . . ." Tears gathered in her eyes. "How could anyone, even a vampire, do that?"

He chose to ignore the insult. "The one who did this does not deserve to be called vampire. He invaded my territory and committed an atrocity. When I find him, I will annihilate him."

She shivered at the menace in his words. "You police each other?"

"In my territory, I set the laws." He smiled. "But enough of that. Before we leave, I would ask a boon. You could, perhaps, help us find Heather's attacker by giving us access to her house."

"If it means getting the bastard who did this to my baby, with pleasure." She reached into her bag and handed him a set of keys.

He smiled. "I thank you, but we cannot enter without your invitation."

"So it's true?"

"That much is, but don't believe all the myths you hear about us."

"Mr. Roman, in exchange for giving me Heather's whereabouts, I'll invite you into her house and you can stay as long as you want!"

"Lady, I will not reveal my friends' addresses to anyone, without their permission, for their sake, and Heather's. The renegade who mind-raped her is still at large."

"And you think I'd lead him to her?" She looked ready to do injury at the suggestion.

"No, lady, but if he had a way of tracking or following you . . ."

"I'd know if he were. I'd recognize that vampire stench anywhere."

Insult aside, that skill could prove helpful. "Lady, would you take me to her house?"

"The police went over it and found nothing."

He smiled. "They missed the vampire scent, too, I imagine."

She acknowledged his point. "What will you do?"

"Bring several of my older vampires to see what they can find. And if you agree, we'll leave them searching while we set off for Ohio."

She agreed.

The damp in the house wasn't just the cold of a February night. It was the chill of terror. The fright and horror he'd sensed on the two ghouls had its origin in this tidy, desolate house. They entered the kitchen where the screams seemed to cling to the walls. Adela Whyte's face reflected the pain and agony. Remarkably sensitive for a mortal.

"I'm afraid the electricity is turned off," she began.

"We don't need lights or heat," Vlad assured her, as Dawntay and John wandered through the house and back out to the drive. John soon found a faint trail and set off running, only to return when the scent disappeared. "Must have left a car parked in the shopping center. No way I can follow after all this time."

Vlad nodded. He'd expected as much. What he hoped for was some clues as to what breed of revenant he was dealing with. He glanced toward Adela Whyte, intent on his two vampires as they climbed on cabinets and poked under carpet.

Interesting woman. He wondered how she'd get on with Dixie LePage.

Tom held open the door. Mr. Lee's little shop was reminiscent of the set for a TV period drama. Age-darkened shelves and drawers covered the walls, and the glass-topped counter on one side was filled with shoelaces, tins of dubbin, and boxes of buckles. The walls had yellowed to the color of very old paper, and the flagstones on the floor could have been there since Tom was a boy. Two ancient-looking industrial sewing machines sat behind the counter. Over one of them peered a wizened old man who looked as if he'd been there for a couple of centuries.

Rubbish! She was hanging around with vampires too much.

"Can I help you, my love?" He asked in a soft, Devon accent. The machine stopped its whirring, and a face as wrinkled as an old apple smiled at her. Ancient but not immortal.

Angela stepped up to the counter. "I hope so." She slipped off her coat. "Meg Merchant down at Crystals and Dreams sent me here. Someone bought this coat in Totnes, and I'm trying to find the shop it came from. The label says Mariposa, but it seems there's no such shop."

Mr. Lee walked around the counter and took the coat with work-roughened hands. "Nice bit of work this. Leather and tanning once made this town rich. Did you know that?"

Angela shook her head. "No."

"Leather and the wool trade built several fortunes back in the middle ages. We've had a few young people working the leather trade. No tanning." He smiled with twinkling dark eyes. "The town fathers wouldn't like that. Malodorous. But we've several weavers, and even a young man making handmade shoes. Now that's something I never thought I'd see again." Angela wished he'd cut short the reminiscences and answer her question, but she smiled as he went on. "Quality work this."

That she already figured out for herself.

"You recognize the workmanship?" Tom asked.

"Oh yes." Angela bit her lip and made herself wait for him to go on. "I would without the label. Good British leather, none of these far eastern imports, and a lot of hand finishing." He ran his gnarled hands over the surface of her coat. "Ah yes! You don't much see workmanship like this nowadays. Mariposa was one of the few places left doing work like this." With a nod and a smile, he handed Angela back the coat.

"You said Mariposa is a local firm?" Excitement and hope shimmered through her.

Mr. Lee shook his head. "*Was* a local firm, and an old one. They had financial problems but were bought by up by Americans about a year ago. Seemed to be picking up for a while but closed down right before Christmas."

Just her luck!

"Do you know anyone nearby who dealt with

them? Who might know how to contact them. Perhaps about leftover stock?" Tom asked.

"You might try Sara Clandon."

"Sara Clandon?" Angela asked. "Where does she live?"

"It's a ladies' store. Down on Fore Street just below East Gate."

East Gate turned out to be the clock that spanned the street, and Sara Clandon was an upscale dress shop. Angela half-wished she wore something more elegant than blue jeans.

"Mariposa?" the carefully coiffed assistant asked, repeating Tom's enquiry. "We used to carry most of their lines, but not anymore. They went into insolvency a couple of months back." She walked over to a rack of leather and suede garments. "We have other very nice lines. Perhaps there's something here." She perked up noticeably at the prospect of a possible sale. February was obviously not a time of brisk business.

Angela was getting heartily tired of dead ends. Time to break the news they weren't buying. "Thanks, but I wanted a Mariposa garment to go with my coat. If you can't tell us anything . . ." She turned toward the door.

"Darling," Tom said, stopping her, "since we seem to have missed the boat with Mariposa, how about we look at what they have?" Because things here were too darn expensive and she didn't have anywhere near enough money. And . . . "How about this waistcoat?" He held up a vest of butter-soft purple leather. It draped in his hands as if it were heavy silk or fine wool.

She was about to refuse when she caught his thoughts. *Try it on. It'll keep her talking.*

She tried on the purple vest and a soft suede one the color of old teak. She even obliged Tom by slipping into the fitting room with three skirts. While she fiddled with zips and buttons, Tom chatted up the assistant who seemed enthralled by him. Why not? He was a darn vampire, wasn't he? Beat her why he didn't just throw a glamour on the woman and be done with it.

By the sounds coming through the rose velvet curtains, they were both thoroughly enjoying themselves. She wouldn't be surprised to hear Tom inviting the woman over for a snack after dinner.

Was he trying to get her jealous?

"How are we doing in there?" the assistant called.

The patronizing "we" was the last straw. "Fine!" Angela pulled back the curtains and walked out—in leather skirt and vest and not much else. "I still haven't quite decided what I'd like." She walked over to the rack and looked through the hangers. Okay, Tom was only ferreting out information but he didn't have to be so darn charming about it. Angela jangled hangers back and forth, until she spied a pair of black, leather slacks.

"I think I'll try these." Smiling at Tom, just to make sure everyone remembered he was with her, Angela stepped back into the fitting room and swept the curtains closed. She could still hear Tom and the dratted assistant murmuring together. Damn!

The pants were absolutely beautiful, hung like heavy silk, smelled expensive, and fit like a second skin. She sat, twisted sideways, and bent over to touch her toes. The supple leather moved with her. She needed these pants. She fit in them. Or rather, they fit around her. She felt taller, more confident, sexy, and ready to out-vamp any woman alive. The last thought put a grin on her face.

She remembered just in time to pull her sweater on over her bra. "What do you think?" she asked as she swept the velvet curtain aside.

The assistant uttered a genteel "Delightful, madam! Not many ladies could carry those off."

Tom just gaped. When he finally got around to closing his mouth, he said, "We'll take them."

Now it was her turn to drop her jaw. "Tom . . ." Before she could protest, he had his plastic money out and the card was already in the assistant's hand.

"Keep them on."

It took a minute to realize he'd not spoken aloud. Time for a good, long talk about getting into her head, but . . . heck, she loved the pants, and one day soon, she'd have a job and could repay him.

Borrowed scissors snipped off the tags, and ten minutes later, her blue jeans folded in pale blue tissue inside a glossy shopping bag, they were back out on the street.

"I picked up some useful odds and ends from her," Tom said, "Let's stop here, have a cup of coffee, and mingle with the mortals, and I'll tell you what I found out."

"After I take you to Meg Merchant's."

"We could go back to the Royal Oak and sort out our room arrangements."

"What's to sort out? I already have a nice room."

Tom nodded. "Yes, I looked in the window last night. But it's not big enough for two. They have an unoccupied suite overlooking the river. Its mini-bar will be a lot better than the boot of the car for storing your meat."

"How did you see it? Climb up the walls?" Now he was edging back to proprietary and managing and . . .

"Of course, I wanted to be sure you were safe . . . and while I was looking around . . ."

"You played peeping Tom!"

He shrugged. "I ascertained it was a safe and satisfactory place for you to stay."

He did, did he? "And it passed your exacting standards?"

"It will do for a few days."

"Maybe I need to stay a couple of weeks—or months."

"I doubt that."

She took a slow breath and prayed for patience. "Fine! Just keep your doubts with you while I go and pay Meg Merchant what I owe her!" Since he went along with her, she relented a little. It never hurt to be gracious to a vampire. "Afterward we can go back to the hotel and sort out our sleeping arrangements."

He raised one dark eyebrow. "Who said anything about sleeping?"

She ignored that, turning at the corner and marching the few yards to Crystals and Dreams.

The overhead bell jangled as Angela opened the door. Meg looked up from her knitting and smiled.

"Hello, my love! Back again? Returning the cards, are you?"

"Far from it. They worked beautifully. I'm here to pay you."

The door closed behind Tom, and he stepped beside her.

Meg's smile faded. "Need something?"

"No, I'm here with Angela." Tom gave Meg his most charming smile.

It didn't work. Meg actually scowled at him. Maybe she didn't like men. Tom didn't seem any happier. A crease settled between his eyebrows as he looked around the shop.

"How much do I owe for the cards? And Meg, where I can buy a yard or so of silk, to wrap my cards and keep them from outside influences?"

Meg relaxed a little. She smiled at Angela as if trying to ignore Tom's presence. "Up the top of High Street on the left is a place called Fine Fabrics. You'll find good silk there. Or if you prefer, I have some scarves for sale."

Easier and simpler. Angela picked a deep purple one, handed her credit card to Meg, and waited while she rang them up. Tom stayed near the door, obviously ready to leave. Shame that. She'd wanted to browse, hoping something else might trigger memories, but with the tension between Tom and Meg, it would have to wait.

Meg glanced toward the door as she handed back Angela's credit card. "Is he your lover?"

Reticent obviously wasn't Meg's style. Angela stared for a full ten seconds. "What makes you say that?" She should have told her to mind her own business.

"Your aura. Yesterday it was black. I'd never seen one like it, but now you have scattered blazes of light. Without him you had virtually no light." A crazy old woman! It was utter nonsense but made perfect sense.

"Tom and I are close."

"That I can tell." Meg handed her the credit slip to sign and then slipped it, and the scarf, in a small bag. "What is he?" she asked under her breath, not even looking in Tom's direction.

"What do you mean?"

"What I said. What is he? He has no aura. Every living thing has an aura, even if it's dark like yours was. He has none. What is he? The walking dead?"

Chapter 7

Meg's whispered words reverberated in the overheated shop. Confusion rattled against shock as Angela struggled to respond. How? Ignore it as the imaginings of a crazy old woman? Laugh it off as a joke? Agree? Or ask what exactly she meant and feign ignorance of her meaning? She took the bag from Meg. "Thank you."

Meg shook her head. "Think I'm raving, don't you?"

"No." And that was as far as Angela wanted to go with this conversation. Her monosyllable earned an odd look from Meg. Angela resisted the temptation to glance across the shop at Tom.

"He is your lover," Meg insisted, "and you know what he is. I've heard about the power they wield with sex."

This was getting ridiculous!

"Got what you needed?" Tom had crept up behind her. What the heck? With his hearing, he hadn't missed a word anyway.

Sheer, unsullied fear crossed Meg's eyes and was fast replaced with a fierce glare and a set jaw. She muttered something under her breath. Angela couldn't catch the words; she didn't need to. The meaning was obvious.

"Save your curses for those who mean you ill," Tom said, his voice calm and untroubled. Meg's eyes flashed a cross between horror and confusion. His hand pressed Angela's elbow. "If you've found what you need, let's go," he said.

His tension showed in a steady thrum from his fingertips. What in the name of Hades, or the Abel Tom and the others invoked, was going on?

"Yes! Go!" Meg almost shouted, "and remember my warning," she added, looking right into Angela's eyes. "You have power. He will wrench it from you."

"You're wrong about him," Angela said as Tom propelled her toward the door. "I'll be back," she called as Tom opened the door, "later today or tomorrow. I need an athame for the full moon."

The look in Meg's eyes stayed with Angela long after the echoes of the door bell died in the cold air.

"What the hell was all that about?" she snapped, most unfairly. Meg deserved it every bit as much, but Tom had his hand still fused to her elbow and Meg was three shops away up the street.

He didn't stop for several yards, barreling down the hill and taking her with him. She'd had enough! She wrenched her arm free and stood her ground. Tom stopped four or five paces away and frowned back. She was darn tired of everyone glaring at her. What in the name of rain and wind had *she* done? "Tom, will you please tell me what's going on?"

"I might ask you the same."

"Ask me and you'll find out how little I know. I got the distinct impression you and Meg Merchant know a lot more than I do."

He shut his eyes, as if weary or exasperated. "This is getting involved."

So involved it appeared beyond her understanding. "How?"

"Why do you need an athame for the full moon?"

"I don't know. I just knew it. The full moon's in two days." Now it was her turn to feel the confusion closing in. "Beats me how I know, and why it's important. It was another flash of memory. I've given up expecting them to make sense." She was tired, and giddy, and weary, and it wasn't even lunchtime yet.

"You need sustenance." Tom pulled a packet of chops from his pocket. "Let's find a less public place."

They walked the few years down the hill to the castle and climbed up to the keep. It was deserted—small wonder given the cold—and they perched on a ruined wall. Angela devoured the first chop. The second one she chewed more slowly. Either way it was hardly an elegant meal, but given the way Tom fed, he could hardly turn up his nose.

"Feeling better?"

She nodded. "Yes." Tons better.

"What was this about reading cards, and how

did you find out?" He sounded worried. Not surprising after having her go giddy on him and being cursed by a crazy woman. Odd that! Meg seemed rational enough, apart from knowing Tom was a vampire and all her talk about auras.

"I wandered into Meg's shop yesterday, just by chance . . ." she broke off. "Talking about Meg, what was going on in there?"

"I was going to ask you the same thing, after you tell me about the cards."

"Why not now?"

"The cards came first."

Okay, she could be patient. "I went in to get out of the rain. The shop felt friendly, welcoming." Or had when Tom wasn't there. "Meg and I got talking. She made me a cup of tea, and I looked around and bought the cards. On the way back to the hotel I had the encounter with the thugs, ran most of the way back, and arrived ravenous. After I ate, I laid out a spread of cards, and I read my fortune, and yours." She waited for him to scoff. He didn't.

"But you just paid her for them."

"Yeah. That was her idea. She told me to take them, bring them back if I couldn't read them, and to pay her if I could. So I paid her, and bought the scarf. I need silk to wrap the cards in to retain their power—and as for the athame, I don't know where that came from. I don't know what to use it for, but I need one. I can go back on my own if Meg spooks you."

"She doesn't 'spook' me, as you call it!"

"You certainly spooked her!"

"A foolish, fanciful old woman."

"I don't believe so, and I don't think you do either."

He gave a dry chuckle. "Read my mind, can you?"

"Since you seem to be able to get into mine, why not?"

"I have powers you don't."

At least he stopped short of "me vampire—you ghoul." "Yes, and maybe I have powers you don't."

That got him thinking. And frowning. He stood up, ostensibly to throw the bloody butcher's paper in the trash, but just as likely to give himself time to think. Why had her comment hit him so? Did he really think she was inferior? Tom was in for a shock—once she discovered what her powers were.

He crumpled the paper until it was the size of a walnut—no mere mortal could compact it like that—and dropped it in the wire trashcan. He strode back to where she sat. "What powers do you think you possess?" he asked, standing less than a yard away and frowning down at her.

"So far, I can read fortunes in the cards and repel would-be attackers. Not bad for someone who doesn't even know her own name!" That last one was a bit self-pitying, but she was too darn mad to care.

He scowled even more at that. "Seems to me you know a lot more about yourself than you did a week ago in London."

What was that supposed to mean? "Good thing I left then, isn't it? Must be the fresh country air unfogging my memories." Either that or the rain washing them clear. She ran her hand over the soft leather that covered her thigh. She and Tom were spatting again. The man drove her bonkers! Charming and helpful one minute, snippy, picky, and irritating the next. And he was probably reading that in her mind this minute!

She sighed. "Why do we always rub each other the wrong way?"

He looked even more confused than she felt. "I think it's because we're attracted to each other but neither of us knows what to do about it. You've got your past you want to uncover, and I've got to come to terms with the fact you're rational and intelligent."

It took her several seconds to remember to close her sagging jaw. "You didn't expect me to be rational or intelligent?" He needed to revise his opinions about women, or she'd do it for him.

Shock crossed his dark eyes. "I expressed that badly."

"I'd go along with that." On the other hand, if he considered her irrational and unintelligent it might explain . . .

He sat down beside her on the broken wall, his hands clasped between his open legs. "What I meant was, I had this preconceived notion of ghouls— from vampire folklore if you like—and you don't fit the image."

"I see." At least she thought she did. "You believed we were mindless puppets, like automatons in a B movie." He nodded. "Who gave you that idea?"

"Justin, actually."

She couldn't help spluttering. "I must have a word with him next time I see him."

"I think he's probably revised his opinion the last week or so."

"Glad to hear it!" They sat in silence for several seconds. "What about you? Have you revised your opinions?"

"Not in the least."

She'd slap his smug jaw, but she'd break her hand. "Indeed?" A lot of effort went into one word.

"Indeed." Abel, help her! Tom was smirking. It was almost worth the risk to her metacarpals. His hand closed over hers as she started to make a fist. "When I first saw you, I thought you were the most beautiful woman I'd ever seen—and trust me, I've met a few over the centuries—and on the heels of that I decided you were the sexiest creature ever created. You bowled me over, dear. I've never managed to get over it. Not sure if I want to." His hand relaxed over hers but didn't move.

"So I'm a mindless sex goddess, eh?" She liked the idea of the last half of that.

"Mindless, no. As for the other bit, I'd never dream of arguing with a lady."

She let out a near snort. "My memories of our time in London were a bit different. And what have we done on and off since you walked in the hotel this morning?"

"I believe in the diplomatic world they call it 'lively exchange of views.'"

Tom could keep her smiling, if nothing else, but there was more, and she knew it. "I can handle being a sex goddess."

"A goddess in black leather." The look he gave was the next best thing to a leer. "How about we postpone the search for the source of your coat and repair to the Royal Oak to arrange a room for the two of us?"

"You're staying?"

"Try stopping me."

She looked down at his hand covering hers, at the twisted fingers that touched so gently. As his hand slid up her arm, she felt his touch, even through leather and a sweater. His hand reached the crook of her elbow. She shivered. "Cold?" he asked.

She shook her head, doubting she could ever be cold so close to him. He smiled, easing his hand up to her shoulder. His free arm snaked around her waist as he turned her to him. He moved slowly, as if savoring what awaited. Her lips parted in anticipation as he leaned toward her. They just brushed lips at first. Slowly. Testing. Neither of them pushing, content to taste the anticipation between them and the building passion on their lips.

She kissed back. Urging him to open his lips. To take her tongue. To possess her mouth. To absorb her need. With maddening slowness he eased their lips open. She took the advantage and invaded his mouth, pressing her tongue against his, feeling the passion stir between them as he responded to her touch. Now he kissed back, running his fingers through her hair. She was shivering with need and longing. She pressed closer, oblivious to the damp around them and the soft, falling rain. She slid her leg over his, feeling the rub of wool against leather, and male muscle underneath.

Her hand eased inside his jacket, touching satin

lining and lambswool sweater. She'd have delved farther but he shifted her sideways, pulling her against his shoulder. She looked up at dark eyes blazing with heat and need. Her heart snagged. "Yes," she whispered.

He held her steady as his lips traced a slow line from the curve of her jaw to the base of her neck. He hesitated over her pulse, licking her waiting skin. Once. Twice. The third time his mouth closed. She felt the lightest of nips, just before her mind soared and her body yielded. Blood and passion flowed freely. A wild pinpoint of ecstasy burst into a raging inferno. She wasn't seeing stars, she was among them. Flying to gather the light of the universe in her mind and carry it to Earth in her heart. Fire blazed in her body and a chorus of pleasure echoed in her brain as she lost herself in a vampire kiss, floating in a dark and blazing ardor. A whimper came from a distance as the soft touch of his tongue pressed against her pulse.

"Tom!" It was more gasp than speech, but it was the best she could manage.

His arms held her close as the ripples of joy slowly eased to a warm sense of glorious fulfillment. "Think you can walk?"

"Hell if I know!" She wasn't even sure what day of the week it was.

But she could stand, with his arm around her shoulders for support, and walked down the damp grass to the gate and the road beyond. Tom took her along a street of houses, up beyond an old building on the left and the church on their right, and through a narrow walk and down steps to emerge near the bottom of High Street. The Royal Oak was only yards away.

Columbus, Ohio. The same day.

"Marlowe? Hello! Vlad Tepes here." Kit Marlowe gritted his teeth. Vlad had proved himself a gentleman last November, but that didn't mean he had to like the vampire.

"Hello." Say little, commit to nothing, was a good approach when dealing with Dracula.

"I am calling to request a favor."

He should have guessed! "What do you think I can do for you, Vlad?" Dixie would say he was being snippy. Good thing she was out of the house.

"I'm not entirely certain. I'm on my way to Columbus. Should arrive in a couple of hours. I need to see you."

Very good thing Dixie wasn't here. She'd ask him to stay for tea, or a pint of A positive. "We can meet. You're staying at the Southern Hotel again?"

"We will be."

Kit caught the plural pronoun. "We?" Was he moving in with his colony?

"Yes. I need to explain. Briefly. It's . . . unusual."

"I see." A lie. He didn't, but not understanding Vlad Tepes was nothing new.

"I have a mortal with me—a woman."

Bringing a doxy along for the ride? How Gwyltha put up with it, he'd never understand. "Interesting."

A short dry laugh came down the phone. "Interesting indeed, Marlowe, but not in the direction you're thinking. This mortal is Jane's mother."

Talk about dropping bombs! Kit wished he had breath to catch. In the absence of respiration, he shook his head and arched his neck. "Is she genuine?" She had to be; he couldn't see Vlad Dracula driving six plus hours on a whim.

"I have every reason to believe so. Her name is Adela Whyte. Her twenty-five-year-old daughter disappeared three days before I found my two ghouls. I have been to the house. Even after all this time, the walls reek of horror, pain, and vampire."

"Not one of yours?"

"If he were, he would be extinguished. Permanently. No, this was a renegade, a possible threat to all of us."

Bad news. Very bad news. Just as the talk from last November had finally died down. Sewers and storm drains were more immediate neighborhood problems than fanged monsters. And a darn good thing too. "You think he's likely to come here?"

"Who can tell? It would seem he—or she—disappeared, but we both know how easily one can hide when one chooses."

"What if Jane isn't this woman's daughter? She can't be the only missing twenty-five year old."

"True, but time frame and the circumstances of the house aside, I have seen a photograph of her daughter. If I had any doubts, believe me, I would not have driven miles to bring her here."

Kit wanted to tell Vlad to call back. A chat with Dixie was needed. "What do you suggest, Vlad?"

"That we meet—you, Miss LePage, Mrs. Whyte, and me—to debate the best course."

"She'll want to see her daughter." What was to debate?

"Naturally, but we must prepare for any repercussions."

"I see." A lie. What repercussions? This woman was either Jane's mother or she wasn't. But they were exposing their natures to a mortal. Vlad's caution was well founded. "When do you want us to talk to her?" And sweep her mind if need be.

"I'll call when we arrive. Should be within a couple of hours."

"Anything else, Vlad?" He wanted to hang up and think this out, and talk it over with Dixie.

"Nothing that can't wait, Marlowe." He paused. "Other than to alert you that Mrs. Whyte is a professed and practicing Wiccan."

"That's all he told you?" Dixie tossed the empty blood bag in the trash compactor—a new purchase, perfect for destroying leftovers.

"More or less."

"And we don't tell Jane yet?"

"Not until we meet her putative mother."

Dixie frowned as she bit a corner off the second bag. He wished she could bring herself to feed with him, but that was as unlikely as the sun setting in the East. Just drinking blood had been hard enough for her. Twenty plus years as a vegetarian had left its mark.

The second empty bag landed in the compactor.

Dixie wiped her mouth, and smiled. "I should be happy for both Jane and her mother, but all I can think about is how this heaps problems on all of us."

Now he *was* concerned. Dixie seldom acknowledged difficulties or problems. If she was worried . . . "If push comes to shove, Vlad and I can exercise a little mind control."

"What for?"

"What for! She's a mortal who believes in our existence."

"She's a mother who lost her child. Honestly, Christopher! How could you even think that! If Jane really is her missing daughter, we have to bring them together. It's what will happen after that worries me."

"What do you think might happen?"

He'd been on the receiving end of that look before. "It's obvious." As a secret code. "I'm not sure which will be harder. Either Jane doesn't remember her from Lilith and the poor woman will be devastated, or Jane will know her and risk suffering a gigantic memory flash. What if she remembers every detail of her mind rape?" She shook her head. "This isn't going to be easy for anyone."

"If that happens, she has her mother and three vampires on her side. That counts for something."

"It counts for a hell of a lot, but it won't stop the hurt."

"Maybe we should wait until we meet the woman." A prospect he did not relish. "One more thing." Did he even want to say this aloud? "Seems Mrs. Whyte is a witch."

"She's what?" A purely rhetorical question. Dixie stood up, eyes blazing, and grabbed his arm, all ready to save him a second time. Abel, what it was to be loved!

"Vlad was quite clear on the point."

"He'd darn well better check her for Druid knives, and mistletoe, and I don't know what else before you get within a mile of her."

Kit pulled Dixie close, drawing her head against his chest. "Stop worrying, love. I'm at full strength now. She's the one to worry. Facing three vampires must be every witch's nightmare."

"She's a mother worried about her child. She'll face the devil if she has to."

This rapist vampire might be the next, worst thing.

Chapter 8

Totnes.

Tom believed in using his powers. Ten minutes after being told he couldn't check in until after three, they occupied a corner suite overlooking Fore Street and the River Dart.

"Suit you?" Tom asked as Angela looked around.

She grinned. "I believe so." It made her previous room look like a shoe box. "Only . . ."

"Only, what?"

"There seems to be only one bed."

He raised an eyebrow and looked over the carved, oak bed with a hand-crocheted spread. "So there is. Should I call for extra blankets, so you're not cold on the floor?"

"Clever clogs! Who says you won't be the one on the floor?"

"If you ask nicely, I might let you share the bed."

Another time she'd have laughed along with

him, but after two days of Devon drizzle and that odd interlude with Meg, Angela was in no laughing mood. "No problem. I still have my room." She took two steps toward the door.

She'd overlooked how fast vampires move.

And how impossible it was to budge one leaning against a door. She didn't even try. Just folded her arms on her chest and frowned.

Tom frowned back.

"Would you mind moving, so I can get out the door?"

"Yes!"

"You're going to stand there all day and block the door?"

He nodded. "All night, too, if need be."

"You're going to need to feed."

"Not before you."

Unfortunately, he was damn right there. Why was it always like this? Dixie and Kit got on fine, meshing their differences. Stella and Justin worked out their problems amicably. How come she got the awkward vampire in the bunch? "Are we going to stand here all day, scowling at each other?"

"I hope not."

Her mood wasn't helped by the utter certainty that if he chose, he could will her to do whatever he wanted.

To her utter surprise, he stepped aside, just as someone knocked on the door. "Who is it?" Tom asked.

"Porter, sir. With luggage from the other room."

Tom met her eyes and said nothing. It was up to

her. She'd missed him. She was glad he'd come. She wanted him so much it hurt. And he was driving her batty.

"Sir?" the voice repeated.

As Tom stepped aside, Angela grabbed the door-knob. "Come in, and thanks."

The porter set up a luggage rack and swung Stella's borrowed canvas bag beside Tom's leather case. Out of the corner of her eye, she saw Tom's hand go to his trouser pocket. "Just a minute," she said, reaching for her bag on the bed. She pulled out a £2 coin and gave it to the porter. "Thank you so much."

Angela shut the door behind his exhortations to call reception if there was anything they needed. Since peace of mind and restoration of lost memo-ries seemed a bit beyond the capabilities of a provincial hotel, she doubted she'd call.

Door closed, she turned to continue her face-off with Tom. He wasn't there. Water was running in the bathroom.

It would be so easy to grab her bag and go. She had money and credit cards, and a ten-minute walk to the station. But she wasn't going anywhere. Not until she found out something about this defunct Mariposa company, and spoke to Meg again, and sorted things out with Tom. Did she want to spend the night with him? Yes . . . No . . . Oh hell!

"What are you doing?" Stupid question if ever there was one. He was filling the tub, and must have used every complimentary bottle of bath oil. The room smelled like a summer garden in July.

"After that damp walk, how about a nice, warm bath? If I get your clothes off, I'll have a chance at seducing you."

"Tell it like it is, eh?"

"Thought you wouldn't welcome prevarication."

"Why does just about everything you say and do drive me crazy?"

"Haven't we had this conversation before?"

Yes, and got nowhere.

Tom bent to run his hand through the rising bubbles. Satisfied the temperature was to his liking, he started unbuttoning his shirt.

"Taking a lot for granted, aren't you?"

He gave a little shrug, the vampire equivalent of an exasperated sigh. "Maybe. Either way I need a wash after driving down. Would be nice if you'd join me."

"If you hadn't noticed, two minutes ago we were having an argument." She had a hard time keeping her eyes off his chest, and his one visible nipple.

"I had noticed, but making up with wild sex after an argument is a time-honored mortal tradition." His mouth turned up a little at the corners. "We could pretend we were mortals."

She stepped closer and pulled his shirt out from his pants. "Mortal? No way, José! Me ghoul, you vampire! Cut out this mortal crap!"

His eyes sparked as he looked down at her. "Praise be to Abel!"

His lips were soft against hers, but more than confident as they opened her mouth. A wild anticipation stirred deep in her belly. Her body throbbed with wanting as the tip of his cool tongue found hers. She let out a little sigh, wrapped her arms around his neck, and kissed him back. It was a delicious, no-holds-barred, take-no-prisoners embrace. Wild, joyous satisfaction coursed through Angela. In spite of all their differences and wrangling, they shared the same need, and the same fire blazed as they touched. She pressed her tongue into his mouth. His body pushed against hers. As he rocked his hips into her belly, there was no mistaking his interest. She smiled under his kiss and angled her hips even closer. He responded with a heat that matched hers.

She rocked against him, parting her legs. Fine wool brushed soft leather. She eased one hand from his neck and down his chest. His skin was smooth and cool under her heated fingers. She ran her hand over his chest, his nipple hardening under her touch.

Tilting her neck, she opened her mouth even wider, drawing in his tongue and glorying in the passion that stirred between them. Nothing mattered now but the wild joy they shared. Her hand eased across to his other nipple. Tom moaned as it hardened under her fingertips.

"Hold on, Angela," he whispered, pulling back but keeping one arm around her.

She frowned up at him. "Why?"

"Because the damn bath is about to overflow all over their premium broadloom."

He hooked his arm around her waist and pulled

her with him as he reached over and turned off the water. He was right. A thick crest of scented foam ballooned over the vast tub.

"Looks like something out of a Roman orgy scene."

He chuckled. "Wouldn't know. A bit before my time. Now if Justin were here . . ."

"I wouldn't be thinking about stripping him naked." She reached for his belt. "Come on, Tom. What are we waiting for?" He had her leather pants unzipped and halfway down her thighs before she'd even opened his belt buckle. "Unfair advantage!"

"Yes!"

Why complain? He knelt at her feet, running kisses from her knees up her thighs as he pulled her pants all the way down. She balanced herself by holding onto his shoulder. She lost her panties as she lifted each foot in turn to step out of her pants. Her shoes and socks shot across the room.

"How come I'm naked from the waist down and you're still dressed?"

He grinned up at her. "You must be slacking!"

Not any longer! She might not quite have his speed, but his shirt hit the floor within seconds. The rest of his clothes didn't take much longer. He pulled her sweater over her head and unsnapped her bra. She pushed the lace straps off her shoulders and let it fall.

"Are we going to stand here ogling each other? Or are we . . ."

She never finished—rather, she finished with a shocked gasp as he grabbed her by the waist and stepped into the tub. He held her above him, her breasts level with his mouth. He kissed and tugged at them with his lips until her nipples hardened and need throbbed between her legs.

As she threw back her head and let out a slow moan of appreciation, he lifted her higher and ran a line of kisses down to her navel. She glanced up and saw just how close the ceiling was. "Tom!" She looked down at him: his hair rumpled and his mouth headed for the soft skin of her belly. "Put me down! Unless an unconscious woman is part of your fantasy."

His eyes were dark with desire as he raised his head. And grinned. "Would keep you quiet, wouldn't it?" As he spoke, he lowered her, her warm skin sliding over his cool body. She didn't even try to hold back the shiver of excitement.

She was shin-deep in the water, toes reaching for the bottom, when he whispered, "Turn around." Holding her facing away, he sat, taking her with him. Settling her between his spread legs, he pulled her against his chest. Suds and warm water sloshed out of the tub.

She looked over her shoulder at him. "I think we're messing up their premium broadloom after all."

"And you really care right now?"

Not as much as a responsible guest should . . . not when his lips nuzzled the back of her neck and his hands cupped her breasts. The carpet could go hang while his fingers teased her nipples and his cool lips ran a trail of kisses from the base of her neck to her shoulders and down her arm.

As his hands slid down her belly, she leaned

back against his chest, flexing her shoulder blades against his hard muscle and rubbing her back against his soft chest hair.

His fingertips reached the top of her pubic hair. And stayed. Barely moving, except to ruffle her curls. But when Angela rocked her hips to bring his fingers in closer contact to her nub, he moved his fingers higher.

"What are you playing at?"

He chuckled in her ear. "Patience, my love. You're in too much of a hurry."

He reached for the scented soap, and rubbed the lavender foam over her skin before rinsing off with a soft washcloth.

It should have been relaxing.

She wasn't relaxed, and neither was Tom. "Are you sure you want to make this last?"

"You think I can't?"

Another time she'd have taken on the challenge. But not with his arm against her breasts. "I'm not sure *I* can. I don't have your vampire strength."

"Thank Abel! If you did, you'd be uncontrollable."

That earned him a jab in the ribs, and more water sloshed over the edge.

"You're dangerous in here," Tom said, cupping her elbow in his hand. "I'd better take you where I can keep you down."

Her snort became a yelp of shock as Tom stood and lifted her. He jumped out of the tub before she had a chance to think, and seconds later, holding her in one arm, he pulled back the bedclothes and deposited her on the sheets.

"I'm wet!"

Not for long. Somewhere between whisking her out of the tub and rolling her on the bed, Tom picked up a vast bath towel. It was warm from the heated rail and soft against her skin. He rubbed gently, kindling a fire within her as the towel brushed her. She was panting by the time Tom tossed the used towel aside. His skin might have been damp, or dry, or soaking wet—she was too caught up in her need to care. It wouldn't matter if Tom transmogrified, turned green, or self-combusted. She was self-combusting as tiny kisses rippled up the inside of her leg, his lips fluttered kisses over her belly and breasts, and he licked from her breasts to between her legs. His lips closed over her pleasure nub. She sighed, murmured, moaned, and finally shrieked aloud under the caress of his mouth.

As her first climax rippled through her, Tom moved. Lifting her hips, he angled her toward him, and entered. She gasped with joy as he filled her with his vampire power. Tirelessly, he drew her with him back to climax. Waves of sensation crashed through her consciousness, until all she knew was the press of his skin against hers, the wild rhythm of their lovemaking and the heat of the passion they shared.

She felt his mouth on her neck and sighed in anticipation. The nip was lost in the maelstrom of sensation bombarding her. They were together. He was in her head. She opened her mind to him, wanting to sense, feel, know every sensation between them. Wild fire surged through the brain. Need engulfed her. She was aware of cries and shouts around her, within her, and inside her. Of their own volition, her hips rocked harder and faster. She heard a male sound, a grunt, a cry, and a triumphant shout as they came together. An eruption of pristine joy carried her onto a surge of pleasure. She felt Tom's heat and power filling her until she was drowning in joy. She let out a long cry, a moan of perfect pleasure, and collapsed in his arms.

In the glorious aftermath of her climax, wild flashes of perception burst into her still-giddy consciousness, like trails of light following a rocket in the sky. For a few seconds, she was too sated with joy to grasp what she knew, but as her sex-fogged brain made sense of the incredible truth, she sat up.

"Tom?" Angela shook her head to clear the dizziness. "I need to go back to the shop." She tried to unjumble the new revelations from the immediate past. "To Meg Merchant's."

A furrow set between his eyes. "Right now?" His mouth curled a little at one corner as he trailed his hand down her arm.

"Soon."

"Better get your strength back first. I took a good bit of blood both times."

As if she'd not have noticed! "It's important!" She sat up and swung her legs over the side of the bed.

"Hold on!" He caught her upper arm just as she wobbled on her feet. "Sit back down. I'll get you some meat. After you recover, we'll talk."

Since her legs were unlikely to take her even as far as the minibar, she agreed. "How much did you take?" she asked as Tom handed her a steak. The scent of fresh meat was too much to even pretend to listen to his reply. She chomped down and bit off a mouthful, and another, ripping the steak with her teeth. As she swallowed the last fragments, Tom handed her a Kleenex. She wiped her mouth and, just to be sure, her chin as well, and crossed to the bathroom to wash her hands.

The carpet was soaking around the tub, and their clothes were scattered all over the place, but she wasn't about to complain. She'd missed Tom. Horribly. And if he would only be reasonable, she wanted him to stay close.

"Better?" he asked as she came back and sat down beside him. Both of them were still naked, and Tom was ready for a repeat performance.

She couldn't help grinning. She wrapped her arms around him, relishing his cool skin against her still-heated body. "I've missed you, Tom."

His arm curled around her shoulders and pulled her close. "You're incredible, Angela. I can't get enough of you. I went half-bonkers while you were up in Yorkshire."

"I thought it was my leaving Yorkshire that sent you half-bonkers?"

He grinned. "No, love, your leaving Yorkshire sent me full bonkers. I was terrified something would happen to you."

"Right! A lot can happen to a mindless ghoul wandering in the wilds of the West Country." She gave him a loving nudge with her elbow. "A marauding vampire might seduce me."

He nudged back. Harder. And somehow had her on her back on the bed, legs dangling. "Who seduced whom, may I ask? I believe you begged me for more at one point."

"Are you complaining?"

"Not as long as you do it again. Soon."

Looking up at the creases in the corners of his bright eyes, she reached and smoothed the wrinkles across his forehead. Tom looked so much older than the other vampires she knew, but the last months of his mortal life had been so harsh. She did love him, incredibly so. He talked about *her* driving *him* bonkers! Sometimes his attitudes made her want to yowl.

But after such splendid sex and such a wonderful memory flash was no time to dwell on that.

"I love you, Tom, truly I do." She eased herself up to sitting. "I've just remembered something wonderful, but first I have to go back and talk to Meg. She might be able to help."

"Love, why her? What can she do? A nutty old woman with all her talk of auras and Abel knows what else."

Angela sat bolt upright at that, grabbing his arm. "Tom, that's why she can help. She's not crazy, trust me. She'll know how to help."

He shook his head. "Angela. I'm not sure even seeing that old woman again is a good idea."

The man had no idea. "She's just the person I need. Let me explain."

He didn't. "Trust me, my love, after four hundred plus years, I have learned a few things, and honestly, you'd best avoid that Mrs. Merchant—I'm pretty certain she's a witch."

"Yes, Tom, that's why she can help me. I'm one, too!"

Tom's face gave full meaning to thunderstruck. "You can't be! You're not like them. It's not possible!"

"It's perfectly possible, Tom. I just remembered."

He stared at her for several long seconds. "You're not fooling, are you?"

"No." She sagged back against the head of the bed. Tom looked devastated. "What's wrong? Aren't you pleased I got a chunk of memory back?"

"And I thought Kit and Justin faced difficulties over the women they loved." He let out a tight laugh. "This tops any coil they had to unwind."

"What in the name of reason are you talking about?"

She had no idea. Was this just another gap in her memory, or was she truly unaware? "What am I talking about?" Tom sat up, distancing himself a little. "I'm talking about the ages-long enmity between vampires and witches."

Only a brilliant actress could fake her amazed gawp. She stared as if he had grown horns. Mind you, the old witch's reaction earlier this afternoon hadn't been much different. Angela finally took a deep breath. "What enmity?" As she spoke, she folded her arms on her chest, but as if suddenly realizing she was naked, she pulled the sheet up to cover her breasts, and scowled. "What are you talking about?"

This was not a conversation to have naked.

He crossed to the oak wardrobe, pulled out a cream-colored toweling dressing gown, and held it for her. "Put this on."

"Why?"

She would have to ask! "This will take a good bit of explaining. No point in you freezing to death."

She threw off the bedclothes and stood. His heart snagged as he looked at her glorious body. What malign fate wished this on them? He dropped a kiss on the nape of her neck as he put the robe over her shoulders.

"What's the matter?" she asked.

He dreaded having to tell her, but not to tell was unthinkable. Remembering the joy they'd just shared, and meeting her clear eyes as she tied the belt, he could not credit her with harm or mischief in any shape, form, or . . . He caught her hand. "Sit down with me, and I'll explain."

They sat side by side on the chintz-covered sofa. She didn't lean back on the heaped pillows, but turned and fixed him with a stare. Giving him the eye? Impossible! This was Angela, the woman he loved.

"Tom, spill it! You're getting me worried. Fifteen minutes ago we were making love, and now you look as if you're about to pronounce the death sentence. What's this ridiculous 'enmity' all about?"

He wanted to wrap his arms around her warm shoulders, but how could he do that and then tell her what he had to? "It's not ridiculous. It's long standing—goes back to way before my time."

"Your time?"

"The sixteenth century! Don't interrupt!" She leaned back, frowned, and pinched her lips together. He wanted to kiss them, but instead, "I've no idea how or when it started—Gwyltha or Justin might know—but we do not mix with witches, and they have nothing to do with us. That was part of my worry at your coming down here to Devon. We avoid this part of England; it's steeped with magic. At best we keep a very wary distance from witches. At worst, there is destruction."

"Planning on destroying me?"

"Of course not! We are not the side that destroys! You know our code!"

Her gray eyes all but sparked green. "You're suggesting witches do! 'Harm to none' is our maxim in all things!" She paused. "I just remembered that. Oh, Tom! What if it all comes back?"

It would add catastrophe to disaster—or would it? If she never did harm—and he had no trouble believing that—could there be others not bent on destruction? "Maybe it is coming back. Listen." He grasped her hand, needing to feel her skin against his. "One way or another we have a veritable pig's ear to sort out here. There has been ill will between vampires and witches for centuries. I won't question your ethics, Angela, but others don't follow the same standards. Kit . . ." He broke off for a few seconds, remembering. "Let us just say, there are witches who mean us ill."

"There are mortals who'd gladly stake you and stuff your mouth with garlic, come to that!"

"That's myth! I'm talking reality."

She bit her lip. "What you're saying is, there's some sort of vendetta between witches and vampires."

"Exactly!"

"That's ridiculous!" She looked across the bed.

"Did what we just do seem like two people in the middle of a vendetta?"

"Your memory was lacking."

"Yes, and some of it still is, but not my common sense!"

"You don't understand."

"I'll agree with that! How about you explain. Again. This time I might get it."

"Harm has been done to vampires that we will never forget."

"And no harm ever to witches? What about me? And Jane? We were made by a vampire! If what happened to us isn't harm, what is?"

"That was the work of a renegade vampire. Not one of ours, not even Vlad's sort, would have done that!"

"Perhaps those destruction-bent witches were renegade witches. Ever thought of that?" she paused. "What did they do?"

"Try to kill Kit."

"Kit?" Her eyes widened. "Why on earth would anyone want to hurt him?"

"We possess powers that many mortals envy."

"Someone tried to kill Kit because of his powers? What happened?"

"You must ask Dixie to tell you one day. Meanwhile, back to us."

"Okay. Seems easy enough."

"It does?"

"Of course." It was as clear as a nineteenth-century fog. "There's this ages-old feud between witches and vampires, right? We agree that the vast majority of us are ethical, moral, and peace loving. I'm a witch. You're a vampire. It's up to us to end the feud."

He should have expected something this outrageous. "You can't just end it!"

"Why not? Can't see how continuing it is doing anyone any good. Besides, just us being together puts a wrinkle in the old vendetta. Let's go ahead and rip it up."

She was so incredibly pleased with herself, it was impossible not to feel her confidence. But her faith was built on a true heart and ignorance. She hadn't seen what he had. Maybe that was an advantage. Maybe . . . He had to protect her. She was still as naive as a child, and as vulnerable. "I think we need to fill in a few more blanks about you first, Angela. Now we know you're a witch; it has to narrow the field. Now we're looking for a witch who disappeared in Chicago last September."

"Think I'll be listed as a witch in the missing persons?"

Sarcasm made her sound even sexier. Abel, it was a temptation . . . but . . . "Someone has to have missed you. We have to look some more." And he had to learn about witches. Unthinkable! But for Angela, he'd do it.

Angela flopped back on the bed, her eyes fixed on the ceiling. "We're back looking for two nameless persons no one seems to have missed. Sheesh! You'd think someone would have missed me, if it was only my credit card company when the check didn't come on time!"

He felt the pain under her lighthearted words. "Even if no one did miss you before, there are several who would now, and one who'd be broken-hearted."

That earned him a tired smile. Staying was a real temptation, but an odd sense of urgency nagged at him, and in over five centuries he'd learned to trust his instincts. Maybe this Mrs. Merchant could help. He was going to see her. Alone. But Angela was unlikely to agree to stay behind . . .

"Angela, love." He drew her close. "There's no vendetta between us. I love you."

She looked up at him, eyes bright, lips parted. "I love you too," she whispered.

Her lips opened under his. He ran his hand inside the toweling robe, cupped her soft breast, and felt her nipple harden under his fingertips. Heck, they were both ready and more than willing, but she needed rest, and he needed a chat with an old witch.

He skimmed the surface of Angela's mind, holding her close as she responded to his suggestions of sleep. She relaxed, going limp and heavy in his arms. He covered her with the bedclothes, fixed another mind message to sleep at least two hours, remembered just in time to get dressed himself, and slipped out the room and down the stairs.

The front hall was empty, even the receptionist had abandoned her post. Perfect. In seconds he was out the door and up Fore Street. He took the short-cut over the old town walls and past the church, and he made his way toward Meg's little shop.

Chapter 9

Columbus. The same day.

"Here goes," Kit Marlowe muttered as he punched the elevator button.

Dixie resisted pointing out that three vampires were a match for one witch any day of the week, plus this Mrs. Whyte was probably scared witless about the coming encounter. Christopher, quite understandably in light of his experiences last summer, held witches, Wiccans, and warlocks in distinct aversion.

As the doors opened, he stood aside for her. "Keep in mind, she's just a mother looking for a missing grown-up child," she suggested.

"I am. It doesn't work too well! I hope Vlad took seriously my stipulation and frisked her for Druid knives."

The unknown woman had her sympathies. Dixie wouldn't wish on anyone a pat down from Dracula.

"He's got too much sense of survival to take risks. He drove with her for close to seven hours. Plenty of time to suss out any concealed weapons, or nefarious plans." Dixie squeezed Kit's hand. "Don't worry. If she dares even look at you crooked, I'll up and at her!"

It was a weak chuckle and only a half smile but a distinct improvement over his scowl. The elevator stopped seconds later, and they stepped out into the hallway.

The first time she'd been in this hotel, a few months earlier, she met Jane and Angela. Now it was to meet Jane's maybe-mother, and a witch. Life was never dull in Ohio.

Christopher walked down the carpeted hallway and hesitated before Vlad's suite. Their presence was enough. The door opened, and Vlad Dracula ushered them in.

"My friends." He gave Dixie a little bow. "I thank you both. Miss LePage, may I present Mrs. Whyte."

Dixie looked at the tall woman across the room. Vlad had doubted she was Jane's mother! She was an older carbon copy. True, her hair was longer and sprinkled with gray, and her eyes darker blue, but she had the same set to her head and shoulders, even walked the same way as she crossed the room toward them.

"Hello," she said, hesitatingly holding out her hand. "I'm Adela Whyte."

"I'm Dixie LePage, and this is Christopher Marlowe. Most often known as Kit."

For a terrible three seconds, Dixie was afraid Christopher would refuse to take Adela's hand.

She should have known better than doubt him. It wasn't exactly a cordial handshake on either side. Adela appeared no happier about this than Christopher was, and Vlad looked positively anxious.

Heaven give her patience! Witches, covens, and traditions aside, couldn't they see this woman was not of the ilk of Sebastian Caughleigh? Apparently not. Drat it! She had not taken time off to stand here all afternoon while the three of them eye-balled each other. "Adela, what makes you think we have your daughter?"

It broke the ice, even if it did cause Vlad to gape and Christopher to mutter "Dixie!" but she got Adela's full attention.

"Heather disappeared in September. Gone. Just like that. Not a trace. The police tried to find her, but she never turned up. No clues. No body. Nothing. A week later they found her car, stripped of every-thing. The only lead the police had was a postcard from her sister in England that arrived two days after she disappeared, saying she was coming to visit— that was a dead end—and unauthorized charges on Heather's credit card. Until I'd got around to stopping it, someone charged things all over the city." Eyes bright with tears, she looked at Dixie. "Mr. Roman believes Heather might be here."

"What led you to Vlad—Mr. Roman?" Christopher asked.

Dixie would like to know that. Was Vlad adver-tising his vampire condition?

Adela took a deep breath. "After the police let me back into Heather's house, I scoured it, trying to find a letter, a phone message, anything. I kept thinking they had missed something. All I found was a hideous smell—I thought it was chemicals the police had used—and an overwhelming sensation of fear and terror. I didn't mention that to the police; it was hardly the sort of thing they could analyze in a lab, but I did call in help—a psychic witch. Bella spent several hours in the house and told me the place reeked of a predatory vampire."

Adela paused, but after obvious effort to keep herself together, she went on. "We've known for years there were vampires in Illinois. We've deliberately avoided them and presumed they did the same. We've had no incidents, no murders, no savagery. No contact, thank the Goddess! But I couldn't disbelieve Bella. I kept asking, why now? And why my Heather? Was it because of her connection with me? But that made no sense. She wasn't one of us. She scoffed at my faith. But she was still my daughter, a beautiful, honorable young woman, a schoolteacher, for goodness sake, and one of you . . ." she scowled, her eyes the nearest mortal thing to blazing, ". . . destroyed her!"

"Madam." Christopher's measured, Brit tones broke the silence following Adela's impassioned outburst. "One of *us* . . . ," he put definite emphasis on the *us,* "did not commit this heinous act. If you wish our help, you must accept that."

Dixie could have kicked him. The poor woman was all to pieces, obviously as scared as a rabbit in a fox's den, and he was giving her an ultimatum. "Christopher . . ." she began.

Vlad raised his hand. "Forgive my interrupting, my dear Miss LePage, but my friend Marlowe made a very good point." He turned to Adela. "You begged for my help; I offered it. My friends have now made themselves vulnerable. Is it unreasonable to ask your word that you do not seek revenge, that you mean us no harm?"

A tight hysterical laugh greeted Vlad's request. "Me do you harm! There are three of you for a start, and what harm could I do to one of you?"

Christopher went very still. "It has been tried, madam. It has been tried."

"Not by me, or any witch I know! 'Harm to none' is our dictum!"

Christopher looked ready to snarl. Vlad was glancing from him to Adela with something approaching nervousness.

Time for a modicum of commonsense. "Look! Adela, Christopher, can't we all accept the premise that whatever happened in past places and times, right here and now, none of us means any harm to anyone, and we'd all be far better employed seeing if Jane really is Adela's daughter than feuding over past horrors?" She was tempted to tell them all to sit down and put their fingers on their lips, but maybe that was a trifle too school librarianish when dealing with two master vampires and a witch.

Christopher gave her an apologetic smile and even managed a polite nod to Adela. "I can accept that, for the present."

"So will I. I want my daughter. I'm not here for revenge."

That should, at least, get them through the afternoon. "Do you have any pictures of your daughter?" Dixie asked. She didn't really see the need. By looks alone, Adela was obviously Jane's mother, but just getting everyone to sit down and look at a couple of photos might diffuse the rippling tension.

"I have several. One that I showed Mr. Roman earlier, and I brought Heather's own photo album. If she has no memory of who she is, I thought pictures might help."

Dixie only looked at the photo Adela produced for appearance's sake. Christopher's face, as she handed the photo to him, was worth the walk downtown.

"By Abel!" He stared at the picture before asking Adela. "You give us your word this is your daughter?"

"I do. You have Heather?"

"We don't exactly 'have' her," Christopher replied. "She works for us. Helps Dixie out in the shop."

"She has a job?" Adela seemed to be questioning her own perceptions as much as Christopher's word.

"Yes. We have a shop in German Village, the Vampire Emporium. She works there."

Adele looked from him to Vlad in obvious confusion. "I understood from Mr. Roman she was severely brain damaged from the attack."

"She was," Dixie replied. "When Vlad found them, they didn't even know their own names. Their memories were blank, yes, but it was as if someone erased the tape but left the recorder running. They both learned. Fast. Jane—sorry, Heather—is a great employee."

"I want to see her." She wasn't asking. Her voice

and attitude clearly announced she'd take out both Vlad and Christopher if they tried to stop her.

"Of course you do." Christopher handed her back the photo. "The question is, should we announce you or not?"

Adela frowned. "You mean warn her I'm coming?"

"Something along those lines. Your just walking up might be a bit of a shock."

"You think a shock would be harmful?"

He shrugged. "Truly, I have no idea. My experience with ghouls is limited."

"I thought vampires were experts in these matters!"

"Other vampires." Vlad said quietly. "As I explained earlier, madam, we do not make ghouls. In all my vampire years, I have known three. Your daughter and Angela are two of those three."

Dixie couldn't help wondering about number three, but it could wait. "Christopher and I have known two. So you see, we're all pretty clueless when it comes to background knowledge. I suggest you walk into the shop, say 'hello,' ask her if she remembers you, and play it by ear from there."

"I'm not sure that's a good idea," Christopher said. "What if it sends her into shock?"

"Why should it? She's had snatches of memory return without going into shock, and this is her mother, after all."

"Maybe some preparation would be advisable. Madam, bear in mind, your daughter is not as you remember her," Vlad said.

"You told me that so many times; I had night-mares she was a vegetable, and now I find her earning her own living."

"She's a long way from vegetable," Dixie said. "Even in her worst state, she and Angela weren't that, but she needs support still. She can handle working in the shop; it's not too busy at the best of times. But you mentioned she was a teacher, and she's nowhere near able to stand up in front of a class . . . not yet."

"That's irrelevant! I want to see Heather. If it sends her into shock, I'll handle it."

Both Vlad and Christopher had the good sense not to argue.

Adela went into the adjoining room to fetch her coat. As they stood, Christopher knocked the photo album on the floor. He bent down to retrieve it, and he stared at the open page. "By Abel! Dixie! Look at this!"

Two little girls in shorts and sweatshirts stood barefoot on a beach. Arms around each other, they grinned at the camera. One was a a dark-haired little pixie, a much younger Jane. The other had wind-blown, long blond hair. Her face was shaded with a pink sun visor, but it looked like . . . "Angela!"

"Yes," Christopher said. "She must know her."

"Know who?" Adela said from the open door-way.

"Who's this?" Dixie asked. "The book dropped and fell open at this page. Who is she?"

"You expect me to identify her to you?"

"Hardly an unreasonable request," Vlad pointed out.

Everyone was too damn prickly! "It might be important for Heather," Dixie said.

Adela relaxed a tad. "That's my stepdaughter, Elizabeth Connor. Interesting you should pick her." Adela gave a wry smile. "She grew up to be a very powerful witch."

That left Christopher and Vlad speechless for a few seconds.

Dixie asked, "Were she and Heather close?"

Adela frowned. "Is this important?"

"I'm pretty sure it is. Very important. Were they close, and do you have a more recent picture of her?"

"Yes to both, if it's the least relevant."

"Please show us."

There was no doubt. The two young women seated at a sidewalk cafe were Jane and Angela—or rather Heather and Elizabeth.

"Okay!" Adela said as she took back the album and snapped it shut. "Now can I see my daughter?"

"There's something you have to know first."

"What?"

Dixie told her.

Give Adela credit, she went pale as the cream-colored sofa and sat down rather heavily halfway through the telling. But she listened, her eyes widening with horror as Dixie told what they knew.

"Lizzie, too," Adela whispered as Dixie finished.

"Yes," Christopher said. "She's safe now with friends of ours."

"Vampire friends?" She raised her eyebrows, but the earlier antipathy was missing.

"Yes," Christopher replied. "Old and trusted

friends. She's staying with a friend since my mortal youth: Tom Kyd."

Adela stared for several seconds, her eyes wide. "Heavens! I get it. Christopher Marlowe, Tom Kyd." She turned to Dixie. "I suppose you're Aphra Behn."

"No one so illustrious, I'm afraid. I was a librarian, but Christopher and Tom are who you think they are." Thank Abel, she hadn't asked who Vlad was. Elizabethan playwrights were one thing, medieval warlords another. "Ang . . . I mean Elizabeth, is safe. Did she and Heather live together?"

Adela shook her head. "We might as well all sit down. This will take as long as your story. I was married for four years to Lizzie's father. A big mistake, but we won't go there. Lizzie and Heather got very close. Both only children. About the same age. It was natural enough. In fact, it was Lizzie who kept me married to Piet Connor as long as I was. I hated leaving and splitting up her and Heather. But in the end I had no choice." She sighed. "To cut a long and agonizing story short, Piet and I divorced but Heather and Lizzie stayed close. In the last few years, jobs took them apart but we all stayed in contact, and I helped Lizzie develop her gifts. Sometime last summer, Lizzie went to work for her father, in England. She spent Oak Festival with me and left a few days later.

"Some of it makes sense now, but not all. After Heather disappeared, and the postcard from Lizzie turned up, the police asked who she was. I told them and called Piet. He was, for him, surprisingly sympathetic about Heather but said Lizzie was in England, had changed her plans the last minute, and wasn't coming over. But if Lizzie did come back, perhaps stopped to see Heather on her way to her father's, and was with Heather when they were attacked . . ."

"It seems an incredible coincidence," Dixie said—more than that seemed wrong somehow—but . . . "Where is Lizzie's home?"

"Oregon. Her father owns a chunk of land on the coast. It's where Lizzie and Heather lived as girls."

"Chicago would make a reasonable stop on the way," Christopher said.

"This young woman's father has not missed her?" Vlad sounded skeptical. Dixie didn't blame him.

"He said Lizzie was staying on and seeing Europe on the money she'd earned. I was disappointed she hadn't called or sent a postcard or e-mail—unlike her. But I was too occupied worrying about Heather to think much about Lizzie. He needs to know what happened. He's no candidate for father of the year, but . . ." She looked up at all three of them. "You're certain this Angela is Lizzie?"

"Yes," Vlad replied.

"And she's in London, with Tom Kyd?"

"No," Dixie said. "She's with Stella and Justin. I spoke to Angela a couple of days ago. Justin is a physician," she explained to Adela—no need to say exactly how long he'd practiced. "He has a clinic in Yorkshire. Angela worked for Stella for a short while, here in Columbus, babysitting their son. She went up to Havering to visit." No point in complicating this as to why Lizzie/Angela had walked out on Tom. This woman had quite enough to worry about without learning her Wiccan protégée had just had a lover's tiff with her vampire boyfriend.

"I need to call Piet and tell him: Later. Right now I want to see Heather."

"If I may, I will drive you there," Vlad said.

They all took him up on the offer.

Jane Johnson dusted off the near-spotless counter and tidied the bargain books on the table by the door. They often had a few browsers come in from downtown during their lunch hours, and it paid to be ready. The morning had been quiet. Few people wanted vampire paraphernalia or books in February. They'd been busy on Saturday, when they hosted a signing for a local vampire romance author, but since then it had been quiet as a tomb.

She chuckled to herself. Not a thought to share with Kit, he tended to tetchiness over some things.

Wandering over to the door, she straightened the OPEN sign and looked down Fifth Street. From her vantage at the corner, she watched two youths stroll down the street. At the intersection with Jackson, they paused, glanced at the houses on either side, and turned left.

Not that surprising, but when they walked past her window a couple of minutes later, she wondered if they were looking for somewhere. The maze of streets in German Village could be confusing. She stuck her head out the door to call to them, but they were nowhere in sight. Funny, they'd been strolling, almost ambling, before. They must have decided to hoof it up to Livingston. She shut the door and was back behind the counter when she heard a thud. Then a barrage of knocks, as if someone was trying to kick down a door.

Next door! It came from Marie's Massage Zone. In seconds, Jane was out her door and into Marie's waiting room. The door to the work area hung askew. Jane opened her mouth to call to Marie, but a sense of danger left her silent. She took a cautious step forward and heard sounds of drawers and papers being tossed about and a muttered "The bitch must have money somewhere!"

She took a silent step toward the shattered door. Marie was lying face down in a crumpled heap.

How dare they attack Marie, her friend, who'd shoveled snow off the sidewalk with her just the other week and made them both cocoa to warm themselves up. Just a half hour ago, she'd popped her head around the Emporium's door and suggested they meet early one morning for breakfast, and now she lay, inert, on the floor.

Without stopping to consider the danger, Jane ran past Marie and into the small office beyond.

The two youths she'd noticed were ransacking the place. Marie's beautiful temple wall hanging was ripped off the wall, her delicate mother of pearl screen was thrown aside, and laundered sheets and towels were tossed in all directions. Even the glass vase with a single orchid lay in a damp patch on the carpet.

"How dare you!" Her yell reverberated inside her skull, and the two punks turned.

"Well, shit. A visitor," one sneered. He turned to his cohort. "Think this bitch has money?"

"Let's ask . . . nicely," he replied, and pulled a gun out of his jacket.

Her brain froze as a wild fury rose from deep within her gut. "No!" she yelled, and leaped forward, knocking the gun out of his hand.

His jaw dropped. His eyes popped. "Shit! Shit! Shit!" he screamed as he backed away and tumbled onto the heap of linen.

"What the hell?" the second one asked. Jane swiveled around to face him, anger engulfing reason. How dare they! How could they! "You hurt my friend! You came in here to steal! I'm stopping you!"

"No!" he whimpered, his face going ashen.

He turned to run.

She beat him to the door, grabbed him by the collar, and dragged him back, dropping him on top of his pal. "You're not going anywhere!"

"Don't hurt me!" he whimpered. "Didn't mean no harm . . . just joshing!"

"Yeah! Right!" It came out with a snarl. He screamed and started crawling away toward the back of the room.

Why not? The door to the small bathroom was open. "Move it!" To encourage him, she nudged with her foot. He scuttled like a crab, and when he was halfway in the room, she grabbed the second one and dumped him in there too. She gave the tangle of legs an extra shove and slammed the door on them. Still wild with fury, she pulled the metal filing cabinet over to block the door. They were darn well not going anywhere anytime soon.

Then she ran back to Marie.

As Jane reached out to feel for Marie's pulse, she noticed her own hand was covered with rough, gray skin. Both of them were. What on earth? Her arms too. As she watched, her skin faded back to normal.

Had she looked like that all over? Was that what had scared the two thugs? No time to worry about that now! Marie had a pulse, but her breathing was shallow. Jane grabbed the phone and punched 911.

It was hard to hear the dispatcher, with outrage still buzzing in her ears. "On the corner of Fifth and Jackson," Jane managed. "There's been a robbery . . . or at least they tried to rob. and Marie's hurt . . . she's unconscious. You'll need an ambulance too. Please hurry."

"They're on the way, ma'am."

"How long will they take?"

"Not long, ma'am. How many assailants did you see?"

"Two."

"Is it possible they're still in the vicinity?"

"Yes. They're in the bathroom."

There was a pause. "You said in the bathroom, ma'am?"

"Yes, I was so angry when I saw what they'd done to Marie, I lost it and shoved them in the bathroom."

"Juveniles were they, ma'am?"

"Oh no. Twenties I imagine. Didn't really look that closely, and it all happened so quickly."

"Not armed, ma'am?"

"Not anymore. At least I hope not . . . one did have a gun."

"Where is it now?"

"On the floor." She could see it: hard gray metal lying among the shards of a glass dragonfly.

"Don't touch it."

She had to be kidding! Jane could smell the cold metal. It radiated malevolence. "When's the rescue squad coming?" The thugs in the toilet could wait, but Marie . . .

"Soon, ma'am. They're bringing backup."

As if on cue, a siren sounded outside, getting louder until flashing red lights lit the ceiling overhead and cast bloody strobe-like shadows on the floor and Marie's still-inert body.

The police were here! Jane ran out through the waiting room, headed for the front door, and stopped just in time to avoid colliding with the officer who stood on the sidewalk, gun drawn.

Chapter 10

"You okay, ma'am?" the officer asked. She was about Jane's height and had *Petit* inscribed on the silver nameplate on her white shirt.

Jane looked into concerned brown eyes. "I'm fine, but Marie's hurt!" Two police cars blocked the intersection. A third pulled up, and two more offices got out. There were now five of them, watching her. "You've got to help Marie! They hit her on the head."

"Yes, ma'am, the rescue squad's on its way," a tall, male officer said. "Was it you called 911?"

Jane nodded. "They were trying to steal from Marie, and I didn't want them to get away." Her head spun and the brick sidewalk shifted under her feet.

Officer Petit steadied her with warm hands. "I think you need the medics too."

Jane shook her head. It hurt to think, but she

knew there was a good reason not to let a doctor check her. "I'm fine."

"The suspects are still in there?" another officer asked.

"Yes. In the bathroom." That sounded ludicrous. "There was nowhere else to put them." Even worse. "Please get them. I'm scared they'll get out and hurt Marie."

"Sure you're okay?" Officer Petit asked. Her alert, dark eyes watched with an alarming intensity.

"Dead certain!" Jane stifled a giggle.

"Please step back, ma'am, behind the cars," Officer Petit said. Odd name—she wasn't French or small, not really, she was . . . Jane shook her head. She was beginning to ramble and needed to stay alert. She was bone-weary, was lightheaded, and kept wanting to look back at her hands.

"Want to sit down?" Officer Petit asked.

"No. I'll be fine." She'd will it so. Holding onto the hood of a parked car for support, Jane got behind the nearest police car.

Resting her arms and chin on the roof, she watched as two went around the alley, and two entered the Massage Zone. Petit covered the front door until an officer stuck his head out and called, "We need you inside to cover us, Petit. It's going to take two of us to move this filing cabinet."

Minutes later, they emerged, half-dragging two sniveling robbers. Talk about changed attitude! The taller one, who'd called her "bitch" was begging them to keep the "monster" off him. The other was mute, aside from the occasional whimper.

"Must be high on something," Petit said, as they tucked one each into the back of the two nearest cars. "Talking trash and muttering about monsters and devils!"

At that point the rescue squad arrived—more uniformed people asking Jane if she was okay. "It's Marie who was hurt! Not me!" It came out as a shriek, but she was too exhausted to care. They carried Marie out on a stretcher minutes later. "She's coming around," one of them said to Jane. "We'll just check her out." Marie was pale, and she mumbled a little as they carried her past Jane.

"We're going to need a statement," the taller officer, Jones, said.

"Better call robbery," one labeled Muller said. "They might want to see this, since we've got everything, weapon and all, intact." He looked at Jane. "Beats me how you moved that filing cabinet on your own."

Jane gazed at the maze of vehicles parked at all angles, the uniforms, and solicitous faces. "I don't remember moving it." But she clearly remembered looking down at leathery, gray hands.

"You sure there wasn't someone with you?" Petit asked.

Jane sighed. She felt as weary as if she'd run to Cleveland and back. "No. I work next door." She nodded toward the Vampire Emporium. "The shop was empty. That's how I heard the noises through the wall, and went to check on things."

"I see, ma'am."

She got the distinct impression they didn't believe

her—and didn't give a damn. Her head throbbed,
her body ached, and if she didn't have five minutes quiet, she might just burst into tears.

She crossed the road to the open ambulance.
Marie was strapped to a gurney but conscious and
complaining. "I don't need to go to the hospital! I
need to check on my business. Someone needs to
lock it up." She caught sight of Jane. "Jane, will you?
My keys are in my purse in the bottom drawer!"

Easier said than done. In the twenty seconds
she'd been talking to Marie, they'd wrapped the
front of the Massage Zone with orange tape. They
wouldn't let her into a secured crime scene but
agreed to fetch Marie's purse. After several minutes,
Officer Muller emerged, carrying Marie's purple
bag.

"Thanks!" Jane smiled and was rewarded with a
broad grin.

"Anything for a lady who can disarm punks."

Drat! Kit and Dixie advocated staying unobtru-
sive the way preachers urged temperance, but how
could she have stood by and done nothing? Too
late now. She crossed the road back to the ambulance.

"I assume this sort of obstruction is not custom-
ary," Vlad said as they slowed almost to a standstill.

They'd turned off Livingston onto Fifth. Just
ahead, a van was trying to back up. The next block
was crammed with an ambulance, cop cars, and
police officers, all illuminated by flashing lights.

"What on earth can it be?" Dixie asked. "An accident?"

As the van turned left down Blenkner, their view cleared. A police car blocked the road and two other were parked askew. The back doors of the ambulance stood open and arguing with one of the medics, and a police officer was . . .

"Jane!" Kit said.

"Heather!" Adela was out the door and racing down the brick street. Vaguely aware of the three vampires behind her, she stopped a few feet from the crowded scene. "Heather?" she repeated.

Jane turned. She was pale, but her eyes were the same clear blue they'd always been.

"Heather?" Adela took a deep breath. "Do you remember me?"

Adela barely breathed as her daughter handed a small purple purse to the figure on the gurney and took a step toward her.

Heather paused, frowning as if trying to understand, until recognition lit her eyes. "Mom!" She ran the last few paces and, as Adela caught her, collapsed in her arms.

"Jane." Kit put his arm on her shoulder. "Don't permit yourself to faint."

Adela frowned at him. "She's ready to drop!" Did he think Heather could control collapsing? And he'd better start getting her name right.

"You can't have the EMTs trying to take your blood pressure," he said. "Jane, hang on a few minutes. We'll get you out of here."

"She's called Heather."

"Don't confuse her," Kit replied. "She's had more than enough already."

"And you told me she was fine!"

"She was this morning," Dixie said. "Whatever happened here upset her."

"Excuse me, sir and ma'am." A police officer walked over while Adela and Kit argued. "This is a crime scene. You have to move your car."

"Crime scene" set Adela's mother antenna oscillating. "What is going on?"

"Nothing to worry about," Officer Muller replied.

"There most certainly is! And you'd better tell me! Whatever happened has upset my daughter! What is going on here?"

Kit stepped forward, as if prepared to put himself between her and the officer. Had she really been threatening an officer of the law? Between a vampire, a long drive, more vampires, and finding Heather in the middle of a crime scene, it was entirely possible. She'd needed a cycle of serenity and calming spells to settle this turmoil.

"We'll certainly move on, officer," Kit said, "and take Jane with us."

"Sorry, sir, but Miss Johnson needs to stay. We have to get her statement."

"Why do you need her statement?" Adela said. She was snapping, but . . .

"She's our witness, ma'am."

"Mom," Heather said, "it's okay."

It wasn't. Heather was shaking, and her skin was the color of dirty parchment.

"Officer," Dixie began. "Jane's ready to drop. If you don't need her this instant, how about we go wait in the Vampire Emporium? I'm the owner, Jane works for me."

Officer Muller hesitated. He was very young. Uncertain. "We can't do that, ma'am, we need . . ."

Kit stepped up. "Officer." The man looked him in the eye. "There's no need for Jane to stay out here. You can fetch her from the Vampire Emporium when you need her."

The man blinked and looked from Kit to Heather. "No need for you to hang around here, ma'am. We'll come and find·you in the Vampire Emporium when we need you."

Adela didn't have a chance to think about the impossibility she'd just witnessed. "Come on, Adela," Dixie said, "let's go." Dixie took one arm, Adela the other, and propelled Heather across the street.

"Get her inside and feed her," Kit said. "I'm going to park the car with Vlad."

In different circumstances, the little shop would have fascinated Adela. This was where her daughter worked, the place she'd been spending time while Adela searched, worried, and confronted vampires. As it was, Heather collapsed on an overstuffed chair between two rows of bookshelves. She was even paler, if possible, and shaking.

"Mom?" it came out like a reedy whine.

"Pull the blinds and lock the door," Dixie said. "I'll get her something to eat."

Adela didn't stop to ask what Heather ate. As Dixie disappeared into a back room, Adela slid both heavy bolts home, turned the sign on the door to read CLOSED from the street, and pulled down the blinds.

When she turned back, Heather had a ripped-open package of meat on her lap and held a raw steak in her fingers, ripping off mouthfuls with her teeth and chewing and swallowing like a starving animal. While Adela watched in horrified fascination, Heather disposed of two large steaks and licked the last traces of blood off the plastic tray before wiping her mouth with a paper towel.

"Feeling better?" Dixie asked.

Adela had no doubt she was. The awful paleness faded as color returned. She looked—almost—like the daughter she remembered. "Heather."

Heather smiled and reached out her arms. "Mom, you look so worried. I'm fine now, but there's some things I have to explain."

"Yes, my dear. I think there are."

"Well, Mom . . ."

"Christopher and Vlad are back," Dixie said, and unbolted the door to let them in.

"You look better, Jane," Christopher said as he closed the door behind him.

"Better!" Adela snapped. "She's still dazed and weak."

"I'll be fine, Mom. Don't fuss."

"Fuss!" Adela snapped. "Heather, you disappear without a word. Your house is left open and empty with traces of blood in the kitchen, and I find you, four months later, in the middle of a crime scene surrounded by cop cars and ambulances. All this time, you've been living and working for a bunch of vampires, and you tell me not to worry!"

"There was only one ambulance."

She suppressed the smile, she couldn't help it,

and as she hugged Heather to her, the tears she hadn't shed for four months came in a torrent. The pair of them were boohooing and wailing like a couple of banshees, and Adela didn't give a damn. So what if they were giving the vamps amusement? She had her daughter back, safe . . . or almost. "I've come to take you home," she said through her sniffs.

"Mom, we need to talk. I can't go home right now."

"Why not?" She nodded thanks to Dixie for the box of Kleenex. Considerate woman for a vamp. As they'd all been, but . . . "You have to come home."

"No, Mom. Not yet. And even if I wanted to, the police need me as a witness. I saw those thugs go into the shop. I saw them searching Marie's office and trashing the place. I'm going to see them behind bars."

"Yes dear, but . . ."

"Forgive the intrusion," Vlad said, "but I'm afraid, madam, your daughter is right. Chicago would not be a good place for her at present. If the rogue vampire is still lurking, she could fall back under his control."

Adela shuddered. "You said your people"—she didn't want to think what and who his "people" were—"were hunting him."

"We are, but meanwhile your daughter needs protection. That was why I brought her and Angela here."

"You think she should join Angela in England?" Kit asked.

"Wait a minute . . ." Dixie began. "Before you hustle Jane—sorry—Heather—out of the country, don't you think she needs to spend time with her mother? There's some things they need to catch up on."

Sensible young woman. Or was she young? For all Adela knew, she was as old as Vlad.

"Someone approaches," Vlad said.

Seconds later there was a knock on the door. "Ms. Johnson? It's Officer Petit. I need to get a statement."

Heather stood up. She was steady on her feet and looked nine hundred percent better than ten minutes earlier, but Adela wanted to tell the damn police officer to give her baby a break. "Sure you're okay, Heather?"

"Yes, Mom. For now." She gave her a quick hug. "I'll need to eat again soon. I'm ravenous, but I can wait. Better get this over with."

After the door closed behind her, Adela looked around at the three vampires. They looked harmless enough but . . . "Why does she eat so much?"

Dixie shrugged. "Stress, I think. Her metabolism is faster than a mortal's, but she doesn't normally eat this often. Two or three steaks and a couple of chickens last her all day as a rule."

"She just eats raw meat?" She wanted to ask Heather this, but Dixie was here, and approachable.

"Mostly. She can eat cooked food, and does when she needs to pass as mortal, but raw meat, as freshly killed as possible, holds more nourishment." Dixie sat down beside her. "Anything else you want to know?"

Volumes! "I think Heather should be the one to tell me."

A knowing smile twitched the corners of her mouth. "You still don't trust us one iota, do you?"

She wasn't stupid! But they had protected Heather, or so they said. "An iota, yes. You have looked after my daughter; I'll be ever grateful for that, but old prejudices die hard."

Dixie smiled. "Didn't we agree to bury the hatchet?"

They had. "You mentioned ills done to you by witches."

Dixie nodded. "It's in the past. What matters now is Jane's—I mean Heather's—future, and letting Angela know who she really is."

Adela agreed, and then noticed Vlad and Kit concentrating on the door.

Dixie noticed too. "How's she doing?" she asked them.

"Holding her own," Vlad replied. "The police officer is inclined to skepticism and seems convinced our young friend had assistance in confronting the perpetrators, but Jane is unwavering in her account."

"You're listening!" Could they hear through walls?

Vlad inclined his head. "We felt it necessary. We cannot permit them to intimidate or distress your daughter."

Adela wasn't about to ask how he'd intervene. The little scene she'd witnessed outside convinced her this bunch didn't let much thwart them. She suppressed a shiver. "You're saying Heather's fine?"

"Weary, by the sound of her voice," he replied, "but certain and consistent. Seems she does not care for anyone to hurt her friends."

Yes, that was Heather. She'd ended up bloodying a little boy's nose in first grade when he'd called her best friend "smelly four eyes."

She was woozy and every muscle ached, but Jane knew this had to be got through, and so far, so good. Officer Petit seemed less intimidating than the others. Seated in her patrol car, a clipboard balanced on the steering wheel, Officer Petit listened and wrote down everything. From Jane first noticing the two youths loitering up and down Fifth Street, to hearing the noise through the wall and walking into mayhem. Petit wrote in neat square handwriting and handed the completed sheets to Jane to read and sign.

"Tell me something," Officer Petit said after she tucked the forms back in the clipboard. "Have you had martial arts training?"

Had she? Jane looked at the long-fringed dark eyes and shook her head. "I don't think so."

Petit raise her neatly plucked eyebrows. "You don't know for sure?"

Why hadn't she just said no? Because she couldn't lie to a police officer. "I had an accident, a few months back, and lost my memory. It's come back in snatches. I don't remember learning martial arts, but perhaps . . ."

"If you haven't, Heaven alone knows how you took care of that pair single-handed."

"I'm not sure myself." Petit's face inspired confidences. "They talk about people seeing red when they get angry. It's true."

"They were armed. You took a terrible chance."

Armed? Yes! "I saw the gun in his hand. I think I knocked it away."

Petit smiled. "I think you did too. We found it way across the room. You took a hideous risk. Don't make a habit of it. Next time you might not have weenies so easy to scare."

"I hope there isn't a next time!" Not if it left her this weak.

"Sure you don't need the EMTs to give you a once over?"

And have them need medical attention for shock? "I'm fine, really. Just shaken up. I'm closing the shop and going home for the rest of the day." To talk to Mom and hear the rest she had to say. Mom! Talk about surprise on top of shock.

"That's it, then . . ." Officer Petit said. There was something so safe and confident about her. Something akin to envy curled in Jane's heart as she looked at Petit, and it wasn't her long eyelashes. It was another envy. Jane bet Officer Petit knew exactly where she'd been born, gone to school, lived all her life.

"Need anything else?" Jane asked.

"I doubt it. This is as straightforward as they come. We've your evidence, and Ms. Worth's once we get to talk to her. The two of them were caught right at the scene of the crime. Shouldn't have any trouble with this one," she paused, smiling as she shook Jane's hand. "If we need you again, or if the detectives need to speak to you, we know where to find you. You need to take it easy. Shock's often delayed."

Nothing delayed about it! "I've got good friends here, and my Mom's visiting." It sounded so normal and ordinary, she had to stifle a giggle. She opened the door. "I'm glad it was you who took my statement. The others are a bit intimidating."

Office Petit grinned. "They stuck me with it because they couldn't handle facing a woman who disarms and intimidates roughs like those two. You unnerved them."

Jane didn't try to hold back the laugh. "Think they'll let me off the next time I get stopped for speeding?"

"When this gets out, you'll be a local heroine."

That would bring on another whole set of problems. "I hope not."

Jane crossed the road and paused to watch the activity around the Massage Zone. The mess and mayhem behind the doors there was nothing compared to the fragmented chaos of her own existence. Just when she was beginning to get a handle on being Jane Johnson, she wasn't! She was Heather someone or other, had a mother, and another life, and heaven alone knew what.

Before she started a second life, she'd better sort this one out.

"That was unexpectedly tactful of them!"

Kit had gone to the hospital to pick up Marie. Dixie was checking on something in the Vampire

Emporium. (And no doubt eavesdropping on the remaining cops.) Vlad eased out of the scenery after requesting Adela call him whenever she needed transport back to the hotel. Jane faced a mother–daughter tête-à-tête, and so far her mother's attitude toward Kit and Dixie and Vlad was getting up her nose. "Why so surprised? They're considerate people."

"So I'm beginning to realize, Heather." Adela sighed. "I'm doing this badly: upsetting you by mistrusting your friends."

"Vlad rescued me and Angela from the streets. Kit and Dixie's colony gave us identities, jobs, and homes. Why are you so suspicious of them? If they were going to harm us, they'd have done so by now!" Heaven help her, she was arguing with her mother, and it felt so familiar.

"You're right, Heather. Even a myopic old witch can see that. I as good as stalked Mr. Roman, and in return he drove me here to meet you. It's just that I have a long tradition of antipathy and mistrust to overcome. You never had any time for my religion, or you'd know that. Lizzie would understand."

"My sister?" She had a whole hidden family to come to terms with.

"Stepsister, to be precise. I was briefly married to her father. Your relationship with Elizabeth endured when mine with Piet's . . ."

"Petered out?"

Adela chuckled. "It was more of an explosion. He married me to make use of my power, and I declined to be used . . . but never mind that! Just a minute." She went into the dining room and came back with a thick book. "Another example of your friend's thoughtfulness, I left this in the suite and Vlad fetched it while you were with that police officer." Adela set the book—Heather now realized it was a photo album—on the coffee table. "I brought these pictures, in the hopes it might help trigger memories. Look through and see if you recognize anyone."

Why not?

Jane turned the pages. Recognized herself as a child, in a bunny costume carrying a plastic pumpkin, wrapped up in a snowsuit, standing by Niagara Falls, and a few years older in DC with the Capitol in the background. The next page, she was on the beach, hair blowing across her face, her arm around a fair-haired girl. A very much younger . . . "Angela!"

"Yes." Adela smiled. "Your friends said the same. Look at a few more photos to be sure."

She didn't need to but . . . she turned the page and saw them in party dresses, parkas, and ski boots, and riding side by side on a pair of ponies. There was even a picture of her sitting by Angela, sporting a cast on her leg. "What's her real name? Not Angela, right?"

"Elizabeth Connor. We all call her Lizzie."

"Tell me about us."

"You're my daughter, an elementary school teacher, and a part-time potter. You have a small house in Chicago. Still there, as it happens, but standing empty. Lizzie does things with computers. She is," Adela hesitated, "a witch like me, but more powerful."

"What about her mother?"

"She died, when Lizzie was two. A car accident."

"Her father?"

"Is still very much alive. I should call him and tell him what happened The fool believes she's backpacking around Europe."

"What's he like?"

Adela's mouth twisted in a crooked smile. "A very rich man, incredibly successful in business, and a pathetic excuse for a human being."

"I see."

"And no, Heather. That is not the spite of a scorned woman. He carries ambition to the point of obsession. I left him because he wanted me to use my powers to further his business goals and defeat his rivals. I refused. I warned Lizzie never to let him know the extent of her powers or he'd try to use them. She's always been desperate for his approval. It would be hard for her to refuse him."

"He wanted you to cast spells to knock out the competition?"

"That was the gist of it. Silly really. He's managed quite well without me. The man owns businesses all over the place. He's as rich as Croesus, and as miserable as a ten-day dirge. How that man produced a lovely woman like Lizzie has always amazed me."

All this was giving her a headache. "I need to call Angela, or Lizzie as she really is, and tell her this."

"First I should call Piet. He's a sorry father, but he is her father. She's in England, right?"

"Yes. She's smitten with Kit's friend Tom. She went to be with him. He lives in London."

"So Dixie mentioned. Lizzie's with him now?"

"Not exactly. She called me a couple of days ago. They had a falling out and she went up to Yorkshire to stay with Justin and Stella. Two other vampires."

"More vampires?"

She nodded. "Mom, if it weren't for vampires, Angela and I would have died weeks back on the streets of Chicago."

Adela sighed. "I'm beginning to appreciate that. It's obviously something I've got to come to terms with. Meanwhile . . . just tell me where Piet can find Lizzie."

"No. I will not speak to Mr. Radcliffe! Tell Piet Connor this is Adela Whyte, and this is urgent! It concerns his daughter. And whatever he's doing *can* be interrupted." Adela wanted to spit. Try calling Piet out of humanity and consideration and you get the runaround from a blasted aide. And the twerp thought she'd be palmed off with that creep Laran Radcliffe! What Lizzie had told her, on more than one occasion, was quite enough to put her off him.

"Adela?"

"Piet?"

"Yes, since you insisted."

"I insisted for good reason. I'm not sure you want the office staff to hear this before you."

"Hear what, Adela? If you're fussing about Lizzie again, she's in Europe and has no idea where your daughter got to."

"Piet, Lizzie is in Europe, yes, in England, as it happens. But she's not exactly well."

"What the hell do you mean?"

"Sit down."

"Adela, I don't have time . . ."

"Yes, you do! Back in September, when you thought Lizzie had canceled coming over, she hadn't. She did come. To Chicago."

"What are you talking about?"

He sounded worried. About time. "She stopped off to see Heather. Most likely on her way to see you. That I don't know. But while she and Heather were together, they had an accident."

"What sort of accident?" He actually sounded scared.

"No one is too sure." If she told him it was a renegade vampire attack, he'd hang up on the spot. "They both lost their memories and ended up staying with friends. I just found Heather in Ohio, and I discovered where Lizzie is."

She heard a gasp, the line went silent, and a clatter suggested Piet had dropped the phone. Moments later, he asked, "You're certain?"

"Piet. I'm not calling to play April fools. I'm sitting in Heather's apartment, and everyone recognizes Lizzie as the other victim in the accident."

Another silence. "Where's Lizzie then?"

"In England. Seems she met a young man . . ."

"Where is she?" Darn him, he was snapping at her!

"Staying with friends in Yorkshire. A village called Havering." She gave him the address: Havering Clinic, Havering seemed simple enough to find.

Quiet again. "Thanks, Adela." His voice was brisk now. Worry didn't last long for Piet Connor. "I'll be in touch with her."

"I might be able to get her phone number."

"Don't bother, Adela. I have employees to do that sort of thing."

Bastard! Wondering, for the nth time, how Piet produced a wonderful soul like Lizzie, Adela hung up. Still, she'd done her bit. When Heather next called Lizzie, she'd speak to her. Meanwhile, she had her own daughter to worry about.

"You heard that?" Piet frowned at Laran.

"I did."

"You swore you wouldn't hurt her!"

Laran's strong hand rested on Piet's shoulder. "I didn't. I had a chat with her and met Heather. I gently took any memory of meeting me away from both of them, and knowledge of the UK problem from Lizzie, and left immediately. If something happened later . . ." Laran shook his head. "They were going out that evening, clubbing. Made it clear they wanted me to go so they could leave. You know these clubs. . . . Maybe they got into drugs or something. Didn't you say Heather was a bad influence?"

Had he? Piet shook his head. "What now? If Adela is right, and the damn woman always had been, Heather is getting her memory back. What if Lizzie's returns? What if she remembers what she found? We've rolled up most of that operation, but it's not all taken care of yet."

Laran ran his fingers up Piet's neck, caressing a dark bruise near his collarbone. Piet let out a little groan of anticipation. "Don't worry, Piet. Lizzie isn't going to remember anything." He bend his head and bit gently.

He drank deeply. He'd need it with a transatlantic flight ahead.

Piet was unconscious when Laran dialed Alan's extension. "I need the company plane as soon as possible. I'm going to DC. And book me on the first flight I can connect with."

Chapter 11

Totnes. The same afternoon.

There were two mortals inside the shop. Tom walked a few meters up the hill and waited until they left: a pair of teenage girls chattering and nattering how they'd now tell each other's fortunes. Foolish mortals! Dabbling with witches! He couldn't help his mouth twitching. He'd done a great deal more than dabble with 'a witch, and was about to confront one. To use young Sam's expression, Gwyltha would have a cow when she heard. Meanwhile . . .

Tom grabbed the brass knob and opened the door.

Meg Merchant looked up as the bell over the door jangled. Her face drained white. "You!"

Tom closed the door, slipped the bolt home, and turned the plastic hanging sign to CLOSED. "Yes, me."

He paused, hoping he could calm her fears. "I mean no harm."

"Harm is all you can bring! Bloodsucker! Killer! Destroyer!"

"Have a seat." He indicated the rocking chair. "We need to talk."

"You'll learn nothing from me, vampire!" She all but spat the last word out.

"Please sit. And I truly mean you no harm."

"Harm is your middle name!"

"Angela mentioned you keep a kettle in the back room. May I make you a cup of tea?"

"Why would I drink tea with you?"

"Because I sensed in you a certain fondness, perhaps anxiety, for Angela. Her safety matters more than my own existence, and I believe you can help us both."

"Why is her safety so important to you?"

"I love her."

The old witch's cackle cut through the warm air. He sensed mockery and panic in her tight laughter. "Pull the other leg, vampire. It's wooden."

He admired her courage. "Wood does not harm us as much as some believe." Unlike ancient Druid knives. "And I do not jest about Angela. Please sit." She'd never relax standing.

She agreed to sit but took a stool behind the counter, not the rocker. "What do you want, bloodsucker? I'm losing customers while you chatter."

He took a handful of notes out of his wallet and laid them on her glass-topped counter. "Will this compensate you for your lost business?"

She'd counted them as he put them down. They both knew it was far more that the profit from a few stray customers. "Blood money?" she asked.

Mind control would be so much easier but impossible faced with her antagonism and mistrust. Abel help him! Who else around here might have her knowledge? "Not blood money. A goodwill advance."

Her eyes flickered as her mouth twisted on one side. "You want my goodwill?"

"For this afternoon, yes. To help the woman I love."

Meg Merchant glanced at the money, folded her arms on her chest, and looked him in the eye. He sensed, rather then felt, her power. She was old and strong in her skills, but he was vampire, and patient. She frowned at him. "What happened to her, and what are you doing with her?"

Dammit! He'd come to ask questions, not answer them, but if it helped the old witch trust him . . . "May I sit down?" At her grudging nod, he took the rocker, imagining Angela's warm body relaxed against the cushions. "What happened is, someone stole her memory."

"And?"

Fair enough. He couldn't get full truth without offering it. "And made her into a ghoul." After a few moments silence, Meg nodded, and he went on. "I don't know much else. Her memory is returning in fits and starts. Your shop attracted her yesterday and stirred memories. This afternoon she realized she was a witch."

After an interminable silence, Meg nodded. "That explains that." She stood up. "Tea sounds like a good idea. I'll put the kettle on."

He followed her into the little room full of boxes and shelves, containing himself while Meg filled the kettle and plugged it in. He bit his lip while she measured out the scoops of tea, and exercised patience while she put cups on the tray, but it was the scrambling in the biscuit tin that finished him. "What was explained?"

She looked up from peering inside a packet labeled Jaffa Cakes. "Her aura, of course."

"What about it?"

"You don't eat biscuits, I imagine?"

Was she toying with him? "No, thank you. Could you please be more specific about Angela's aura?" Abel help him! Was this what love did to you? For Angela, he was discussing auras, of all things, with a witch!

Meg smiled as if reading his mind. Darn her, she probably could. She might be summoning hoards of support this very minute. Survival dictated he walk out now, but on the off-chance she could help Angela, he'd have a cup of tea with the old woman and watch her nibble Jaffa Cakes—whatever they were. She looked over her shoulder at him. "You know what an aura is?"

"Tell me." Getting her talking could only help.

She put the packet of biscuits on the tray. "A manifestation of life force, the emotions, the spirit inside. You don't have one. Hardly surprising. Your Angela's is black, where she has anything. Shocked me at first. She seemed too young and had such honest eyes to have so destroyed her soul. I saw a few pale sparks of light when she picked up the cards, or fingered that locket of hers, but no real life, except when she was with you. I thought about it all night, wondering what it meant." She broke off as the kettle began to boil, warming the pot, putting it on the tray, and pouring the water.

"You thought she was a vampire?" Tom asked.

"Oh no." Meg put the lid on the pot and added a small jug of milk from an old-fashioned clay cooler. "It was as if someone had taken the life from her."

"Someone did."

Meg paused, tray in her hands, and looked. At him. Through him. "You?"

It was a fair-enough question. He'd control his rising fury. "No, not me, old woman."

She seemed to accept that as she carried the tray through the narrow doorway. He took the cup she handed him. "You were saying about Angela's aura?" Darn the woman, she couldn't stop here.

Meg nodded and set her cup and saucer by the register. "That's the really interesting part. When she's near you, she lights up with a glow of deep rosy pink. Not hard to believe you're lovers." She paused to test the heat of her tea and, hesitating, put the cup back in the saucer. "Do you control her?"

He doused himself with tea at that. After he'd accepted a towel to mop himself up, he said to Meg, "Fancy yourself as a comedienne, do you? I couldn't control Angela if I wanted to! She goes haring around the country on a whim, and I'm chasing after her to make sure no harm comes to her. She thinks she has ties to Totnes. Probably slight. Perhaps she came here on holiday, but she insisted on coming here. So far she's remembered a few details, telling fortunes with cards for instance, the big one being she's convinced she's a witch—like you."

"Has she convinced you?"

"She's convinced me that she believes it."

The only sounds were the slow tick of the old wall clock and the occasional slurp as Meg sipped her tea. Had he been an unmitigated fool? Admitting what he was to a mortal—and a witch at that? Probably! He should have talked this over with Justin. When had he had the chance? He was in love with a witch! There'd be hell to pay when Gwyltha found out. He hoped Angela had no objection to a life in exile.

"Where are you staying? The Royal Oak?"

Meg's question brought him back to the here and now. "Yes." Tactical error no doubt, giving the enemy his whereabouts . . . but . . . "I'm not sure how long we'll be there."

She smiled as if aware of his caution. "You never told me your name."

"Tom Kyd." Now he understood why Vlad used a traveling name.

She grinned, showing a chipped front tooth. "Well, Tom Kyd. Never thought the day would come when a vampire came to me for favors."

"I never thought I'd ever go to a witch asking one, and I've had much longer than you to think about it!"

She chuckled. It was almost a cackle. "And what do you think I can do? If I choose to?" She threw it at him like a challenge.

"I'm not sure. But if Angela is right about herself, perhaps you can help her remember . . ." He paused. "She mentioned needing something for the full moon."

Meg nodded. "An athame. It's part of the rite."

"You have them for sale?" Abel help him! He was preparing to purchase the tools of witchcraft!

"No need," she replied. "Angela can share mine. The night after tomorrow night is full moon. She can join me."

"Where Angela goes, I go." She'd throw a wobbly at that, but he wasn't having her go off alone with this old witch.

"Were you invited, vampire?"

"I'll bring her."

Meg grinned, showing her broken tooth. "Got it bad haven't you?"

"If this can help Angela . . ."

"We can invoke the Goddess's power. But undoing evil such as your Angela suffered . . ." She hesitated. "You have no idea who defiled her?"

"My concern now is to help Angela get back her lost memory. The one who did this we will take care of later."

"It was one of you, wasn't it?"

"Not one of us. A force of evil: a twisted vampire."

"Some of us say all vampires are twisted."

"And some vampires say all witches bring harm."

"You don't?"

He did, until about an hour ago. "Angela has worked hard to convince me otherwise."

Meg smiled. "The night after tomorrow, vampire. Do you have a car?"

When he nodded, she took a notepad from beside the register. "Here," she said after writing a few minutes. "My address, and a map from the Royal Oak. The moon rises at eleven. Be there well before then. Angela may join with me. You"—she paused— "as an unbeliever, have no part in our ceremonies."

She needn't worry about that. "I'll bring Angela." And stay damn close to make sure nothing happened to her.

"Going to open up my shop so I can stay in business?"

He did better than that. As he unbolted the door and turned the sign, two women strolled by and paused to look in the window. Tom wished them "Good afternoon," and when they looked his way, he planted the suggestion in their minds that there just had to be something inside they needed to buy.

He restrained himself from racing back to the hotel and settled for a brisk walk. He needed time to think. Somehow he had to bypass the problems this would bring up with the colony. Angela was his first concern. Meg was darn right! He did have it bad. And despite what she said, he was sticking like glue to Angela.

Back in the Royal Oak, he walked past the deserted reception desk, and stopped. There, on the polished counter, was a room key. A room key with his room number on the brass tag. Why? He'd left the key upstairs with Angela. He grabbed it and took the wide stairs three at a time. He was down the corridor in seconds and all but forced the door open. The bed was empty. Angela had gone.

In seconds, he ran into the bathroom, where the carpet was still damp, and back to the deserted sitting room. Empty! Her toothbrush and makeup were still in the bathroom, and her discarded clothes littered the floor. She hadn't left him, but where in tarnation was she? Abel give him strength! He'd start aging, after centuries of perpetual youth, if Angela went on like this. Why couldn't she have stayed asleep? Why hadn't she? With the strength of glamour he'd put on her, she darn well should have!

She'd stuck a sheet of notepaper to the TV screen—with soap, he realized as he pulled it off.

"Tom," the note said. "One. Don't ever try that vampire mind trick on me again. I have a worse headache than after ghouling thugs. Two. I'm off to do some research in the library. Three. Don't follow me. You went off on your own. It's my turn. Four. I love you."

What did she expect? That he'd sit here and wait for her to come back, while she went off on her own? Which was exactly what he'd done an hour or so ago. Hell!

He sat on the bed, ran his hands over the now-cold sheets that smelled of Angela and loving, and decided to wait for her return.

His resolve lasted thirty-seven seconds. He counted.

He couldn't sit there, not while he worried about her getting lost, confused, or attacked. All right, the last she could take care of. He laughed. A woman who scared off muggers might give him gray hair but was unlikely to get lost. Come to that, his hair wasn't likely to go gray anytime either.

He had to summon his patience, let Angela do her research, and welcome her when she returned; meanwhile he'd better find something to do to stop him from going around the twist.

He phoned Justin.

He was in the clinic, doing rounds.

"Everything okay?" Stella asked, in a voice that implied she expected otherwise. "Is Angela there?"

"Not right now, she's off in the library doing a spot of research."

"I see." She obviously didn't.

"I just got back from checking something else. We split up to cover twice as much ground." It sounded reasonable.

"Smart man! Found anything important?"

"Hard to tell. Angela's remembered a few fragments. The tricky thing is piecing it together." And deciding if he really wanted to attend a full moon ceremony with a coven of witches. How he wished Justin were here! He'd tell him not to even consider it and confirm all his doubts.

"If there's anything there, you and Angela between you will find it." He loved Stella's optimism. "Give her my love, will you?" He agreed to. "And I'll tell Justin you called. I have to go now." She paused. "I'm dropping off a cake for the Women's Institute."

And that was, no doubt, another first for the colony.

He wasn't sitting there waiting for Justin to call back. Tom scribbled a note on the bottom of Angela's, saying he'd popped out for a while and would be back, and yes, he promised, no more "vampire mind tricks."

It was only after he crossed the road and headed toward a florist he'd noticed earlier that he hoped the chambermaids at the Royal Oak didn't come in to turn down the beds.

He bought a potted lavender bush, the scent dredging up memories of old linen presses and summer afternoons, then headed for the butcher by the river. Angela had cleaned out her supplies before she left. She'd need to feed when she got back. She seemed permanently hungry these days. Was it the magic in the air down here? The place gave him the willies. If he had any sense, they'd leave for London the minute she returned from her "low-tech research."

But did he have the right to make that choice for her? Hell, he'd tell her about Meg's invitation and hope to Abel Angela decided it wasn't worth her while.

He removed all the little bottles in the minibar to make room for the meat, put the lavender bush on the bedside table, sat down on the bed, and wished she'd come back soon.

He missed her so much it hurt. He needed to think over the implications of refusing, or accepting, a witch's invitation, and he really should try to get Justin again. But all he wanted was to slide under the sheets and rest his head on a pillow that smelled of Angela.

No. He had to do something, but what? Feeding might be a very good idea. He could hardly take more from Angela, but in his haste to get down here, he'd neglected to bring blood bags. He took the note off the mirror, folded it beside the lavender plant, just in case the chambermaids were more attentive than he expected, and set off.

Somewhere there had to be a needy soul to unwittingly trade a warm pint for a little extra money.

He found him in the all-but-deserted cemetery beyond the town—an old man seated on a bench, absently stroking a bleary-eyed spaniel.

"'Afternoon," he said as Tom sat beside him.

"Good afternoon. Peaceful here, isn't it?"

The man nodded. "Right you are there. Come here most days, I do. Seems I know more people here than out there." He nodded in the direction of the road beyond.

"It's hard to see friends go," Tom replied.

The old man raised bushy gray eyebrows. "I've seen more go than you have, lad."

Tom smiled. "It's not the numbers, it's the depth of the lost friendship."

That earned him a speculative look. "Aye," the old man said at last. "Right enough." He went silent.

Tom took his chance and cast a full glamour on the old man. The dog whimpered, but Tom calmed him until he settled down, his nose resting on his paws. With a quick glance to make sure they weren't overlooked, Tom eased the old man's threadbare jacket open and pulled down his collar. He bit and drank swiftly. The man was old and frail, but his blood flowed strongly. Tom took particular care to seal the punctures well, eased back the collar, and reached inside the jacket for the man's wallet. As Tom expected, it was almost empty. He slipped a couple twenties behind the other notes, hoping it would seem as if the old man had miscounted, and tucked a bundle of carefully creased notes deep into the outside pocket of the coat. The old codger was in for a pleasant surprise.

Pausing only to wipe his own mouth with his linen handkerchief, Tom lifted the glamour.

The old man smiled. "Must have been day-dreaming again." He stood up slowly. "It's getting a bit damp here for my old bones. Time to get Roger home." At his name, the dog looked up, wagging his tail against the gravel path.

"Mind if I walk with you to the gate?" Tom asked. He hoped to heaven he hadn't taken too much and left the old man weak.

"Don't mind if you do."

Beyond the gate, Tom waited with the old man, leaving only after he'd seen him safely on a bus home, before turning toward the open country to run.

He looped south of the town, across well-tended fields and ancient hedges. He came back to the river sooner than he expected, slowing his pace as buildings appeared. He passed warehouses and small factories, walking now, but at a fast pace. Until a sign caught his eye. MARIPOSA. QUALITY LEATHER. Underneath the sign was spray-painted "Closing Down Sale."

He restrained himself from whooping. This had to be the business that old Mr. Lee mentioned. Not quite defunct yet. He sensed human heartbeats within the breeze block walls. Did this ordinary building hold a clue for Angela? Or was it no connection except coincidence? One way to find out.

Tom opened the door and walked into a small office. They were closing down all right. A bare desk was pushed against the wall, there were boxes everywhere, and an unplugged computer sat on the floor. The human heartbeats were beyond the closed door opposite. He crossed the room and tried the door. Locked. He raised his hand to knock on the frosted glass panel when a voice behind him said, "What do you want?"

Tom turned.

The man was well over six four, built like an ox, and had a spitting snake tattooed on his right forearm. "What do you want?" he repeated without a trace of courtesy. "This is private property. Get out!" He took a step closer, presumably to encourage Tom's departure.

Tom stood his ground. "I wanted to inquire about the closing down sale."

"That was last week. We're all sold out now, dummy." Charm was obviously not part of the package.

"I see." Tom met the man's beady eyes and contemplated staring him out, but why waste the effort with childish games? "The sign is still outside. An omission I'm certain."

He should have kept to words of one syllable. The hulk scowled. "Omission, eh? Scarper! This is private property." By way of obvious encouragement, he closed a beefy hand over Tom's left bicep.

Smiling, Tom eased his arm from the man's grasp faster then his shifty eyes could ever see. "Good afternoon," he said, and walked out, deliberately slowly.

Sensing the hulk eying him from the doorway, Tom walked down the road and past the corner of the next building. Looking over his shoulder to check that he was alone, Tom leaped onto the roof, crept along until he reached the edge, and jumped across to the Mariposa warehouse. If big-bicep snakeman wanted him out that urgently, there had to be something interesting going on.

Tom stretched flat on the roof to remain unobserved and listened.

". . . just some yuppie poking around. Said he was asking about the sale. He scared off easily enough. You know the sort. Would never hit anyone in case he'd mess up his manicure."

"Sure it was a yuppie, Mike? All we need right now is some plainclothes police sniffing this lot out." That voice was educated, not university but more likely to do a crossword than snakeman Mike.

"Stop jawing!" A woman's voice this time. "You finish packing this lot."

"What if that Radcliffe chap comes back and sees we didn't sell it all off?"

"Why would he come? Bigwigs like that don't oversee liquidation sales. Hell. He told us to dis-

pose of the last of the stock." She laughed. "We
are. Now you keep an eye out, Mike. Anyone else
comes around, see they make themselves scarce."

Tom remained in place hoping the group below
would leave and give him space to explore further.
Something definitely interesting, and presumably
underhand, going on. At best an attempt to de-
fraud the owner. The light was fading. He'd been
up here ages and the little trio inside were as busy
as ever. Drat! He had to get back. He was here to
help out Angela, not indulge in vigilante enforcement for an unknown business owner being ripped
off by his supposed employees. They were probably just nicking a few leather coats to flog in Exeter
market.

He jumped down to the ground, childishly let out
the air from the tires of a motorbike he guessed
belonged to Mike, and ran the rest of the way to
the Royal Oak.

Angela was already back, sitting on the chintz
armchair, feet propped on the bed, and looking
extraordinarily pleased with herself as she sipped
tea. She grinned. "Hi. Thanks for the lavender.
How did you guess I was in need of calm and
serenity?"

He walked over and kissed her. "Glad you like it,
and I'm glad you're back. I stocked up the fridge
too. I missed you."

"But you didn't sit around missing me."

"I needed to feed."

"In broad daylight!"

"I was careful. I've had lots of practice, you
know."

She rolled her eyes. "Smart-ass!" But she smiled and blew him a kiss. "Want to hear what I found out?"

Might as well let her start. "Go ahead. You first, then I'll tell."

"I've spent the afternoon in the library, first looking at back issues of the *Totnes Times,* then street and business directories, and maps." She grinned. "I found where Mariposa is. It's on the edge of town. I tried to call them but got a machine. Tomorrow I'm going to check it out."

She wasn't. Snakeman Mike was not even getting a glimpse of Angela. "Not a good idea, love."

"Why ever not?"

"I've already been there, Angela."

Chapter 12

Angela listened. Her mind and heart quickening as Tom told of his meeting with Meg. Goddess, bless him! He'd ignored his deep-seated prejudices and met with a witch because he wanted to help her.

She couldn't help smiling as she hugged him. "How marvelous of Meg. I'd love to share a Full Moon ceremony with her. Try as I have, I can't remember all the rituals, but with her to guide me . . ." The waves of skepticism from Tom's direction were so strong, she could almost taste them. He looked quite capable of obstructing things. She took a slow, centering breath. "Will you come with me the day after tomorrow?"

His expression suggested he'd be impossible to stop. "If you insist on going."

Darn him! Bring wonderful news and grouch over it. Men! "I do, Tom. Since you don't understand, just please accept it means a lot to me."

"More than us?"

The question came like a dousing of icy water. How dare he try to make her choose between discovery of herself and him! And how dare he wind her up like this! She deliberately deepened her scowl before smiling sweetly and kissing him on the cheek. She was tempted to slug him around the jaw. "Tom." She gave an exaggerated sigh, well aware he couldn't echo that. "How can I answer that, when we still haven't worked out what exactly is between us?"

"You know what's between us. You're just denying it."

Brother, was he spoiling for a fight? Too bad she was determined to eschew negative energy in preparation for the Full Moon ritual. "As you're denying what I am?" So much for eschewing negative energy! She was generating it.

Tom's shoulders sagged. He looked the closest she'd ever seen a vampire come to weary. "Maybe you're right. Accepting you as a witch means discarding centuries of belief."

"Centuries of superstition and fear!" She crossed over to where he paced in front of the empty fireplace. He'd brushed the dried eucalyptus arrangement in the hearth, and she caught the scent as she reached out for him. "My first encounter with a vampire was so horrific even the traces left of that memory have me shuddering. If I can accept you, Justin, Stella, Dixie, and Kit, and the rest of the colony, as different from that vampire, can't you see me as more than a medieval superstition?"

For several hideous, gut-twisting seconds, she feared he'd say no.

"Will 'I'll try my best' be good enough?"

The plea in his voice was impossible to refuse. "How about, 'try until you twist yourself in knots for me'?"

His laugh came from deep in his belly, rich and sexy. Pretty much like him. "Angela, I'm already twisted up in knots over you. You hadn't noticed?"

She glanced down. "That's not all I'm noticing."

He grabbed her waist and pulled her close. Mmm, she'd been right. She pressed her hips into him. "Woman," he growled, "don't you think of anything but sex?"

"It's a bit difficult when you're holding me this close."

"Good!" Her lowered his lips to hers and kissed. His cool mouth tasted of the damp evening, and his touch stirred the heat between them. She whimpered with anticipation as he opened her lips. With a burst of need, she pressed her tongue into his mouth and caressed. Determined to lead, if only for moments, she curled her tongue against the roof of his mouth and slowly eased along the surface of his tongue, tasting his need as she felt his cool hands easing her closer to the promise of his erection.

As she slowed to better savor the joining of their mouths and minds, he took over, lifting her so her toes skimmed the carpet. In seconds, he had her across the room and flat on her back on the bed.

He was half atop her, his chest flattening her

breasts and his thigh alongside hers. Her body responded to the heat of passion under his cool skin, his touch, and the power of the vampire beside her. She rolled onto one hip, pressed herself off the mattress, and swung her leg over Tom. In seconds she straddled him, rocking herself over his erection. "Why are you wearing all these clothes? Better take care of that." She reached for his shirt buttons.

"No need!"

No time!

He had her wrists grasped in one hand, and no way could she free herself from a vampire's hold. Faster than her eyes could register, he freed his cock, pulled aside her clothes, and lifting her easily, impaled her on his erection. The gasp came involuntarily. The sigh was pure pleasure. Wild spirals of sensation blocked out further conscious thought as they both climaxed in minutes.

Angela toppled, gasping onto the bed. As she bounced against Tom, he grinned. "Got any more good ideas?"

"Let me get my breath back first!"

He positively smirked. "Must be such a disadvantage."

She was too relaxed to even nudge him for that. Her nagging headache had eased, and she felt blissfully content. "So, you had tea with Meg. Anything else?"

He told her.

Made her session in the library pretty pointless. Except . . . He described his eavesdropping from the roof and . . . She reached into faded memories, and the murkiness in her mind parted. "Was it a cinder block building?" She closed her eyes, the better to scour up the images, and missed his searching glance.

"Breeze blocks, you mean? Yes."

"With a little office off the side with pebble-glass windows?"

"You've been there?" She couldn't miss the excitement in his voice.

"I worked there. I don't know when or how long, but I used to sit at the gray metal desk in the corner while I was . . ." Damn! While she was what?

Tom slid his hand under hers. His cool skin seemed to anchor her jumbled thoughts. "I worked on the computer, installing a program . . . and something was wrong."

Very quietly Tom said, "There was a computer on the floor, ready to be packed up."

"A Deltium 2000?"

His fingers meshed with hers. "Yes."

In the ensuing silence, she went on. "Mine had two phone numbers written on the frame around the monitor."

"Yes."

She looked at him. "Could it really be mine?"

Tom shrugged. "Time I found out, I think."

She caught the pronoun right away. "You? I think this is where *I* should go looking."

He was quiet a good minute. Heck! She could see the arguments assembling behind his eyes. What pitiful excuse was he going to fob her off with this time?

"Will you plant me a facer if I suggest you stay behind?"

"Most likely."

"Good thing I heal fast. Try not to break too much. Wouldn't want you to do your hand or wrist in."

He deserved an uppercut to his smug jaw. Angela sighed and made it as long and drawn-out as she could, just to underscore she could do one thing he couldn't. "I'm supposed to stay behind like a piece of left luggage?"

He waited, obviously summoning his specious arguments. "Angela," he began, "from what you told me about yesterday, you do have abilities we've not yet discovered, but I don't think during a breaking and entering is the time to test possible powers. Alone, I can get there and back in a quarter of an hour, maybe less. If I get discovered, I can move fast or transmogrify. If I get injured or shot"—she shuddered at the thought—"I heal." He met her eyes and gave her a rueful smile. "Maybe you can do all or any of those, but we don't know for sure."

Plus, she could slow him down, get in the way, or royally screw things up. She indulged in another sigh. "Okay, Tom." She'd have to agree more often. The look on his face was priceless.

"You're staying here?" It was obvious he still couldn't quite believe her easy acquiescence.

"Sure. If you take too long, I might go down to the bar to scope out the local talent, but other-wise . . ."

A definitely worthwhile kiss broke off the end of the sentence. While her head cleared from the ex-citement, Tom was out of bed, clothes straightened and zipped, and he'd even changed his pale shirt for a black turtleneck. "Thanks," he said, whether for the sex or her cooperation, or both, she didn't ask.

"Take care." It didn't make sense to worry—he was a master vampire for goodness sake—but she sensed something important was about to happen.

"Of course I will. I've you to come back to." He gave her a quick hug and a soft kiss on her lips. "I'm leaving via the stairs, but after I'm gone, open the windows wide, just in case I have to make a hasty return. Don't want to shock the establishment by dive-bombing their bow window."

He was gone, his light footsteps hastening down the carpeted hallway.

She opened the window, imagining Tom flying through like a bloodsucking Peter Pan. As she glanced down, she saw him stopping at his car. He unlocked the trunk, reached in, and slipped something in his pocket; handy-dandy house-breaking tools perhaps? He looked up at her, two floors above, and waved. In minutes he disappeared in the dark along the river.

Not much else to do but wait until he got back. Angela switched on the kettle, preferring a cup of instant coffee to the company of chatty locals in the bar, and decided to see what the cards had to tell her this time.

She hadn't finished shuffling them when the phone rang.

"Angela?"

"Hey, Jane! What's up?"

Jane told her.

Angela listened, interrupting a couple of times to ask a question, but most of the time she listened to the most wonderful and most utterly unnerving news. "You met your mother, my stepmother?"

"Yes. And recognized her. She has photos of us as little girls. I'm Heather Whyte, and you're Elizabeth Connor."

Heck! She'd only just got used to being Angela the ghoul, now she had to be Elizabeth, the rich girl. At least she no longer had to worry about being dependent on Tom for money. She had bank accounts and credit cards of her own. She just had to lay claim to them. And get to know this anonymous father. Jane—no, Heather—was thrilled at finding her mother. Why did she feel so cautious at the prospect of meeting her father?

"Mom's going to call you," Jane went on. "I'll give her this number. I just got it from Stella. I thought you were in Havering."

"I'll be here a few days." At least until after the Full Moon ceremony tomorrow, and . . . another fragment of memory stirred. "Your mother's a witch, right?"

"Yes." There was a pause. "She says you are too."

Just what she needed: someone to advise her about Full Moon ceremonies, and everything else she was trying to remember about her religion. "I know. I remembered that this afternoon. I need to call her."

"I think you should call your father first. He's probably been trying to call you in Yorkshire. He and Mom are divorced, but she spoke to him earlier and he was shocked to hear about our accident."

"Okay, I'll call; let me get a pencil and give me his number, and your mother's."

After Jane rang off, Angela sat very still and thought until her mind ached. So, Jane was Heather. And she was Elizabeth. Supposedly they had known each other since childhood, but all Angela remembered were the few months since Vlad found them shivering in the park. They'd been two employed professional women, and something had reduced them to cringing wrecks. Why? She reached for the phone and slowly punched in the numbers. She had no idea what to say to her father. Heck, she couldn't even picture his face. She'd better not share details of Tom's nature. If her putative father was anxious already, he'd have a hissy fit at the prospect of his long-lost daughter having brilliant sex with a vampire. The phone rang the other end, oddly familiar, but so different from the *brrr-brrr* of a Brit phone.

"Connor residence."

"This is . . . Elizabeth Connor." She made herself say the name with conviction. "Please put me through to my father."

An astonished gasp came all the way from Oregon, via fiber optics. "Yes, Miss Connor. He's in the Portland office. I'll patch you through."

After a few minutes of elevator music, she heard her father's voice—and didn't recognize it. "Lizzie? Where the hell are you?"

"I've been worried" would have been nicer. "So

glad you're okay" a little more welcoming. But in a sudden flash of awareness, Angela knew tenderness was not part of her father's nature. "Hello, Dad."

"God help me! When Adela called it gave me the shock of my life. What have you been doing all these months?"

"Falling in love with a vampire" wasn't a good response. "Living with friends, in Ohio, and now I'm in England."

"Adela said you were in the north of England—Yorkshire."

"I was, but I'm spending a few days in Devon."

"Where?" he snapped. So much for loving, paternal concern.

"In Totnes, a lovely old town."

"You're staying there? Where?" She told him, and added the phone number. "What made you pick Totnes?"

It was on the tip of her tongue to explain about the coat, but she didn't. "Just looking around. I think I might have been here before." Why the hell did she say that?

After a long pause, he replied, "You were. I bought a small company there. Never did anything. It's kaput now."

That made sense of her research and Tom's discoveries. "What sort of firm was it, Dad?"

"A useless one, Lizzie. Laran acquired it, but it turned out to be a dud, so I closed it down."

She only half-heard the end of his reply. The name Laran reverberated in her mind. He was important, she knew, but . . . "Who's Laran?"

"You *have* lost your memory, Lizzie. Laran Radcliffe is my right-hand man. Couldn't run my business without him. You staying there a few days?"

"We plan to." The "we" went unremarked. Good thing, too; she wasn't up to explaining her new relationship with Tom. She wasn't sure she could.

"Talk to you later, Lizzie."

Angela stared at the silent phone in her hand. Her memory might be shot with holes, but surely that wasn't the usual sort of conversation between a man and the daughter he'd thought missing or dead for six months! Tom might have tried to chew her up and spit her out, but at least he worried about her. All her father seemed interested in was the hotel she was staying in.

She set the phone back on the cradle. Whatever was or was not between her and her father, it wasn't a deeply affectionate or loving relationship. Made her doubly grateful for Tom.

She glanced at her watch. Already twelve minutes. He should be home soon.

With a glance over his shoulder at Angela outlined against the lighted window, Tom walked a few yards before setting off at full vampire pace. The streets were all but deserted; besides, who'd notice a passing gust of wind on a February evening?

He reached the darkened warehouse. Not a sign of life. Good. He strolled around the back and leaped up to the roof. No apparent alarm system. The only security was a lone guard who, to judge by his heartbeat, was fast asleep and well over retirement age. Better be doubly careful, he'd hate to give the old codger a heart attack.

Back on the ground, Tom made for the door that led straight into the office. Taking a small lockpick from his pocket, he had the door unlocked and closed behind him in seconds. The computer wasn't on the floor where it had been earlier. Damn! Had they taken it out already? He looked around at the metal filing cabinets, the two chairs upended on the gray metal desk, and the boxes stacked against the wall. There hadn't been that many earlier, he'd swear to it.

The computer was packed and sealed in a carton. Ripping off the brown tape, and making more noise than he wanted to, he opened the box and pulled out the computer. It took only a couple of minutes to unscrew the plastic cover, loosen the hard drive from the housing, and refix the panel. After he'd resealed the carton and tucked the hard drive in his pocket, he looked around. Were there other computers? Records? He couldn't carry off stacks of paper and make a quick getaway, but disks maybe. In the chaos of cleaning out, and the big clearance sale, who'd miss a few floppies?

The filing cabinet was empty. Ditto for the desk drawers. The other packed boxes contained desk lamps, coffee mugs, phone books, and . . . Drat! The night watchman was awake, and coming toward the office.

Leaping upward, Tom braced himself diagonally across the corner above the door and the small window. He hoped the man wouldn't look up. If he did, the old chap would lose the memory.

A cursory flash of a torchlight beam skimmed the empty room before the door closed. But the light in the small room beyond went on, and by the sound of things, the man was making himself a cup of tea. Tom didn't grudge the old codger a warm drink on a cold night, but Angela was waiting and most likely chewing her nails.

Tom jumped down, keeping ears alerted to the sounds on the other side of the wall. Patting his jacket to reassure himself he still had the hard drive safely pocketed, he unlocked the street door and stepped out into the path of a slow-moving police car.

Double damn! Tom leaped to the warehouse roof, jumping from building to building in the dark, leaving behind the flashing blue lights and the shouts. He was far enough away not to be discovered, but he had run in the wrong direction.

He was in the middle of a residential section and perched on the roof of a pub. Judging by the beery-cheery sounds in the street below, it was closing time. Drat! Too many darn mortals about. He paused to get his bearings, saw the dark ribbon of the river to his right, and crept down the shadowy side of the pub, landing in a dark yard between dustbins and stacks of crates. He leaped over the back wall, avoiding the metal spikes that looked as if they'd been protecting the place since Victoria's time. The alley was quiet, the patrons all walking merrily along the street at the end.

Tom was about to saunter out and join them when he felt a sharp jab in his back, and a voice said, "Give us yer wallet then!" and an arm, covered with a dirty-smelling sleeve, wrapped itself across his windpipe.

Enough was enough. He was pressed for time and feeling a trifle testy.

He broke the stranglehold, pushing his assailant to the ground. Tom paused just long enough to notice the accomplice lingering in the shadows, seize him by the lapels, and dump him on his pal. While they scrambled to their feet, Tom grabbed each one by the collar and hoisted them over the wall. By the sound of things he'd aimed correctly. They both landed among the dustbins. The ensuing clatter and yelling had lights blazing on the other side of the wall, and a burly voice demanded to know what was going on, then.

Nice. The pair would have an interesting time explaining things to the landlord and the police. And if they tried telling the truth, they'd be laughed all the way to the police station.

Grinning with satisfaction, Tom brushed off his hands. The pub's customers could now stroll home unmolested. He now understood why Kit had so much fun thwarting potential criminals in his neighborhood in Ohio. He'd have to try it some more. Another time. Angela was waiting. He patted his pocket to reassure himself he hadn't lost the hard drive among the empties and the crates. He'd no idea where he was, so he walked rather than ran through the maze of narrow streets and terraced houses, eventually finding his way to the top of High Street.

He indulged in a leisurely stroll down the hill, half-hoping he'd be accosted by the nasty bunch that harassed Angela. But the street was deserted, no more crime fighting tonight.

Tom hoped the hard drive had the information Angela wanted. Too bad he only had a laptop with him. If he knew Angela, she'd want to check the contents of the hard drive right now, this minute. Never mind, they could be back on South Audley Street in a matter of hours.

He paused at the reception desk just long enough to mention they would be leaving shortly but returning the day after tomorrow, and yes, they would keep the room, before taking the stairs two at a time.

"Thank goodness you're back." Angela got up from an armchair by the window. "You said fifteen minutes. It's been nearly forty."

"I got held up a bit, and got lost on the way back." She crossed the room and hugged him, all soft and warm with the scent of lovemaking still on her skin.

"I'm glad you're safe, and back, but where's the computer?"

"Here." He produced the hard drive with a flourish. A bit theatrical but, under the circumstances, forgivable. "It's all we need, and less likely to be missed than a whole computer."

"How are we going to read it?"

"Easy. I've a couple of Deltiums at home. We can nip up there, have a look-see at whatever secrets this holds, spend all tomorrow at it if need be, and be back in plenty of time for our rendezvous with Meg Merchant and company."

He loved the look of amazement on her face. "Planned it out, have you?"

"Someone needs to." She growled deep in her throat but otherwise ignored the bait. "Let's go. The sooner we leave the sooner we find out what's on this hard drive."

They drove toward Exeter and joined the stream of traffic on the M5.

"Anything happen while I was gone?" Tom asked.

She told him.

"Ah!" Tom replied after she finished. "Do you want to go back to the States and see your father?"

"No!" That was too abrupt. "Not now, Tom. Maybe later. I don't think my father and I have a very good relationship. I have this feeling we disagreed a lot."

"I see." He was silent for several miles. "I do understand, I was a sore disappointment to my parents."

"You, Tom! You were a famous playwright."

"That was the trouble. My parents were very concerned about appearances. My father was a scrivener, a copyist. He wanted me to follow in his footsteps. I let him down, followed my own stars, and took up with disreputables and actors." He paused. "My father insisted I'd come to a bad end. He was right there. At least by mortal measure. If

I'd stayed home I'd no doubt have lived to a ripe old age."

Angela reached over and squeezed his hand on the steering wheel. She wasn't sure what to say. He'd never before talked about his mortal life, or his less-than-happy death.

He meshed his fingers with hers. "Yes," he went on, "I'd have died at forty or fifty of appendicitis or measles, or typhoid from the foul water. Never have met Kit or Justin, and never had the chance to know you." He leaned over and kissed her. "All in all, with all due respect to my father, I'm damn glad I chose my own path."

"You didn't choose to be a vampire, did you?"

He chuckled. "That just happened. A bit like it did to Stella. I'd met Justin a couple of times, with Kit. They were both part of Walter Raleigh's coterie, far too high-flying for me. I shared a room with Kit for a while. We used to read each other's writing. The one who had the most errors bought a jug of ale. Kit was fine company, but always busy, always in a crowd. He moved on, to more exalted things, I thought at the time.

"He told me later, it was because he didn't want me caught up in his web of deception and politics. They seized me anyway. The heavies Walsingham sent mistook me for Kit, and once they had me, they decided to make me talk." He went silent. Angela shuddered at the thought of how they made Tom speak. His twisted fingers still bore the marks. "You wouldn't believe the lies I told them in an attempt to make them stop. When they did, I lay in the straw racked again with guilt for having denounced Kit. When I heard he was dead, I wanted to die myself. But I lived.

"When they released me, my parents wanted nothing to do with me. I was disgraced and dying, and they couldn't stand the shame. Maybe it was fear too. They didn't want to risk guilt by association. I found lodgings in a hovel, and a few weeks later, Justin found me and carried me away to a house in Sussex. The rest, as they say, is history. I died sooner, and I learned later, than they expected, and Kit transformed me. Waking was bit of a shock. Back then, vampires were considered creatures of the devil."

"Sort of like witches?" She hadn't meant to interrupt. But . . .

He laughed. "Touché."

"What about a ghoulish witch?"

"What about her? I love her. You know that, don't you? You can't conceive how glad I am Kit brought me into his life. Instead of moldering to dust in a pauper's grave, I lived on to meet and love you."

She wanted to squeeze him in a bear hug, but he was driving, and even a vampire needed to concentrate on the road. "I love you too, Tom, and didn't mean to interrupt."

"Not much more to say. Just thought you ought to know about my disreputable past. Sure you want to love a man who's been in gaol?"

"Dead certain!" Good choice of words that!

Beyond Bristol, they joined the M6 and drove eastward into the dawn. The sky was streaking with

the new morning as they pulled into the mews behind his house. They made a beeline for Tom's
study. Angela turned on lights while Tom twisted
wires and wielded his little screwdriver. A few minutes later, he plugged in a cable and smiled as the
screen lit up.

"Ah," he said. "Now, let's have a look at it and
see what we have here."

Chapter 13

Yorkshire. That afternoon.

"I'm worried about Angela."

Justin dropped a kiss on Stella's forehead. "Don't be. Tom's long there by now. He was leaving right after I spoke to him."

Stella wanted to shove him hard in the ribs but was as likely to hurt her elbow as make any sort of impression on him. "That's what I'm worried about!"

Justin's jaw dropped. "You think Tom's going to harm her? Never! He was furious last night, yes, but that was worry. I'd feel the same if you went off without telling me."

"Justin Corvus! We're married! Angela is a free agent. I never imagined Tom would harm her, but he's perfectly capable of bulldozing in and trying to take over."

"And?" he asked, with a wry smile. The raised eyebrow was a complimentary extra.

"And if he does, it will piss Angela off no end. I'd like to see them get together at the end of all this, not split up." He reached out and pulled her against him. "Trying to distract me with sex, are you?" Not hard since he was as naked as she was.

"Of course." Darn him! "Listen! Before I get completely carried away. I warned Tom to proceed as if walking on eggs. I made a point of repeating Dixie's maxim about the effectiveness of vinegar versus honey for catching flies. Plus, I told him if he were patient enough to stand back and let Angela follow her instincts, he would find it most illuminating and highly arousing."

"How very male!" She was tempted to throw a pillow at him but he was sprawled on both of them.

"Why not?" His grin spread halfway to his ears. "Look what watching you get wound up has done for me!"

"Looks as though you need taking in hand."

"What a brilliant suggestion." He rocked his pelvis and waved his erection at her.

She closed her fingers around him, circling his warmth and strength, sliding her hand up and down his shaft. He hardened even more under her touch. She couldn't hold back her chuckle. "You really need taking care of."

"Think you can manage that?"

"Oh yes!" She slid closer, easing toward him until her breasts hung over his cock. Leaning lower, she cupped her breasts and, catching his cock between them, enclosed his erection.

"By Abel! You are so soft!" He tilted his head back, almost shaking with the effort to lie back and enjoy it. She kept up the gentle rhythm, and the blatant seduction, until she felt the moisture ooze from the head of his cock. He was as ready as she was! "Stella!" It came out as a sharp groan.

"Yes?"

"Trying to drive me bonkers, are you?"

"Of course, I love seeing you go bonkers!" As she spoke, she shifted onto her knees and straddled him. "In fact, I'm not sure I can wait much longer." Smiling, she lowered herself until he was sheathed deep.

"You're asking for it, woman!"

"You bet I am! If I say please, will you come?"

"Only after you!"

There was a challenge in his eyes she knew she couldn't meet. No matter how she aroused or teased him, he could always outlast her. She tightened around him, watching his face as she eased herself up and down. His eyes widened as she rode him, his hands clasping her hips and his pelvis moving with her rhythm. She sensed he could keep this up all day and into the night. One day, she'd put it to the test, but this was stolen time, between his rounds and Sam coming home from school.

She sped up, moving more swiftly than ever she could as a mortal. Pressing herself down onto his magnificent body, lifting and lowering herself so fast as to cause a heated breeze between their bodies, she was close to coming now. She closed her eyes to shut out the room, the walls that enclosed them, and the rumpled sheets. All she wanted to sense was his hard heat and her coming climax. She moved even harder and faster. A mortal man would be injured. Justin rode along with her. Her hands pressed against his chest as she climbed the peak of her arousal. With a great cry, she came. He held her steady as the ripples of orgasm invaded her mind and body, holding her close, until her climax eased. Then he took up the rhythm, pumping and pressing upward until she felt the vibrations of his coming climax, the further hardening in his cock, and the sudden jerk inside as he filled her. Only then did he ease his grip and let her topple forward onto his chest.

Her breasts were flattened against him. She nestled her face against his neck and draped her arm across his shoulders. "I do so enjoy your habit of coming by in the afternoon."

"So do I." His hand stroked her short hair. "Alone in the house, we can really let go. A yell like the one you just let out would scare young Sam to death. He'd think I was hurting you."

Life had changed since she met Justin, and not for all the world would she go back.

"I'm relieved."

That made her jump. "Stay out of my mind!"

"Veil your thoughts." He pulled her back to him and dropped a kiss on her hair. "Has it been that hard? A new country. A new existence. Helping Sam cope with all the upheaval."

Had it? "In some ways, yes, but others." She kissed him back. "It still seems a bit unreal. I half-expect to wake up one morning and see the old cracked ceiling overhead and find myself back in Mom's house on Lubeck Street, with the wonky furnace and the bathroom window that doesn't fit properly."

"Oh, this is very real, my love. And don't knock that bathroom window. I found it handy."

He'd confessed that little incident a while back. Under the circumstances . . . "Darn good thing you were honest and honorable. A vampire cat burglar or safe breaker would be quite something."

"One reason for our strict code. Vampires taking their strengths and powers on the path of crime would confound most mortal police forces."

She shuddered at the thought. All that power turned to harm! She'd had a small brush with crime in Columbus, and thanked heaven, and Justin, for the safe haven of Havering. "I'm so glad Sam settled so easily." She'd been so scared he'd find the move from Columbus hard, but he settled into the local school right away. "Playing soccer really helped." Would she ever get used to calling it "football"? Sam had.

"I had a couple of thoughts about Sam." Stella rolled to look up at Justin. "Football was a great icebreaker. It might help if he can do the same this summer. Mike, one of the lab assistants, plays on the village cricket team, and his brother is captain. They agreed to give Sam a few lessons before the season opens and coach him along if needed. That way he won't be the only one with no idea what's going on."

She couldn't help it. She gave Justin a great hug. "You think of him so much!"

"He's my responsibility. I brought him over here. I can't not take care of him."

"You do a darn good job! He all but worships the ground you tread on."

"Right now, he's still dazzled with the idea of a vampire as a stepfather. He hasn't a thought for the difficulties a few years down the road. We need to plan ahead."

"The 'not-aging' problem?"

"Most mortals would never see that as a snag! But yes, what do we do in a few years? I've been here seven already. Ten is optimal, fifteen pushing it."

That would make Sam between eleven and sixteen when they had to up tents and move on. They'd talked about it briefly but never as an immediate possibility. "What do we do? Just jerk Sam away from his school and friends?"

"No. We arrange things so he keeps his friends, even if we have to move."

"I'm not leaving him here!"

"Of course not. We're fine for several years yet. I can bleach a few white hairs on my head if need be. But sooner or later we'll have to move on, and if Sam has a circle of friends from beyond the village, he'll be able to keep them wherever we end up."

"You're not making much sense, Justin. Where will he find these friends?"

"At school." He brushed the hair from her face. "I've given this a lot of thought and talked with other families. Sam's bright. He's only got a couple of years here at the village school. He'll have to move on when he's eleven anyway. I suggest we send him to a private school in York, St. Aidan's. He could start as a day pupil, then when we need to move on, he can stay on as a boarder. He can keep his school friends and come wherever we are over the holidays. They have a lot of pupils whose families are overseas. He wouldn't be the only child in the same boat."

"We can't go overseas." Not with her dependency on her native earth.

"No, but we need to find a spot far enough way that we can set up new lives."

Justin was right, but . . . "I don't like the idea of sending him away to boarding school."

"I didn't think you would, but think about Sam. He's mortal, needs mortal friends. This way he could keep them, most likely go to university with some of them." Private boarding schools! University! Life had changed. "Just think about it. Nothing's carved in stone. We might come up with a better idea."

She doubted it. It made good sense. "I don't want Sam to know we're thinking of it . . . not yet."

"I agree. That's why I waited until we were alone. We've got time. Sam seems to get on well with Jim Hall's son."

"Peter? Yes, he's a nice kid."

"All the Hall boys have gone to St. Aidan's. Peter will join his brothers in a couple of years. Might help Sam to know someone there."

It might help Sam; she wasn't so sure about herself! But neither could she see jerking Sam around the country just as he'd settled and made friends. Maybe, in the coming months, they'd come up with a better alternative. Being a mother didn't get any easier as a vampire. She kissed Justin and cuddled close. How could she not love him when he worried about Sam as much as she did. And thinking about Sam, he'd be home soon. Better get some clothes on.

"Mom, could I have some more Ribena, please?"

"Sure." Stella handed Sam the refilled glass. He'd wasted no time switching a taste for grape and orange juice to the blackcurrant drink. "Got much homework?"

"Not too bad. Some maths, and history, and some spelling. I'll do that after tea." She had to smile; he no longer ate "dinner" in the evenings and seldom asked for "cookies." "What's for tea?"

"Fried chicken." She planned on fixing a batch and freezing it for days she was rushed.

"Kentucky Fried Chicken?" he asked with a grin. He'd been tickled to find how popular that was among his new friends.

"How about Ohio Fried Chicken?" She didn't want him forgetting everything about Columbus.

"It's the best, Mom!" His hug put her in grave risk of baptism by Ribena, but so what? Clothes washed. She held him tight. "Oh, Mom, I need to talk to John as we're on the same technology project. Okay if I give him a bell?"

Sam was getting positively bilingual. "Sure."

He took the portable phone upstairs. Stella rolled the chicken in milk and flour and heated the oil in the pan. As the aroma of frying chicken filled the kitchen, she felt a nostalgic hankering for a couple of bites of crunchy crust and moist meat. She knew better than to indulge that yearning.

As the chicken spluttered and sizzled away, she

fixed Sam a small salad and defrosted a couple of biscuits in the microwave. She set one place at the table and called Sam.

He was tucking into his second piece of genuine Ohio Fried Chicken when Justin came home.

Sam looked up, a smile lighting his face. "Hi, Dr. Corvus!" She understood the pleasure in Sam's face. She felt the same, and when Justin stepped close and kissed her, pleasure rippled through her, as her body remembered.

"Doing all right, love?" Justin asked. "Hello, Sam." He ruffled Sam's hair. "How's the world of compulsory education?"

Sam grinned through a mouthful of chicken. "Okay. We have a football match against Scarborough next Saturday."

"Let me know the time, and I'll arrange rounds so I'm there."

Justin would too. It was as if he'd dedicated himself to filling the gap in Sam's life. Maybe Justin was right about boarding school—later.

Justin joined them at the table. Having an audience while he ate never bothered Sam. He split his remaining biscuit and covered it generously with honey, took a bite, chewed, and looked up. "Something weird happened coming home today."

"What?" Her anxiety meter shot way high. She'd agreed to let him bike home with a group of boys who lived in their direction. Sam enjoyed the company and the socializing, but Stella hadn't yet got over her city-bred conviction that danger lurked. True, there were no crack houses in Havering, but . . .

Sam shrugged. "Just this bloke." Justin nodded

but said nothing. Stella tamped down her appre-
hension and followed Justin's lead. Sam chewed
for several seconds and went on. "It was just before
we turned up the bottom of the lane. He looked
mean. He asked the way to Havering Clinic. I told
him it was back through the village on the Whitby
Road. I was scared Jimmy or Peter would argue
and tell him the truth, but they didn't. They thought
it was a joke."

A schoolboy joke. She didn't find it very funny.

"What made you think he was mean?" Justin
asked before she could get in her spiel about truth-
fulness.

Sam thought, biting his lip. "Don't know really.
Just knew he was. He had nasty eyes, like the people who broke in our house in Columbus and tied
up me and Angela." Sam was unlikely to forget
that dire afternoon in a hurry.

"Did he do anything? Say anything else? Ask
who you were?"

Justin's concern had her worried now.

Sam shook his head. "No. Just wanted to get to
the clinic. I thought afterward maybe I'd been wrong.
Perhaps he was a visitor, but I . . ." he broke off and
frowned.

Justin reached across the table and squeezed his
shoulder. "You did right, Sam. In things like this,
follow your instincts. Understand?"

Sam nodded, obviously relieved. Stella bit back
the questions burning her tongue. Justin seemed
to be handling this. Maybe she should let him.

"Was he driving a big car?" he asked.

Sam nodded. "Yeah, a Rover with new number plates. Had a dent on the front bumper."

"Like Dr. Morgan's?"

"No, his is bigger, and this one was green."

Justin nodded. "And he went off toward Whitby?"

"Yes. 'Course when he realizes he's going in the wrong direction, he'll ask someone else."

"You're right, Sam, but I'll have my security people look out for him. Was he wearing an anorak?"

"No, a sweater, a black one, and he had black leather gloves with holes on the knuckles."

"Was he bald?"

That had Sam thinking a minute. "No, his hair was brown and shiny."

With a few more questions, Sam gave Justin a pretty good description of the stranger and his car.

But it wasn't until Sam went upstairs to shower that she had a chance to ask, "What's going on?"

"I don't know. But I'm willing to go along with Sam's instincts."

"It could just be a boy's fancy. What if it's a patient or a visitor?" Was she playing devil's advocate to reassure herself? Who would be lurking around here?

"Unlikely. We give patients maps and very precise directions, and they have copies to give visitors. Same for reps and salesmen. We don't have signposts for a reason: our patients pay for privacy and discretion. Most likely it's a reporter for the scandal rags trying to find out which celebrities are having face-lifts or tummy tucks this week."

"But you don't think so?"

"I don't know, my love. But I have a pretty good

idea what our chap looks like; I'll reconnoiter the area tonight. If he's looking for us and hasn't found us, he's presumably staying nearby. There aren't that many Rovers in Havering."

"You're just going out to look?"

He caught her meaning right away. "It still bothers you that I feed?"

It shouldn't but . . . "Yes, but I know you need to, especially if you're flying. It's just . . ." She reached out to him. "I think it's called jealousy."

"Stella, if I could still feed from you, I would. You do understand . . ."

She understood. Vamps didn't feed from vamps, just mortals. It was another tenet of the blasted vampire code. The code she now lived by. She kissed him. "Take care."

"I will. I won't go until after Sam's asleep. He needs at least a veneer of normal family life."

After Sam was tucked up and asleep, Justin left, launching himself from their bedroom window. Stella watched him disappear into the night sky and closed the window, not for herself, but to keep the warmth in the house for Sam. February on the edge of the Yorkshire Moors was cold. She double-checked that Sam was still asleep and went downstairs to have a couple of blood bags while she watched a video and waited for Justin to return.

The video ended and she was half-dozing, wondering how much longer before Justin returned, when the phone rang.

"Stella!" It was Angela. "Do you have time to talk?"

"Plenty. Sam's asleep and Justin's on the prowl." No point in mentioning why he was out scouring the village and the surrounding countryside.

"Did Jane tell you much when she called yesterday?"

"No. Just asked for you, so I gave her your number. She seemed excited but wanted to talk to you more than me."

"Don't take it the wrong way, Stella. I know she didn't mean to snub you or anything, but it was something she had to tell me. Listen . . ."

Stella listened. It was incredible. But no more amazing than Stella Schwartz ending up a vampire. "So you're not Angela, but Elizabeth Connor." And apparently a rich woman. "What's going to happen next?"

"I've got to figure out what to do. I called my father. He was . . . polite is the best word to use. Didn't sound as if he was pining for my company. Tom may drive me nuts, but he loves me." She paused. "That's sounds a bit sad sack doesn't it? But it's true. And Stella, things are working out between us. I'm certain."

"So am I."

"Bless you for that vote of confidence!"

"How is he?"

"Right now, bent over a computer with Toby Wise." She went on to tell about Tom's "liberating" the hard drive and their return to London.

"You know," Stella replied, "this seems to get more complicated at every turn."

"My life at least. Yours seems beautifully settled."

"It hasn't always been."

"I know. I just hope ours works out half as happily."

Angela rang off. Yes, Stella thought, their life was settled. The biggest excitement seemed to be Sam's soccer matches, and she liked it that way. She hoped this reporter incident wouldn't bring trouble.

Stella hung up the phone and noticed that Sam had left his homework on the kitchen table; she gathered up his books and slipped them into his backpack. Since she was up and in the kitchen, she thought she might as well fix his lunch for tomorrow. She'd wrapped two pieces of chicken in plastic wrap and was cutting a couple of carrots into strips when Justin returned.

The instant he walked in the door, she knew something was majorly wrong. "What is it?"

He shook his head. "I have been reckless and careless." He pulled her close, holding her head against his chest. "I'm sorry, Stella, my idiocy . . ." He broke off. "I have to make some calls and avert what's coming. Will you trust me?"

"Of course I trust you! If you stop talking doom and disaster, and explain."

"Later. I need to call Gwyltha and anyone else I can find. Will you do what I ask? Please."

The worry in his eyes seeped into her heart. Her chest clenched and she shivered. "What's wrong?"

"Something you are not experienced enough or powerful enough to face. Your job is to protect Sam; you both have to leave. Pack enough clothes for a couple of nights, and enough food for him. Take all the spare blood bags. You're going to have to hide."

"I can't leave you!"

"You have to! Trust me!"

If Sam was in danger, how could she hesitate? But she wasn't about to leave without knowing why. "I've already started on the food." She waved her hand at the carrots on the chopping block and Sam's open lunch box. "You can spare a minute to explain."

He nodded. "Sam's instincts were right. I found the creature he mentioned, staying at the Queen Victoria over in Hallerton. At least his car and luggage were there. I found him feeding off an old sot in the churchyard."

"Another vampire? Why didn't Gwyltha mention it?" New as Stella was to vampire custom, she understood the courtesies necessary to cross another's territory.

"I doubt he cared to ask."

Justin's voice made her look hard at his face. He was worn and drained. "What happened?"

"I faced him, challenged him, and lost." He shook his head. "Understand that, Stella? He bested me! I took a roundabout route back here, but if he picks up my trail and follows, I can't protect you and Sam! I have to call the others to join me, and you must take Sam away."

"You expect me to walk away when you need me?"

He shook his head. "I must face him again. With Gwyltha and anyone else I can find." He held her face between his hands. "Let me at least know you and Sam are safe. Do this for me, Stella."

It sounded too much like a permanent farewell. She wanted to stay with Justin. She needed to take care of Sam.

"Where are we going?"

"A safe refuge we use in times of need. Go get ready. Food, clothes, books for Sam. It should only be a couple of days. Do that while I call for help."

She forced herself to count out undershirts and socks for Sam while her mind whirled through a hundred imagined horrors. What really had happened? How had Justin confronted this strange vampire? And what sort of creature was this that could overcome Justin's two millennia of strength? She shuddered as she folded a spare blanket and added it to the bag. She'd no idea where they were going, but Sam needed to be kept warm.

Back in her own room, she added extra underwear to the bag, dressed in blue jeans and sweatshirt, and added some books, a deck of cards, Sam's precious Game Boy, and all the spare batteries she could find, when she sensed someone near.

She turned. Sam stood in the doorway rubbing his eyes. "What's going on, Mom?"

Chapter 14

Being vampire couldn't stop a mother's heart from snagging. Hers downright twisted as she looked at Sam's bright eyes etched with worry and questions. "Why are you packing my clothes, Mom?"

It took her five seconds to decide what to tell. Sam had proven himself well able to cope with upheaval and the unexpected. "Honey, we have a problem. We're going to have to leave and . . ."

"I'm not leaving, Mom!" His little chin shot up, and his jaw set like concrete.

"Son, we have to . . ."

"Why do we have to leave Dr. Corvus? You said you loved him!"

Abel, help her! Sam sure had the wrong end of the stick. She rested her hands on his stiff shoulders. "Honey, we're not leaving permanently. I do love Justin, but we have to go away for a few days. He wants me to take you someplace safe." She paused. "There's been trouble."

His face relaxed, slightly. "What sort of trouble?"

She'd like the answer to that herself. "I don't know all of it, Sam. Justin went out a while ago. When he came back, he said he wanted me to take you somewhere safe."

"It's to do with that man I saw this afternoon, isn't it?"

She couldn't lie. "Yes, honey."

His face scrunched up with thought. "I knew there was something sneaky about him." His brows furrowed. "What about Peter and Jimmy? They were with me! What if he goes after them too? Mom, we have to warn them."

"I think they will be fine, Sam. This is vampire trouble. We'll ask Justin to check, but I don't think you need worry about them."

"Can I help get ready?"

"How about you get dressed in warm clothes while I finish packing. We can't take much. I have your Game Boy, some books, and a deck of cards. Anything else you want to bring?"

"My homework?"

"If you like. We may be there a couple of days."

"I'll bring my new torch and extra batteries, in case it's dark. You can see in the night, Mom. I can't!"

Sam had adapted all right. A few months back he'd have needed a flashlight. Just as well he was so accommodating. How many kids had to leave home in the middle of the night to hide from a rogue vampire? She hugged him tight. "Get ready as fast as you can." She felt his fear like a cold tremor—it matched hers.

As he nipped back to his room, Stella added another blanket to her bag. It was heavy, but that wasn't a problem anymore. She picked up her long, cloth coat—it would make another cover for Sam if need be—and tugged on walking books. Wherever they were going, she bet it was across open country. Where was this safe place? Not far presumably. She wished Justin was coming with her. Even more, she wished to Abel she knew what exactly was going on.

After checking she had toothbrushes and Kleenex, she carried the duffel downstairs to find Sam, already dressed, making sandwiches with Antonia. Stella couldn't help feeling awkward and gauche beside her. The elder vampire was so graceful, so groomed, and so darn stylish. Beside Gwyltha, the colony leader, it was worse. But now wasn't the time to wallow in inadequacies.

"Hi, Mom," Sam said.

"Good evening," Antonia said. "Justin summoned me to help, but seems Sam has everything under control."

He put a completed sandwich on the stack and reached for another slice of bread. "Think you'll have enough?" Stella asked.

He grinned. "No point in going hungry." He paused. "Mom, I put all the spare blood bags in my book back. There aren't many, you know." Her heart snagged again. What had she done to any chance of a normal life for Sam? But she was alive. The alternative was to be dead. No point in going there.

"That should be enough. There's the leftover fried chicken too. We'll not be gone long." She hoped. "If you're okay here, I'll have a quick word with Justin."

She heard him as she crossed the front hall.

"He is my responsibility, Gwyltha, as much as if he were my own get!"

Gwyltha's response was quieter, but Stella caught the word *mortal.*

Stella pushed the door wide open.

Justin and Gwyltha stood on opposite sides of the red Turkish rug. Justin was grasping the back of a wing chair so tightly the upholstery appeared in danger of permanent damage. There was a flattened spot on the carpet where Gwyltha tapped her foot. And if Stella could still breathe, she'd be in danger of choking on the tension between them. "Something wrong?"

Justin looked her way. "So it seems."

"Perhaps," Gwyltha replied.

Gwyltha, the leader of the colony, usually unnerved Stella. She was so educated and aristocratic, and downright powerful and old, plus had once been Justin's lover. But since the only mortal in the house was Sam, seemed he was the cause of the argument. For Sam, Stella would take on anyone, living or undead. "What's the problem, Gwyltha?"

"Not a problem, exactly." Gwyltha inclined her head but didn't smile. "More a difficulty."

"I see." She damn well didn't but was a good guesser. "What's the difficulty?"

"Don't worry," Justin said, stepping away for the chair and crossing to stand beside her. "Did you get things packed for Sam? Why not go wake him?"

"He's already up, dressed, and making sandwiches in the kitchen with Antonia. What's going on?" Since Justin was beside her, she looked right at Gwyltha.

"Once again, Stella, you turn our colony on its ears."

She sounded friendly enough, but Stella wasn't taking any chances. "About Sam, you mean?"

Gwyltha inclined her head again. "Let us put it this way—in two millennia, no mortal has ever set foot in our safe haven and now . . ."

That was easy enough to fix. "Don't worry about it! I'll take Sam somewhere else."

"No," Justin said behind her. "There is nowhere as safe."

"Not much use if Sam isn't welcome."

Gwyltha shook her head. "It's not that, Stella. We've kept this secret since long before my birth."

"And you think Sam can't keep it to himself?" She almost snorted but stopped just in time. "Never mind! There are other places."

"Nowhere as safe," Gwyltha replied, "and I did not refuse Sam haven." Now Justin got the full glare of the colony leader's dark eyes. "With the menace afoot, there is nowhere else you can go."

"Maybe everyone should go there." That way she wouldn't have to worry about Justin.

Gwyltha smiled. "We have to stop him, Stella. No vampire can enter our territory unchallenged."

"This isn't just a vampire straying into our territory, is it?"

"We fear not. Hence Justin's concern for your

safety. You do not possess the strength to face this malevolence. It will take the combined power of Justin, Antonia, and myself. He's right to hide Sam."

"But you don't want him in on your ancient secret? Hell, let's blindfold him, then. He won't know where he's going or been, and he'll be safe."

Gwyltha nodded. "I felt sure you would have a solution." She bestowed a wry smile on Justin. "Mothers always have an answer." She turned back to Stella. "Can you be ready in five minutes?"

It took them four. Sam, bless him, tucked the last of the sandwiches and, she couldn't help notice, a very large packet of Penguins into his bookbag, zipped it up, and grabbed his parka and gloves. "I'm ready, Mom," he said, his mouth smiling as much as his eyes. "Where do we go?"

Stella met Gwyltha's eyes. "I'm waiting to find out."

"To a safe haven that vampires have used for thousands of years," Justin replied.

Sam was suitably impressed. "Thousands!"

"Yes, it's a big secret. So big, in fact, we're going to have to blindfold you. No mortal has ever been there."

"I'd never tell, but if you have to blindfold me . . ." He shrugged. "I know rules are rules. But how can I see to walk?"

"It's too far to walk," Gwyltha said. "Antonia is going to carry you while your mother takes your luggage."

"Sure you can?" Sam asked, looking at Antonia. She was barely five feet and perhaps weighed a hundred pounds soaking wet.

"I think so," the daughter of one of Arthur's chieftains replied. She held out her slim arms. "Give your mummy your things and off we go."

Still doubting, Sam handed over the duffel but hitched his bookbag more securely onto his shoulders. "I'll carry this," he said.

Antonia smiled as she picked him up and held him close to her chest. "This way you won't get the wind in your face," she said. "Hold tight."

As he settled, still uncertain with her arms around him, Justin stepped forward. "Sorry about this, old chap. We know you'd never betray us, but as you said, 'Rules are rules' and even Gwyltha and I have to keep them." He tied the silk scarf securely but comfortably, gave Sam one last hug, and held Stella tight. "Take care."

She couldn't help the strained laugh. "You're telling me to be careful?" He was facing a rogue vampire that had already bested him once. Next thing he'd be telling her not to worry!

"Take care of your mother," Justin said, ruffling Sam's hair. "I'll see you soon." *I love you,* he thought to Stella, *and Sam. Keep him safe.*

"You bet. And watch out for yourself!"

He grinned and blew her a kiss.

There was nothing else to say. She might not be able to cry anymore, but a lump like a fist jammed in her throat. She nodded, checked the balance of Sam's backpack, hoisted the duffel on her shoulders, and with a nod to Antonia, they were off.

Running first at almost mortal pace, they skirted the shrubbery-edged drive that led up to the clinic, turned down the lane, and crossed the fields south

of the village, leaping hedges and gathering speed
as they ran. Once they hit the open moors, they let
loose.

She'd done this twice—both times with Justin
when Sam had been sleeping over with friends,
but that had been for the sheer fun of speed. This
was a vampire run to safety. The wind was in her
face, her body cut through the cold air, and her
muscles pumped with the joy of immortal power.
To her right, cars snaked along the main road,
headlights piercing the dark. They outran them.
Pity Sam couldn't see; he'd be grinning at leaving
the traffic behind.

But this way he remained in ignorance and pre-
served the colony's safety. He carried more than
enough for one little boy. He didn't need any
weighty secrets. He seemed content, head resting
on Antonia's shoulder. He looked asleep. Stella
guessed he wasn't.

She did wonder where they were headed. As
they ran, Stella's vampire sight gleaned the darkness for clues. East, yes. But where? At the rate
they were going they'd hit the North Atlantic before long.

Whitby? she thought to Antonia.

Yes, fledgling, she replied. *We were here long before
our Romanian friend.*

Stella restrained a smile. She bet Vlad's uninvited
arrival had shaken up the colony. Antonia veered
to the north, avoiding the scattered lights and
darkened houses of Robin Hood's Bay.

Be careful along here, Antonia warned as they

started along the cliff path beyond the village. *The cliffs are weak and give way easily.*

I'd better be on the outside. That's my kid you're carrying!

If I slip, I can fly. Stay where you are.

Good point.

They ran the last few miles in minutes, pausing only when the dark outline of the ruined abbey loomed ahead.

Stella slowed after Antonia and walked back the few yards. "Where now?"

"Now we disappear." She gave Sam a pat on the shoulder. "Still all right?"

"Of course. I'd like to get down, if I may."

"Soon, lad. Hold on another couple of minutes." She looked at Stella. "I'm taking Sam down first. Then I'll come back for the luggage, and bring you down last."

"Okay." It wasn't true, but what else could she say? She almost screamed when Antonia leaped sideways off the edge and down out of sight. Stella told herself that Antonia was ancient enough to fly and Sam was perfectly safe. She repeated it, like a mantra, until Antonia returned.

"Toss over the bag."

Stella tossed it. Watching her clothes and Sam's spare socks disappear was nowhere near as nerve-racking.

Antonia was back much faster this time. "Want to climb down or jump?"

She opted for climbing.

Twenty yards down, a sheer face was quite enough

excitement on top of everything else. After scrambling after Antonia through a cleft in the rock face and down a narrow passage, they came to a wide cavern cut into the cliff. Sam was already making himself at home, blindfold removed, a blanket spread on the earthy floor, and rustling in a packet of smoky bacon flavored potato chips.

"Hi, Mom!" He jumped up and hugged her. "This is neat!"

"Neat?" Antonia's voice held a note of amusement. "I hope you realize you're the one and only mortal ever to set foot here. This has been our safe haven for thousands of years."

Sam nodded. "Yeah. It's neat."

Stella wanted to laugh but she hadn't the strength. The tension of the past few hours slammed hard. She felt almost mortal.

Antonia grabbed her arm. "Sit down."

She did, but the sight of Sam's worried face helped clear her woozy head. "I'll be okay, really."

"You need to feed. That run took most of your strength."

"I'll get you one, Mom." Sam rummaged in his backpack and produced a blood bag. "Here you are."

She'd never fed in front of him. Ever. But she was worn out and needed sustenance. Telling herself he couldn't see that well in the scant light from his flashlight, Stella bit off a corner of the bag and gulped it down. It restored her in minutes.

"That's better," Antonia said, offering a handkerchief for Stella to wipe her mouth. "You've had a rough evening one way or another. Stay in here so you don't get lost. We'll be back just as soon as we take care of our problem."

"You mean the bad guy?" Sam asked.

Antonia nodded. "You'll be safe here."

"There's one thing . . ." Sam began.

"What?"

"What if I need to go to the bathroom? I mean the loo. There isn't one." Of course not. Vamps had no need for one. Small boys did.

Antonia thought a minute. "Stella, when Sam needs to relieve himself, guide him down the entry tunnel to the opening."

"Sam," she said, looking at him. "You mustn't let anyone see you. Be careful, and try not to soil the tunnel itself."

"Don't worry," Sam said. "I'll just aim straight out and it'll hit the ocean,"

Antonia obviously hadn't been around many small boys. She gaped. "Yes, that should work."

"We'll be fine," Stella told her. "I hope all goes well for you."

"With Justin and Gwyltha, we have ample strength."

She was gone seconds later.

Stella helped Sam make a bed with the blankets and coats. The cavern was dry and the floor smooth, worn so by centuries of use. She took him to the end of the passage. Sam gaped at the sheer drop to rocks and the steel gray North Sea below, but manfully peed over the edge, at Stella's suggestion, aiming away from the wind.

Back on the blankets, he chomped down two

ham sandwiches and three Penguins—stress hadn't affected his appetite—and suggested she feed again.

"We only have one more," Stella said. "Maybe I should keep it for the morning."

"We won't be here long, Mom. Dr. Corvus will take care of the bad guy."

How could she argue with such blind faith? How could she consider the alternative? Especially since she barely knew what they were facing. But as insurance, she put the last blood bag aside.

At Sam's request, she read to him as he snuggled under the blankets and settled to sleep. Once his breathing changed, she flicked off the flashlight to save the battery and watched in the dark. She couldn't rest, not until she knew Justin was okay.

Chapter 15

Between the echo of waves breaking on the rocks below and the closer, more intimate sound of Sam's breathing and heartbeat, Stella was lulled half-asleep when she heard movement outside.

She was fully alert in an instant and in seconds on her feet and heading for the opening, ready to stop anyone or anything who was after Sam.

"Stella, don't be alarmed."

Gwyltha! "Are you alone?" Where were the others and . . .

"Come and help us. Antonia's here."

Where was Justin?

Stella was at the opening in seconds. It was still pitch dark, but she could see only too clearly. Gwyltha and Antonia clung to the ledge. Between them they held a blood-covered body: Justin!

Stella swallowed the scream that rose in her throat. "What happened? Is he dead?" she demanded. Dumb question if ever there was one. And what if she'd awakened Sam? She listened frantically for sounds of him waking, but he never stirred.

"Help us!" Gwyltha said.

Stella was out on the ledge and reaching for Justin. Between them they brought him through the narrow passage and into the main chamber.

"What in the name of hell happened?" The man she loved, Justin the strong, the powerful, her protector, lay unconscious, his throat ripped out and his clothes soaked in blood.

"We were attacked by a vicious power," Antonia said. "Justin took the brunt of it."

But not all of it. Both she and Gwyltha were covered with blood, and Gwyltha had a mark on her face that bore clear teeth marks.

"We're healed or healing," Gwyltha said, "but I fear for Justin."

She wasn't the only one.

Stella's heart clenched and twisted as she knelt by Justin's inert body. "We have to do something!" she snapped up at Gwyltha.

"We brought him here," she replied, her voice taut and strained. "The earth will help him heal, and you have blood. He needs it."

She only had one bag! Why on earth had she guzzled the other? She hadn't really needed it, and now . . . Sam was still deep asleep, thank heavens. She pulled the lone bag from his backpack and knelt by Justin. His head rested in Antonia's lap. Gwyltha knelt at his side. "Feed it to him, Stella!"

"How?" He couldn't move. How could he feed? "I get it!" She punctured one corner with her teeth.

The opening wasn't much larger than the nipple on a feeding bottle, but even so, precious drops of blood dripped out on his tattered shirt as she held the bag over his mouth. Stella tried very hard not to look at the gaping wound in his throat as she eased the cut corner between his still lips. She squeezed the bag to speed up the flow, and blood dribbled out of his mouth. He wasn't swallowing! Drinking blood was instinctive for a vampire, and Justin couldn't. Her hand was shaking. She had to calm down, think, and somehow find a way to force blood into him. He had to swallow.

The "holding the nose" trick worked on a breather. How? Abel, how? She remembered helping old Mrs. Zeibel, her next-door neighbor in Columbus, give worm tablets to a puppy. Not a flattering comparison to Justin, but what the hell? "Gwyltha, will you hold the bag? Please. I'm going to work the blood down his throat. Antonia, tilt his head up a little."

Neither vamp paused to question. As Gwyltha squeezed the blood drop by drop between Justin's pale lips, Stella massaged his neck from below his jaw to just above the hideous gash. She kept up the downward movement, praying he'd catch the taste of blood and start swallowing.

His throat was still gaping open, but looking closely, she realized his windpipe and gullet were intact. The tear, bloody and ragged as it was, was just in the flesh and sinew, but the sheer size of it had caused his blood loss and weakness.

"You did it! He's swallowing!"

Antonia was right. Justin was swallowing, slowly

and with effort, but he was drinking. He would be okay, now. Stella stopped massaging and held the ragged edges of the gash together. If he was feeding, he would heal. He had to.

It had to have been the slowest feeding in history, but eventually, he drained the last drops from the bag. Gwyltha set it aside. "You take the next bag, Antonia. I'll hold his head."

"There isn't another."

Stella's words echoed in the cavern.

"Why the hell didn't you bring more?"

Gwyltha swearing was a measure of her anxiety. Stella had never heard as much as a "darn" or "drat" pass her lips. "I was low at home. Justin was going to send over more tomorrow as I only had two left. I had one earlier." Something she'd regret for eternity it seemed.

"I'll fly back to the clinic," Antonia offered. "Know where they keep them, Stella? I don't mind a bit of burglary for Justin."

"There isn't time," Gwyltha said, her voice dull with resignation. "He needs it now. He's too weak. I thought the earth would heal him, but evil from that creature has tainted Justin. His only hope is blood."

"Perhaps we should ignore the taboo on taking from each other," Stella said.

Gwyltha shook her head. "No."

These damn Brits, and their stupid code of ethics! "Why not? He's going to die otherwise, right? You'll just sit here and let him die when we've got blood and to spare!" Angered, Stella pulled off her sweatshirt. "If you lot won't feed him, don't try and stop me!"

"Stella!" Antonia touched her shoulder with a gentle hand. "It wouldn't do any good. He needs living, mortal blood to sustain and heal him. Ours is neither living nor mortal."

"There is a reason for that taboo, fledgling." Gwyltha spoke quietly, but the edge was clear in her voice.

Okay. Did that make it worse or better? Neither. Justin was still dying.

"If I fly there and back, I might do it in time," Antonia said.

Gwyltha shook her head. "You're weakened too. I doubt either of us could fly. We used almost all our strength getting him here."

Despair hovered like a choking fog between them. Stella reached out and stroked Justin's face. His eyes flickered open and then closed. She wasn't even sure he recognized her. "There has to be some way we can get him mortal blood!" Stella said.

"I'm mortal."

Sam! All three of them turned in shock. In their preoccupation with Justin, they'd forgotten Sam, asleep at the end of the chamber. Only he'd not been asleep, but listening to every word.

"Sam," Stella began, with no idea what to say next. "Go back to your corner of the cave" seemed all wrong, but he didn't need to be in the middle of all this.

"Sam," Gwyltha said, "you are too young. We do not feed from children."

"You don't have much choice, it seems to me. You said Dr. Corvus was dying and needs mortal blood. You telling me I can't let him feed from me? Try stopping me!"

She should speak to him about his attitude. Later.

"You're young and still growing," Antonia explained. "It would weaken you too much. There's a reason for our rules."

"Sounds like a silly rule to me!" Sam stepped forward. His eyes were red and swollen with unspilled tears, but his jaw was set for an argument. "It might be your rule"—he included all three of them in his frown—"but it's not mine! And you can't stop me. He loves Mom, and me. We need him. He's the only dad I've ever known, and I'm not letting him die." He yanked his sweater over his head, threw it on the ground, and stepped forward.

"Sam, I'm not sure . . ." Stella began.

"I am, Mom. I don't want to sound rude," he said, "but this is another stupid, grown-up rule that makes no sense." He started undoing his shirt buttons. "Don't anyone try to stop me!"

No one was stopping him. But what if it did harm to Sam? Heaven help her. What woman wanted to choose between her lover and her child? But how could she let Sam take this risk? "Sam!" Stella reached out for him. "You're only a kid. Justin might take too much and harm you." She had to say it. She couldn't let her child get hurt. She shuddered as she pulled Sam close. "Sit on my lap and we'll stay close." No, a child had no place at a death watch either.

"Mom, that's silly, and you know it! Dr. Corvus would never hurt me. No way!"

Ignoring her, he undid another two buttons.

"Sam! No!" It was time to assert her position as parent and make him listen.

"Wait, Stella," Antonia said. "Maybe Sam is right. Even weakened, Justin has some control, and the bond between them." She looked at Gwyltha as if expecting to be contradicted.

Gwyltha nodded. "Three of us are more than a match for Justin in his present condition." She looked at Sam, muddy knees, tousled hair, and the little flashlight tucked in his pocket casting a narrow beam across the underground room. "Are you always this persistent and argumentative?"

He shook his head. "No, my mom would get me if I was."

Gwyltha smiled. "Roll up your sleeve. Blood comes more easily from your wrist, and if we do have to pull you off, we can grab your arm. When we tell you to stop, you stop, understand?"

"Yes, ma'am."

Sam calmly rolled up his sleeve.

He gasped when he saw the gash in Justin's neck. "Who did that?"

"The one who tried to kill him, child," Gwyltha replied.

Sam swallowed, his face paling at the sight of Justin's injuries.

Stella wasn't sure she could let this happen. But

how could she refuse? Sam wanted to do this. So she had to sit her and watch her baby offer his blood.

"It's okay, Mom," he said, hugging her. "Really it is. You really think Mrs. Gwyltha would let me if it were dangerous?"

Stella hugged back, and she would have held him longer, but he wriggled out of her grasp and knelt down by Justin's head.

With a quick glance up at Gwyltha, Sam pulled up his sleeve and all but bashed Justin in the mouth with the inside of his wrist.

"Drink, please drink," Sam whispered.

There was no movement from Justin.

"Please," Sam said.

Stella's throat tightened with anxiety and hope. Should she forbid Sam? How could she?

"Please," Sam repeated. "Please, Dad."

Justin's lips pressed against Sam's wrist but there was no other movement as they all waited. In the silence, Sam's heartbeat echoed off the rock roof. Prayers to several gods rose to the heavens above. If Justin did not drink . . .

With a jerk, both his hands grasped for Sam's slim arm and held tight. Sam winced as Justin's fangs pierced his skin, but he didn't make a sound, just knelt there, leaning forward, smiling.

Stella glanced at Gwyltha. Would she really know when enough became too much? What if Justin went hunger crazed and they couldn't stop him? Why had she ever agreed to this? A vampire was feeding off her Sam! Her lover was taking from her baby! Her son was saving his father's life!

"Enough, Justin, enough!"

Justin responded to Gwyltha's command instantly. Why not? She'd transformed him, hadn't she?

He pushed Sam's arm away and sat up, shaking his head and opening his eyes to look around. He looked dazed and confused but was no longer dying.

"Gwyltha," he said, "what the hell happened? That creature . . ."

"Is gone," she replied.

Stella could have hugged her for the interruption. Sam had seen more than enough tonight. She wanted to know what had happened and what sort of creature could do this to Justin, but no way was Sam knowing all that.

Justin sat up. "Who gave me blood?"

"I did!" Sam grinned and landed a bear hug on Justin that almost had him flat on his back again. "I did! They said I couldn't but then said I could. I'm so glad I did. I didn't want you to die."

"Sam!" Justin hugged him back but cast a near-panicked look Stella's way over Sam's head. *Did I really take his blood?* he thought.

Stella smiled and nodded. They'd have to talk about this later.

"It's okay, really it is, Dad."

That silenced Justin. Sam had never called him Dad to his face before. "Son." He pulled him close, sitting Sam on his lap and holding him tight.

"We've got the same blood now," Sam said. "Just like Pete and Billy and their dads. You're not my stepdad anymore. It's neat."

It was. And emotionally racking, but she couldn't dampen the joy in Sam's eyes. And the incredulity in Justin's was nothing to be missed either.

"I hate to break up this family moment, but Sam needs that blood replaced very soon, and you need more, Justin," Gwyltha said.

"There's plenty in the clinic."

"But we need to get there," Antonia said. "We flew here but getting back . . ."

"I could run back and drive the car over," Stella offered. She'd driven to Whitby often enough. It would take time, but . . .

"You've had one run tonight," Antonia said. "You'd risk draining all your strength before you get there."

"It's worth a try."

"Mom," Sam began, "I'll go with you."

"Mortal child," Gwyltha said. "You're not going anywhere until we replace that blood you gave."

"Oh!" Sam pushed out his lip but didn't argue. Not surprising. He was white about the gills.

"I'll call a taxi," Gwyltha said, pulling out her cell phone.

Summon a taxi in the middle of the night to a vampire's lair. Why not? This was Whitby after all.

"You are flippant, fledgling!" Gwyltha said with a frown in Stella's direction. "We need to leave as soon as possible. Sam, gather up your things. You're coming with us." She paused to speak to the dispatcher at the other end. "I need a large car. For five people, at the Black Swan. In thirty minutes. Wait for us if we're not there." Snapping the phone shut she looked around. "We don't have long. Stella, you help Sam pack while we get changed."

While she and Sam stuffed the blankets and spare sweaters into the duffel, the other three disappeared into the darkness at the end of the cave and returned, in typical vamp style, just minutes later, clean and in fresh clothes. Gwyltha and Antonia were as neat and stylish as ever, and Justin, other than tired lines around his eyes and mouth, looked his usual sexy self.

"Your neck's healed!" Sam said as Justin bent to pick him up.

"Yes, son. Thanks to you." He kissed Sam on the forehead.

"There's blood between us forever, Sam. Never forget. I'm in your debt. I owe you."

"You really owe me?" Sam asked. "Like in owe and payback?"

"Yes."

"But not like in 'owe you a new bicycle or a new Game Boy,'" Stella said.

"Aw, Mom!"

She ignored his rolling eyes. They'd have to talk all this out once they got back, but most of all she wanted to be sure the invading vampire had been totally disposed of. Waiting until Sam was back in bed would half do her in.

"Time to go," Gwyltha said. "Sam, hold your mother's hand and don't let go. We're going out a different way from the one we came in."

"Can't my dad carry me?"

"Not yet. He's still not completely recovered.

That's why we need to get back as soon as possible."

"Okay." With a smile, Sam slid down to the ground and settled for holding both their hands as they made their way through a maze of tunnels that eventually emerged inside the ruined abbey.

"Cool!" Sam said. "It looks different in daytime."

"Hush," Gwyltha told him. "We aim to pass unnoticed, not announced to the entire town by a noisy, mortal boy."

Sam got the message. He was silent as they crossed the grass, and Antonia and Justin hoisted him over the fence. They took the quick way down to the town, taking the steep, curving lane with its hundreds of steps. A left turn at the bottom, a quick walk over the cobbled street between shuttered shops, and they came out opposite the Black Swan. And the waiting taxi.

It was close to two by the time Sam finally fell asleep. Stella sat by his bedside. She looked strained and worn, and she was visibly anxious.

"He'll be all right, love," Justin said. "I gave him more blood than I took. A good night's rest and he'll be right as rain."

"Certain?" Stella asked, glancing up. "Gwyltha and Antonia acted as if hideous consequences waited if you took from him."

"If I hadn't replaced his blood, yes. He's a child, still growing, and his body immature, but I gave him three pints. He'll be his old self by morning.

He can sleep late, take it easy over the weekend, and be raring to go by Monday."

"You really mean that?"

"I wouldn't lie to you, Stella. I wish to high heaven I hadn't had to feed from him, but . . ."

"He wanted you to. You've done a lot for him these past months. He wanted to pay you back."

Yes, Sam was as honorable a son as any man could wish for. A noble offer, but . . . "There's something you must do, Stella."

"What?"

"Rake away his memories of tonight. He's a child, Stella. Do you really want him keeping memories of Gwyltha and Toni bloodied by that creature? And me with my throat torn out?"

"You still don't trust him with your secret hideaway, do you?"

Unfair, but understandable. "I trust him, Stella. He already knows my secrets and yours, and I believe he'd never divulge our refuge. But do you want him waking in the night with memories that are the stuff of nightmares?"

"No. But if that goes, so does his knowledge of what he did for you."

"Yes, but I will know for eternity." He put his arm around her. "I wish I hadn't had to take from him."

"It was Sam's choice. If you hadn't, you'd have died. Just as I'd be a corpse in the ground if you hadn't transformed me. It was the only chance, and Sam knew it."

"But he mustn't know it when he awakes. You realize that, don't you?"

She nodded, her eyes on her sleeping son. Justin watched with her. Young mortals were so fragile, so weak, and so alive. Justin thought briefly of his half brother Lucius. He'd been about this age when he last saw him. Lucius was long dead, even his bones would be dust by now. And Sam . . . Stella would have to watch him age and die. But not for decades yet. And meanwhile, they had to protect his boyhood. "It won't get easier by delaying it, love."

"I know, it's just . . . Hell! You do it! You're expert at this."

"My powers are still diminished, and you're his mother."

"Yeah! And I saw what that vampire did to Jane and Angela's brains. What if I bugger up and leave Sam like them?"

He hugged her, hoping to absorb her fears in this. "He was a rabid creature bent on destruction. I know. I met him last night."

"It was him!" She looked ready to battle a legion of rogue vampires.

"We have every reason to believe so, hence the meeting gathering downstairs. You must do this. Now. You love him. You will not harm him. Just skim his brain, as I taught you to do after feeding. Take away the memories of our refuge, and my attack, and his brave gesture. That's all."

Still hesitant, Stella agreed, had the memories skimmed in seconds, and left Sam sleeping as they went downstairs.

"Now, will you tell me everything that's going on?" Stella asked as they reached the bottom of the stairs. "And what's this about the same vampire that mind-raped Jane and Angela. Did you ever think I'd like to be told these things?"

"I did, and I just told you, Stella. We haven't had much chance to talk before." She nodded, conceding the point. "Now we have to. The others are waiting in the kitchen. We have to make plans and prepare for the next attack."

Chapter 16

It wasn't every day you found vampires clustered around your kitchen table. While Justin gave Sam his transfusion, Gwyltha and Antonia had been snacking on blood bags. The leftovers sat in a heap in the middle of the scrubbed-pine table, staining the surface no doubt.

Stella scooped them all up, tossed them in the compactor, and pressed the button before grabbing a bunch of paper towels and the cleaner and wiping off the table.

"Stella, couldn't that wait?" Justin asked.

"Yes, but since pretending to Sam that nothing out of the ordinary happened tonight is so important, don't you think a heap of empty blood bags waiting at breakfast might be a bit of a giveaway? He knows how many I drink a day." Snippy, yes, but she had just about had enough. This was her kitchen, and if they didn't like it, tough cookies—

assuming Antonia and Gwyltha knew what cookies were!

Stella tossed the used paper towels in the trash and sat down.

"I take it you took care of Sam's memories," Gwyltha said.

"Yeah, I did."

Gwyltha's perfectly shaped eyebrow rose just a tad. "Reluctantly?"

Was it? "No." Stella shook her head. "He doesn't need to remember all that went on. I just hate the thought of messing in his head."

"It's for his safety and protection."

"And yours."

"True," Gwyltha said, "but Sam's safety, like it or not, is linked inexorably with ours. When Justin took responsibility for him, we all did. I won't say 'don't worry, you're a mother,' you will, but Sam is not in danger."

"How can you be so sure?"

Gwyltha frowned. "That creature came searching for someone else."

"How do you know that?"

"He told us," Antonia said.

"Just like that?"

"Not exactly!" Justin rubbed his neck. Stella winced for him as he swallowed slowly. "But he made himself clear."

"What happened?" It was about time she knew.

"In a nutshell," Gwyltha began, "we confronted him on his prowl. I asked why he'd not asked courtesy of passage. His reply was he came merely to regain his property. A mind slave. He wanted the one known as Elizabeth, and in . . ."

"Ohmigod!" All three glared at Stella's interruption. "Sorry." Another rule she'd obviously broken.

"In return we could keep the other for whatever purpose we chose. I told him we had no Elizabeth and no slaves. He lunged for Antonia, but it was a feint before attacking Justin. It took the pair of us to tear him away. Even then he was demanding this Elizabeth." Gwyltha gave a shudder. "He is a monster, with vampire powers. He's yielded for now, but I fear he will return. We must prepare."

"Should we call everyone here?" Antonia asked.

"Before we can plan defense or attack," Justin said, "we need to know what sort of creature we're dealing with."

"Yes," Gwyltha agreed. "While Antonia was out reconnoitering, I called Etienne."

"No!" Antonia turned and stared at Gwyltha in shock. "You can't have!" Antonia looked almost green. If vamps threw up, she was about to.

"Easy, Toni," Justin said, reaching out to clasp her shoulder. "Peace. Listen. Would Gwyltha do this if she were not desperate? You saw what that creature can do. We need all the help we can muster."

Stella would have given the chance to taste chocolate again to know exactly what was going on. Justin had a lot of questions to answer later.

"With all due respect to your sensibilities, Antonia, the needs of the colony must come first. Etienne Larouslière knows more about other vampires than anyone else undead," Gwyltha said.

Stella took advantage of the uneasy silence. "As it happens, we do know Elizabeth."

That got everyone's attention. She told them about Angela's call. It wasn't often a fledgling got to leave three masters speechless . . . if only for a few seconds.

Justin looked up at the ceiling, ran his hand through his hair, and muttered, "Damn!"

Antonia stared but looked a lot less green.

Gwyltha raised both eyebrows and asked, "If you had mentioned this before, it would have helped."

"If there had been time, I would have, but Justin came in, called you, and I was rushing around packing things for Sam. We never stopped to talk." In the panic and worry, it had slipped her mind completely.

"What difference would it have made?" Justin asked. "We'd still have faced him not knowing his strength. Plus, we'd not have answered truthfully that we knew no Elizabeth. Maybe he believed us and is gone. If not, next time we challenge him, hopefully we'll know his weaknesses."

"I thought you beat him off," Stella said.

"We repulsed him, yes," Gwyltha said. "But he will restore himself. Think how quickly Justin healed. This creature will do the same. What he will not do is find Angela. We must warn Tom to be vigilant, and call in support." She paused. "I do wonder what brought that monster here. He must have had information from someone."

"But we sensed he was a solitary," Antonia pointed out.

"Maybe he has human servants," Gwyltha said.

"Enough conjecture. If Etienne can identify him and pinpoint his weaknesses, we can better defend ourselves next time."

"You're certain there will be a next time?" Stella shuddered at the thought.

"There must be," Gwyltha said. "We will not permit him to remain in our territory. Meanwhile, Justin, call Tom and warn him we're coming down and that Etienne is already on his way. He agreed to meet in London."

"I'll call him," he said, adding. "When do you expect to be there?"

"As soon as we can. We'll transmogrify. Come with me, Justin, if you feel you can leave here. Antonia can stay with Stella and take her and Sam back to the refuge if need be."

Just staying put would have been a lot less trouble, but Sam had needed blood. Justin nodded and turned to Stella. "What about it, Stella? Would you be comfortable alone here, with Toni for company? I truly doubt that creature will return. He mind-probed all three of us and left convinced we didn't know his Elizabeth." Darn good thing she hadn't told them Angela's real name. "I think I can help down in London, if you can do without me."

Hell, this was getting too complicated to keep track of. Monsters, magic, and vampire experts that turned Antonia nauseous. "To be honest, and utterly selfish, I want you to stay, but if your going down there will help things, go ahead."

"Thank you, my love." He kissed her as he stood up. "I'll give him a bell."

And she'd go check on Sam.

* * *

Laran left the two teenagers unconscious in the bus shelter. Serve them right for being out so late at night. But they had provided very necessary sustenance, and out of gratitude, he left their minds intact. He'd contemplated binding them to him, but a couple of ghouls would be more trouble than they were worth and might just clue that trio into his whereabouts. Not that he knew where to go next. Where was Elizabeth? Hell, if he'd only just killed those damn women when he had the chance. When he did finally run Miss Elizabeth Connor to ground, she was toast. He'd had enough of pandering to Piet's paternal sensibilities. Elizabeth was a loose cannon and needed sinking. Deep.

But until he found her . . . what?

Since he was this side of the Atlantic, visiting Mariposa and taking care of the Marshes might be a good idea. They'd served their use, brief as it was, and there would be other mortals, other failing businesses, and other opportunities to set up money laundries. He'd persist. He always had.

Might as well call Piet and see if he had any better information about Elizabeth's whereabouts. Another irritation: his cell phone was useless here but the replacement he'd stolen from the boy would do. Laran flipped it open and punched in Piet's number.

"Laran, don't bother about Yorkshire. Lizzie's not there!"

Now the idiot told him. "I found that out for myself, Piet. Where the hell is she?"

"In Totnes! She's gone to see where she used to work! She called me yesterday."

"You're sure this time, Piet?"

"Yes, yes! I spoke to her. She left wherever she was in Yorkshire." If she was ever there. The bunch he confronted had never heard of her. "She's in Totnes! She's gone to find where she used to work!

"And now you tell me!" The man was losing his brains.

"You told me not to contact you, but wait until you gave me directions." Damn, he had.

"Where the hell is she?"

Piet told him, adding the hotel room number. "She's staying there a few days. Now, Laran, talk to her. Explain things. Emphasize the importance of discretion."

"Believe me, I will."

"You won't hurt her, will you?"

"Trust me, Piet." And the idiot did. Mortals were so pathetic.

Laran pulled out the map and looked at it in the dark. Fucking Devon! About as far away as she could be and stay in the damn country. But he could kill three birds with one stone, or rather one pair of fangs. Made the trip worthwhile. Should he drive the darn car, or abandon it and fly? Living death was full of difficult decisions.

London. South Audley Street.

Toby Wise frowned at the monitor. "Look at this, Tom. Interesting."

Tom glanced at Toby's computer. "Good Lord!"

They'd been mumbling over the computers for

hours. Angela paced Tom's high-ceiling study, pausing by the French windows to look out on the winter-bare garden. She'd been worried Tom had taken a drive from the wrong computer, but no, when they booted it up, there it was: the entire program she'd installed, and the back door she'd found by accident.

Twenty minutes later, he called Toby to come and help. "He knows as much about business as I know about computers," Tom told her. "He can make sense of all this."

Maybe. But apart from muttering it looked pretty fishy, Toby hadn't uttered a complete sentence since he arrived, and now he and Tom were mesmerized by the computer. She followed along with them as far as she could; she might have installed the program, but she'd never actually used it. Just looking at the confusing columns of numbers brought back her father's snitty comments about not being an accountant. But Toby saw plenty wrong it seemed. Her instincts had been right . . . and what did that say about her father's business practices? She stared out the windows at the pock-marked trunk of a bare plane tree and sighed. The less-than-satisfactory recent phone conversation with her father rankled. Had she been too abrupt, or had he? Why were they so distant? Was it over this? Hell, she'd been out of sight for five months and he hadn't missed her. That alone sounded incredible. Her mind wasn't that garbled.

"Blimey! Would you look at that?"

She'd never heard Toby swear, ever. "What is it?"

Tom looked up. "What d'you find?" Before Toby

could answer, the phone rang. Not the sleek gray one on his desk, but Tom's cell phone sitting on the inlaid side table by the window. Since she was nearest, she answered it.

"Angela," Justin said. "Is Tom with you?"

"Right here glued to a computer."

"Let me talk to him, please."

Tom took the phone, his attention still on the scrolling figures and columns on the screen. "Hello, Justin, what can I do for you?" Vamp hearing would have come in handy. All she caught were Tom's occasional "Dear heaven, no!" "Of course." "When?" "You really think it's necessary?" and "By all means" until he hung up and stood chewing his lip.

With great self-control, she let him mull over whatever he'd just learned. He'd tell her when he was ready. Meanwhile, she really wanted to know what Toby just found. "What is it, Toby?"

"Your guess was spot on. The books are cooked, right, left, and center. The file you found was just part of it, the others are all over the place. You stumbled on a very interesting and, I must say, ingenious racket."

"Later, Toby! Sorry, Angela, but that will have to wait. We have a crisis on our hands."

Toby took his eyes off the monitor. "What's up, old chap?"

Tom snapped closed his phone. "Mayhem! Seems Justin, Gwyltha, and Antonia confronted a trespassing vampire. Justin was attacked and badly injured." Angela choked back her gasp of shock. "He's recovered. They put the intruder to flight. But his apparent strength has everyone concerned. Gwyltha wants to know what kind of vampire they're dealing with, so she's called in Etienne Larouslière."

"Bloody hell!" Hearing Toby swear twice in one evening constituted a record, or major stress.

"Who's Etienne Larouslière?"

"A damn frog!" Tom replied.

Seemed unlikely Gwyltha was summoning amphibians in what appeared to be a dire emergency. "Not the enchanted prince variety, I assume?"

Tom's mouth twitched. "No, my love. The sort that comes from France. Gwyltha called on Etienne as he knows more about our kind than any other vampire this side of the Russian frontier. I can't deny the man's breadth and depth of knowledge, but normally, I wouldn't have him in my house. But under the circumstances . . . He'll be here as long as Gwyltha needs him."

"He'd better get a move on," Toby said. "It's only a few hours until dawn."

"Does that make a difference?"

"To him and his colony, yes," Tom replied. "Vampires differ according to bloodline. Etienne, like many vampires on the continent, can wander freely without his native earth, but as daylight comes, he falls into a deep sleep, like a film vampire."

"So there is some truth to the Hollywood version."

"Very little." That was always a sore point with them.

"So, a French expert is coming to help out with this vampire that attacked Justin." She shivered just thinking about the strength of a creature that could overpower Justin.

"There's more to it than that." Tom came close and hugged her. "Seems this one went to Yorkshire to recover what he called 'his property': someone named Elizabeth Connor."

"Ohmigod!" Her knees shook so, she'd have fallen if he hadn't held her.

"Yes." Tom's voice came tight and strained. "We have to find out who he is and overcome him, and Etienne Larouslière is our best chance. A brilliant mind, but a character like a . . ."

"Amphibian?" suggested Toby.

Tom's mouth twisted in a half smile. "Pond scum comes to mind."

"How come I get the feeling you two don't like him very much?"

Toby laughed. "Because, Angela, you are a woman of perception and intelligence. In fairness, Etienne has never done me direct harm, but . . ."

"Just don't let him ever get you alone," Tom growled, "or I'll kill him!"

He was starting up the protective macho act again. "Tom, I can take care of myself, don't worry. Seems to me this Etienne is the least of our worries right now." Someone flirting she could handle, being claimed as "property" she was way less confident about.

"Like it or not, he's coming," Toby said. "After all, he does have his uses, and right now we need him. We'd better trust our leader's wisdom. Meanwhile, want me to open a couple of windows, Tom? I assume they are all flying."

"Larouslière is. I think the others are transmogrifying."

"Very well." He crossed the room and opened the French windows. "You have clothes for the others?"

"In the back bedroom. Be a pal and open the windows up there too. They should be here soon."

When Toby left, Angela looked at Tom. "I'm scared. He's come for me and injured Justin in the process. What if he attacks Stella, or Sam?" It would be her fault.

"It wouldn't!" Damn mind reading again. "Go easy on yourself." He stroked her hair, and she couldn't help herself from nestling against the strong wall of his chest. "Sam was safe, and Justin healed after he fed. No lasting harm was done."

"But it was my fault!"

"Stuff and nonsense! No more your fault than getting made ghoul was. It happened. And if this so-and-so has come for you, he's in for the shock of his miserable existence. He isn't getting you, ever. You're under my protection, and that means the whole colony's protection. No one harms those we claim as ours."

A few days back, she'd have fought the idea of "belonging" to Tom. Now she found security where once it had rankled. "But if I'm bringing danger."

He kissed her slowly, with a long sweet promise for later. "You bring me joy, Angela. Joy beyond my imaginings. Never forget that."

"*Charmante!*" An amused voice announced.

Tom muttered something unrepeatable.

Angela turned, Tom sticking to her like glue. Staking his claim in the most proprietary way: one arm around her shoulder, his fingertips resting just above the swell of her breast, as if he was branding

her with his mark. She found it not in the least un-
pleasant. "Good morning," she said. "Good grief!"
would have done better.

It was hard not to stare. Etienne Larouslière
wasn't tall, but he made up for it in every other
way. Dark, windswept hair fell in curls over a high
forehead. His skin had a pale cast of alabaster, and
his eyes were the purest blue violet she'd ever seen
on a human. His shirt matched them exactly. It
was open at the neck to reveal a wide, gold chain
and a dangling medal. His shirt was obviously silk,
with full sleeves falling over his wrists. His pants
were black leather. He looked like an unholy cross
between a biker and a choir boy. Until he smiled.
Then the seducer came to the fore.

"Morning, Larouslière," Tom said.

"Ah, my friend Kyd, and . . ." He bestowed a
practiced smile on Angela and a raised eyebrow at
Tom. "You will introduce me?"

"I'm Angela Ryan." She held out her hand.

"Enchanté." Bending over her hand, he kissed it
and looked up and smiled. His mouth curled, his
eyes gleamed with promise, and his lips parted,
just so. "Angela. Ange. A perfect name for a perfect beauty!"

Once upon a time, like twenty years ago, she
might have been impressed. "Pleased to meet you,
Mr. Larouslière."

He tried the smile again, still holding her hand.
"Please, call me Etienne, I implore you."

"Hi, Etienne. Glad you got here okay. You beat
the others." She retrieved her hand from his ten-
der grasp. Enough was enough.

"They're on their way," Tom said. "Need to feed after your flight, Etienne?"

Etienne smiled at Angela. His eyes feasting on her neck sent prickly goose bumps down her spine. "That would be delightful. You are ever the generous host, Tom."

If Tom gripped her shoulder any tighter, she'd have bruises. She flexed her shoulders, and he took the hint and relaxed his hold. A little. "I have blood bags in the kitchen," Tom said. "Let me show you the way."

He all but bulldozed Etienne out the door. For once Tom's proprietary illusions were welcome. The door closed behind them, but not before Etienne cast her a final, luscious smile saying, "Later, Ange," before Tom hauled him out the door.

She had twenty seconds to breath deeply, shake her head, and vow never to be alone with Etienne if she could help it, when Toby returned.

"All's set upstairs. The frog arrived I gather?"

"Yes."

"Oh." He smiled, his teeth ivory white in his dark face. "Like that, was it? I take it you were not bowled over with his charm and presence."

She had to laugh. "Decorative, yes, but not my type."

"Bothersome, was he?"

"Not really. Tom didn't give him the chance."

Toby chuckled. "Rather incredible, isn't he? But under all that gigolo act is the most amazing brain. He really does know more about our kind than any vampire alive. Of course he's been around a while. Long before my time."

Toby had been transformed in the eighteen hundreds, Tom and Kit in Tudor times, Justin the fourth century, and Gwyltha much earlier. Where did Etienne fit in? "When?"

"He was, I believe, killed during the taking of Jerusalem, during the First Crusade. You must let him tell you the story of his transformation one of these days. Apparently the French do these things differently."

Someone called from upstairs. Justin and company had arrived.

"Stella's not with you?" Angela asked as he and Gwyltha came downstairs.

"No. A fledgling cannot face this sort of power. She's safer in Havering," Gwyltha replied.

"What if he comes back?"

"She has Antonia to protect her, and I somehow doubt he will. He was looking for someone else entirely," Justin said.

"Yes, Tom told me. He wants Elizabeth Connor and that's me. Do you think he's the vampire who made us both?"

"It would seem so," Gwyltha replied. "And he's powerful. We have our work cut out for us. We have a battle royal ahead of us, unless I am much mistaken."

Chapter 17

When Angela once asked Tom why he bothered with a dining room, he'd replied, "To maintain the illusion of a mortal household with the cleaning service. And I do use it from time to time."

This was one of those times.

Gwyltha took a seat at the head of the mahogany table. Tom sat at the other end. Angela didn't wait to be asked, but snagged the seat next to him. Justin forestalled Etienne's attempt to sit beside her, but now she had him facing her across the polished table. Toby took the remaining seat.

So this was a vampire powwow.

She shouldn't be flippant. Her survival no doubt hung on the outcome here, but it was the contrast between them.

Tom, as always, close, reassuring, and reliable. Angela knew she could trust him whatever happened. He'd gone to a witch to try to help her.

Gwyltha, imperious, strong, and confident of her

position. Etienne, who'd flown all the way from France at Gwyltha's request and was eying Angela appreciatively despite Tom's proprietorial hand on her arm. She'd have to take Toby's word about Etienne's brains.

Toby, the nearest to a compatriot she had here, but history and geography divided them. He'd fled the plantation of his birth and stowed away on a blockade runner during the Civil War.

And Justin, polished and confident, and sinfully good looking. If she didn't have Tom, she'd be a wee bit envious of Stella. But she did have Tom; she had no doubts now. She knew who she was and that Tom Kyd loved her. She just hoped this lot could find a way to thwart the lurking threat.

Her fragments of memory of her creator still gave her nightmares, and if he'd almost overcome the combined strength of Justin, Gwyltha, and Antonia . . .

"My thanks to you, Etienne, for coming so swiftly to our aid," Gwyltha said.

Etienne half-rose and bowed. "How could I refuse? This menace must be stopped. I am at your service, as always."

"You know everyone, I think, except perhaps, Angela Ryan."

She got a courtly bow too. She had to admit, he did have style. "The pleasure is already mine," he said.

"Let's begin," Gwyltha said. "Justin and I can tell of face-to-face experience with this interloper. If Angela can add what she remembers, then perhaps your knowledge will identify the sort of creature we are dealing with, so we will know his weaknesses."

"You aim to destroy him?" Etienne asked, raising a perfectly shaped eyebrow.

"He has attacked us and threatened one we hold under our protection," Gwyltha replied. "He will be offered the chance to return whence he came; if he refuses, we assert the right to defend ourselves and our own."

Etienne nodded, acknowledging the reasonableness of this. "If you tell me what is known, I may be able to help you." He shrugged. "We do not have long."

"Dawn is at 7:45. We have three hours," Tom said. "The secure chamber is yours, Etienne. Stay as long as you want."

"I will trespass on your generosity no longer than I have to."

"As time is of the essence, let us start with what we know," Gwyltha said. "Justin, you encountered him first. Tell us what you learned."

Etienne nodded, leaned back in his chair, and inclined his head toward Justin. "I am all ears."

So was Angela. She'd picked up fragments from Tom, but her attention earlier had been on the filched hard drive, not the goings-on in Yorkshire.

"It began yesterday afternoon. My mortal son told me a man had stopped and asked directions to our clinic. On impulse, Sam misdirected him. I'm glad he followed his instincts. I sought the man out, thinking he was a reporter from one of the scandal rags. When I encountered him, I planned to redirect his attentions; instead he blasted me with incredible power. I retreated, called Gwyltha and Antonia for help, and fearing further attack, sent my wife and son to our refuge."

"You took a mortal to our haven?" Toby asked, but at a glance from Gwyltha, he raised his hand in apology. "Excuse my interruption, Justin. Please go on."

"Together we approached the intruder and asked his business. He demanded return of his property: an Elizabeth Connor. Not knowing the name, then, we denied knowledge of her whereabouts. He responded with full force, feinting at Antonia, attacking and disabling me, and only departing after mind-probing all three of us."

"*Mon Dieu!* Antonia was harmed?" The sharpness of Etienne's tone surprised Angela. His face showed pure worry. "What happened to her?"

"She is well," Gwyltha said. "No more harmed than I was. Justin bore the brunt of the attack."

"She is well but unable to attend?" He didn't need to say "liar." His tone did it quite adequately.

"She is well," Justin replied. "She remained behind in Havering to help protect my fledgling wife and my mortal child. My instinct was to stay and guard them, but Gwyltha wanted my strength here in case of further attack."

"You think he will attack here, in London?"

"Who can tell?" Gwyltha replied. "We know he left Hallerton, where he was staying. Antonia, as we speak, is alerting all the colony to this creature's presence. If he is sensed or sighted, we will know, but finding one lone vampire, if he chooses to hide, is like looking for a worm in the earth."

"*Eh bien.*" Etienne nodded. "Please, proceed," he said to Justin.

"I have little more to tell," Justin went on. "The attack was swift and fierce. He went for my throat, to maim rather than kill, I believe. Once he mind-probed us and discovered we were not lying about this Elizabeth Connor, it appears he left us and the neighborhood."

"And no one knows where we may find this mysterious Elizabeth Connor?" Etienne looked around the table.

"We didn't then," Gwyltha said.

"But now?"

"A great deal has come to light in the past few hours," she replied. "We knew of her all along, but by another name."

"Which is?" Etienne asked.

"It's me," Angela said. Wrong grammar but who cared at this point?

Etienne was eying her more speculatively than ever.

"I think," Justin said, "that if Angela tells her story, it will explain a lot."

"Yes," Tom patted her arm. "Tell everything. The more Etienne knows, the better chance of hitting on the truth."

"Everything?" she asked.

"Yes."

Angela took a deep breath. This was going to get more attention than she wanted. Ever. "Okay."

She started with Jane in the park in Chicago and meeting Vlad. Went on to coming over with Tom, her desire to find out her past, the disjointed flashes of returning memory, the trip down to Devon—that got a few surprised looks—following up the coat clue, the calls from Jane and Adela, and her own conversation with her father. And finished with finding out about working at Mariposa and Tom's appropriating the hard drive. "Toby was helping us make sense of the data, but when we got Gwyltha's call, we stopped."

"Tell the rest," Tom said. "It may be relevant."

From incredible to relevant was quite a boost. "I know I'm Elizabeth Connor. My father lives in Oregon. I used to work for his company. I'm a witch, and according to my stepmother, who is also a witch, I had considerable skill." Might as well go for broke.

If she'd been aiming for utter and total shock, she succeeded. Toby dropped his jaw and left it hanging. Gwyltha stared. Justin let out a quickly silenced laugh. And Etienne looked at her with frank interest that, for once, was totally devoid of any trace of sexual significance. It was a distinct improvement.

"I see." Angela suspected Gwyltha did not but kept that to herself. "Justin," Gwyltha said, "I owe you an apology. I thought introducing a mortal child into the colony was a major upheaval. Compared to this, it was a mere ripple."

At least Gwyltha accepted her as part of the colony. She was over the fence, now to jump into the fray. "Why would my presence be such a disruption? I'm no more a destroyer than you are the creatures of horror novels." If that didn't get her tossed out the window, nothing would.

"I have to concede, Tom," Justin said. "You have me bested. I wonder if Vlad knows what he's set among us . . ."

"He most likely does by now," Angela said, not that it mattered. "Excuse my being blunt, and I don't want to sound oversensitive or anything, but why assume I'm a drag on the colony? Maybe I've got skills that might help you, if not as a ghoul, as a witch. After all, no one wants to see this rogue vampire taken care of more than Jane and me. Jane's not here; I am."

Two stunned silences in five minutes was probably a record. Not likely to show up in the Guinness Book of World Records, but still . . .

"Incroyable!" Etienne shook his head.

Angela couldn't help wondering if he purposely arranged the stray curl to fall over his forehead. "What's so incredible?" Might was well let him know she knew that much French.

"You are ghoul, but . . ." He gave a very Gallic shrug. "You are intelligent. I had expected . . . less . . ." He added rather lamely.

"I'm not that sort of ghoul!"

Toby cackled, no other word for it. "I think, Gwyltha, we might just as well accept what we have in our midst and concentrate on our more imminent problem. After we take care of this menace, then we can worry about having a witch in the colony."

Gwyltha nodded. "Fair enough, Toby. If no one

has any objection." No one had. They looked too stunned to protest. "What can you tell us, Etienne?"

"A few questions first, if I may?" He turned to Angela. "Mademoiselle Goule, what do you remember about your maker? Anything, no matter how trivial."

"Not much, I'm afraid. All I remember is a feeling of utter terror. We just huddled in the park, unable even to think. After Vlad rescued and fed us, slowly our memories returned. They're still sketchy, and a lot of what Jane told me I take at her word. When I spoke to my father, I didn't even remember his voice. I know I worked for him, installing software, but what exactly I did I'm not too sure. I'm certain there was some sort of trouble in the business. Toby and Tom were trying to figure out exactly what when we got the call everyone was arriving—went off on a tangent a bit there. Sorry."

Etienne nodded, all seriousness now, the lighthearted banter gone. "Since you, or rather the person you once were, is this creature's target, maybe it is not a digression after all. Time will tell." He looked toward the end of the table. "And Gwyltha, you and Justin, you sensed power, strength."

"And malevolence," Gwyltha added.

"Incredible strength," Justin said with something resembling a shudder. "Admittedly I was weakened from my first encounter, but he took me down as easily as if I were a puppy! And left me close to done for."

"But you did recover."

"Only after extensive feeding, and even now I'm weakened."

"As am I," Gwyltha added. "He blasted me off my feet for several yards and pinned me to the ground while he attacked Justin."

If he could take down Gwyltha and Justin, who could best him?

"But he did not injure or attack Antonia," Etienne said, as if thinking aloud, "and any vampire with minimal perception would see her as the weakest of the three."

"He started for her, or so we thought, but it was a feint," Justin reminded him.

Etienne nodded. "Or was he repulsed by her? Eh? What was she wearing?"

"Blue jeans and a sweater, and trainers," Gwyltha replied, a bit tersely. "What difference would it make?"

"No jewelry?"

Gwyltha and Justin looked at each other. Gwyltha frowned. "A wrist watch, earrings—small gold ones I think—and something on a chain around her neck."

"A silver chain, perhaps?"

"Yes," Gwyltha replied.

"Hah! Our first pointer. He is repulsed by silver. Without that chain, I conjecture Antonia would have been his first victim. He perceived her relative weakness and attacked her first."

"In that case, we'd best hit the nearest jeweler as soon as the shops open in the morning," Toby said.

Etienne agreed. "Make sure you purchase pure silver. Your survival may depend on it."

"What else?" Justin asked.

"What else can you tell me? Height? Looks? Voice? Did he speak English well, or as a foreigner?"

"Taller than Justin, heavier build. Voice . . ." Gwyltha thought about that. "An accent, could be American."

"Definitely American, I'd say," Justin added. "Dark hair, bad breath."

"And he admitted a connection to Elizabeth Connor, our Angela," Toby said. "Seems we should start there."

"But where is 'there'?" Angela asked. "A park in Chicago? Jane's house? Apparently he—or another vampire—was there. Jane said Vlad's people tracked him. We know he knows me. He most likely was the one who did me in, and he is repelled by silver. That's not a lot to go by."

"Perhaps," said Etienne, "we can add to that. He's only been seen at night, right? Maybe he sleeps during daylight."

"No. Sam first saw him yesterday afternoon on his way home from school. It was getting late but still light. Daylight does not immobilize him," Justin said.

"Great," Toby muttered. "So he has the freedom to move constantly."

"So," Etienne said, "the silver we can take as given. If he slept in day, I'd say we were dealing with a vampire from North Africa, or parts of the East. We know nothing about his shapeshifting or flying abilities. But we know he was driving rather than taking the faster way to travel. That gives us, perhaps, the advantage of speed and mobility. Let us see, immunity to daylight, sensitivity to silver, possibly unable to fly or transmogrify. Any trace of earth in his hotel room? The car?"

"Never thought to look," Justin said.

Etienne frowned a little. "That could go either way then. Still we have something. I'd say he's either from the European part of Russia, or Central America. A wide canvas, I admit, but . . ."

"Weaknesses for either of them?" Gwyltha asked.

"The former are easily weakened by wood—no need to stake, a good bash to the head will do the job. Some of the more barbaric leaders have their human servants put wooden collars on out-of-favor vampires as punishment." He shuddered at the thought.

"And if he's from Central America?"

Etienne smiled at Gwyltha. "Nothing so easy, I'm afraid. They do react to certain herbs grown in the jungles, but other than that, it is said they can be repelled by magic and charms."

"What sort of magic?" Angela asked.

"How should I know? It is not my province."

"But it is mine."

Another shocked silence.

"You are proposing using magic spells against this creature?" Angela couldn't tell if Gwyltha was scandalized or just sarcastic.

"Why not? Tom told me that witches tried to kill Kit. They had power against him. I don't harness power to destroy, but rather to protect. If I can work spells of protection and use them as defense against him, it might help. If it works in South

America why shouldn't it here? Magic is magic."
Magic was also suspect, if not downright taboo, as
far as everyone else was concerned.

"And how would you harness this magic?" Gwyltha
asked, not sounding as shocked as the others.

"Tonight is full moon. Time for rebirth. Power
gathering and sharing." She paused; might as well
go for broke. "I was invited to join a coven for a
Full Moon gathering by a witch in Totnes. With
our combined power . . ."

"Dear heaven!" Toby said. "What next!"

"What have you got to lose? Seems with what
we're up against, you need all the help you can
get."

"Angela, in all my days as vampire, never have
we collaborated with witches." Gwyltha sounded
more stunned than anything.

"A new millennium, a new cooperation, perhaps."

"Incredible," Justin said. "But I, for one, will
trust Angela."

"If a mere observer may offer comment?" Etienne
said. "You already trust Angela with your innermost
secrets. She knows enough to destroy us all if she
so chose. Why not trust in her honor a little further?"

"I trust her utterly," Tom said. "I will go with her
tonight. If the monster strikes earlier, then we
must do as best we can, but if her power can add to
our strength, how can it not help?"

"Is this an ultimatum, Tom?" Gwyltha asked.

"No, Gwyltha. Just a declaration of my trust in
Angela. I do not believe her capable of harm.
Whatever power she draws, she will use to protect

not destroy. Can we afford to refuse any help? If this creature can overpower you and Justin, it seems we need something more than we can muster."

Angela was tempted to jump up and hug Tom but decided to wait until they were alone and she could thank him properly. If only the rest would agree.

No one objected outright.

"So be it," Gwyltha said. She turned to Etienne. "My thanks for sharing your knowledge. We are indebted."

"If it resolves this present crisis, I am repaid. Scourges like this harm us all."

"So," said Justin, "we're looking for a man, taller than I, heavier build, allergic to silver, impervious to light, maybe susceptible to magic, or perhaps wood. He makes ghouls and considers them property."

Everyone shuddered at that, Angela most of all.

"What else? Tom asked.

"Bad mannered, arrogant," Gwyltha went on. "Very focused on what he wants, ruthless, sure of his strength and position, and willing to ride roughshod over anyone who gets in his way."

"I knew someone just like that," Angela said. "I couldn't stand him. He used to work for my father."

Chapter 18

As the flippant words hung in the air, Angela gasped at the hideous possibility. "No! It can't be. It's not possible!" But the musty memory of an overheard phone call and her father saying Laran was going to "take care of her" poked like a barbed echo inside her mind. "No!"

She began shaking, the room wobbled around her, and the figures around the table became pale blurs as Tom's arms caught her.

When she came to, she was stretched out on the sofa in Tom's study. Tom sat beside her; she had a cold cloth on her forehead, and the other four vamps clustered at a distance, looking worried.

Talk about feeling a fool!

"Better?" Tom asked. "You had us all worried there." Angela nodded. Talking seemed too much effort. "You had another memory flash, didn't you?"

"Yes. But . . ." Talk about feeling giddy. Fainting again seemed highly probable.

"She needs sustenance," a distant voice said. "You have food for her?" She caught the French accent.

"In the fridge in the kitchen. Justin, be a pal and grab her something."

"I may be all right." She forced herself to at least sit up. Reclining on the couch was so wimpy. She had to think about this, but her head hurt when she tried.

"Here, Angela." She'd forgotten how fast vampires could move.

"Thanks." She took the pack of lamb chops from Justin and gnawed, her mind clearing as she swallowed. Toby, Justin, and Gwyltha had the tact to wander over to the window. Etienne watched her, fascinated.

"*Mon Dieu,* it is true! I have heard speak of it but never witnessed. Indeed, Gwyltha, your colony is the most fascinating I have ever encountered."

Another time, Etienne's outright curiosity would have irked. Now, she was too worn to care.

"Feeling better?" Tom asked.

"Yes." Better, but not exactly fine. Still . . . "Sorry about that. I get headaches and go lightheaded when memories surface, but I've never passed out before."

"But have you ever had a memory of your father return before?" Etienne asked.

"No."

"Would it be asking too much for you to remember as much as you can about this man?" Gwyltha asked.

No, it wasn't too much, just too difficult, but . . .

"His name is Laran Radcliffe and he works for my father. But I remembered overhearing my father, on the phone, saying Laran was going to 'take care of me.' It must have been then that I ran away. If I went to Jane, and as she's my half sister that makes sense, then . . ." She broke off, her throat tight with horror. "I led him to Jane. All this is my fault!"

"Stuff and nonsense!" Gwyltha said, sounding like an impatient nanny. "Don't talk rot! How can it be your fault?"

"The fault lies upon the vampire himself, and whoever sent him," Toby said.

"That was my father." Cold coiled around her heart at the thought. Finding a lack of cordiality between them was way different from thinking he'd had her ghouled.

"Not necessarily," Toby said. They all stared his way. "Assuming this creature is the vampire we seek, perhaps your father sent him to talk to you, maybe persuade or intimidate you, but never intended a mind rape."

That thought was a lot more comforting. Angela closed her eyes and tried to visualize her father's face. Laran's was the one that sprung to mind. Laran standing by the car before they left for dinner . . . "Damn!" She looked up at Gwyltha and Justin before reaching out for Tom's hand. "It's no good. Laran can't be a vampire. He's a grade A sleaze perhaps. Might well be cheating my father, but not nothing more." A shame that, he fit well into the villain role.

"What makes you say that?" Justin asked.

"He eats solid food. I've seen him. Chews and

swallows. Dad and I had dinner with him the night before I left."

They all looked as if they'd had the solution snatched from their grasp. It had been too easy. Too tidy. Nothing was ever that simple.

"No, no!" Etienne said in the silence that followed. "If we are dealing with a Central American revenant, it makes no difference; they drink blood, yes, and prefer it fresh, but also eat food in limited quantities. Makes it very easy for them to pass as mortal."

"And thus hard to detect," Toby added. "How marvelous!"

"Remember his weaknesses: silver and magic, but," Etienne said, "I regret but I must retire. Dawn comes." Beyond the window, the sky was lightening. "If I may avail myself of your safe hospitality, Tom, then I will rejoin you at dusk."

"Let me show you, Etienne," Tom said, and they both left the room.

Tom went out with Etienne and left her bereft. She was a lone witch facing three vampires. Vampires who'd been friends before she "came out." Now, who knew? And if that wasn't enough for one night, she had to face the distinct possibility, despite Tom's reassuring words, that her father sent Laran to destroy her mind.

"You look exhausted, fledgling," Gwyltha said, "and worried."

"Not surprising, is it? I've been up all night and now wonder if my father did this to me." Tears pricked behind her eyelids.

Gwyltha sat down beside her. "Do you really think that possible?"

"I don't know. I don't know him. I only discovered his existence yesterday. We've had one conversation." Which hadn't gone too well. "I seem to have stronger memories of Laran Radcliffe than I do my own father. That could be because I dislike and mistrust Laran."

"Your instincts are returning with your memories."

"The darn memories are so jumbled nothing makes sense."

"It will."

"Don't we need it to make sense *now?* That creature, whoever he is, is lurking out there right this minute." Angela looked toward the much lighter sky, as if expecting to see an evil face peering in.

"It would help, yes. But even vampires have limits. And ghouls certainly do. You'll be more use rested than worn out. And we need you, Angela."

"I'm not persona non grata?"

"Far from it. If what Etienne says is true, we're going to need your skills."

"My skills are pretty sparse right now."

"They're more than any of us have. This Full Moon ceremony, won't that help restore them?"

Angela nodded. "It should. I'm not sure what I can do on my own. Heck, I don't even know what you want me to do."

"We are all fumbling in the dark, but if magic is the force that can overcome this monster, we need you."

Since this vampire was after her, she needed her skills. "There is always the chance he gave up and went home."

"Do you believe that?" Toby asked.

"I wish! If it is Laran, he won't stop until he finds me. Seems I can't even go home. I can't go anywhere!"

"He won't find you," Justin promised. "If push comes to shove, we have safe places we can hide you."

"I'm not hiding away while he's going after you! He has to be stopped, and if I can help, I will." She thought a minute. "I need to call Oregon. If Laran is there, then we know it's not him." If he wasn't, she'd have a long chat with Dad. A talk to Adela might be a darn good idea too. "Pity I can't call now, but it's the middle of the night there."

"Then take my advice and rest," Gwyltha said.

Wasn't such a bad idea after all.

"A strong woman," Toby said as the door closed behind Angela.

"The best ones are," Justin replied.

"I take your word for it."

Justin grinned. "Do. And talking about strong women, I'd better call mine. I want to check that Sam's all right."

Toby watched him step out the French windows. "Matrimony has mellowed our austere physician."

"He has a good woman," Gwyltha said, "and found contentment."

"What's this about good women?" Tom asked as he came in. "Mine just told me to get lost!"

Gwyltha turned in his direction. "Surely not!" she said, her mouth twitching.

"Said she had a lot on her mind and needed to be alone."

"She does have a lot on her mind, and she needs to rest. She'll need her strength before we're through this."

"You're serious about taking a witch into the colony?" Toby asked, the doubt clear in his voice. "I never thought I'd live to see that day."

"Neither did I," Gwyltha replied, "but Tom vouches for her, and if Angela possesses the skills to help us defeat this menace, then she has a place among us."

Toby shook his head. "I'm not questioning your decisions, Gwyltha, I'm just amazed at them. New vampires, a child, a ghoul, a witch. The colony has changed in the past year."

"It's the twenty-first century, lad," Tom said. "Times change."

"And time's short," Gwyltha said. "We have strategy to devise. We can't leave everything to Angela."

"Everything all right in London?" Antonia asked as Stella put down the phone and walked back into the kitchen.

"Pretty much. Seems they tentatively identified the sort of vampire—never realized we came in different varieties. Apparently your silver chain saved you. Justin had me promise to go into York first thing and buy chains and bracelets for Sam and me. Seems they just held a vampire summit down in London. They don't think he'll be back our way, but no one really knows for sure, of course. Justin has no idea when he's coming home. That worries me; I'm torn between wanting to be with him and being here, to take care of Sam."

"If that animal, I refuse to call him a vampire, is after Angela as he claimed, we should be safe up here. I just wonder how many of us it will take to best him. You didn't see how fast he struck Justin. I did. This animal has power."

"But apparently he can't fly or transmogrify; doesn't, they think, need his native earth; and most likely comes from Central America. This expert they called in from France seems to know a lot."

"Larouslière?" Antonia frowned.

Stella nodded. "Yes, that's his name."

"Oh yes, he knows it all! He's so full of self-importance, it's a wonder he hasn't exploded by now."

"You don't like him very much?"

"Stella. Unless I'm completely mistaken, he's the reason Gwyltha had me stay up here. Not just to help protect you but to protect Etienne Larouslière from me!"

"Oh!" Talk about piquing curiosity. "You don't get on with him, then."

"The last time I set eyes on him, I threatened to cast him out in the sunlight if I ever saw him again. He's French; they can't face the light as we can."

"You meant it?"

"At the time, yes. Would I still?" She shrugged. "No. He really isn't worth the penalty I'd pay, but in a nutshell, I loathe, despise, and abhor him. He's slime mixed with ordure." Having heard this much, Stella had to know the rest. Calm, serene Antonia, who always looked as if nothing could ruffle her, was pink in the face, her eyes blazing.

"What happened?"

Antonia gave a twisted smile. "I was brain addled. I fell in love with him, hook, line, and sinker. To be fair, Justin did warn me about him, said he was fickle, but I was too besotted to listen. I found out the hard way. Caught him in flagrante delicto. And he had the nerve, afterward, to say it was unimportant. He loved me, she was a mere diversion. That was when I promised him the dawn. I might have done it, too, but Gwyltha and Justin dragged me off to Yorkshire." She paused. "That was back when they were together; you did know about that, didn't you?"

"About Justin and Gwyltha being an item? Yes." She wasn't about to be jealous; both she and Justin had pasts, his was just so much longer. "When did this happen?"

"June 1793. A rotten year all around. The king and queen of France lost their heads, and I lost my heart."

Her flippancy didn't fool Stella one minute. "There's no hurt quite like it, is there?"

"You too?"

"Not quite the same. But Sam's father promised me eternal love and adoration, and walked off into the sunset and never looked back."

"After Sam was born?"

"When I was pregnant."

"Men are pigs!"

"Some are. Some are rather wonderful."

"You've got one of those."

"You will one day." With Antonia's style and looks there had to a vampire out there for her.

"No thanks. Once bitten, twice shy." She chuckled. "Literally in my case. No one's ever getting their teeth in me again."

"He fed off you?" Not with the strict taboos, surely!

"Not feed, no, but the French have no constraints about biting and tasting between vampires, not if it's part of lovemaking. Hell, they have no taboos anyway. No sense of fidelity, and as for their much-touted sense of honor, Cain had more!"

Maybe, but under the scorn, Stella sensed deeper emotions than simple disdain. "You haven't seen him in over two hundred years?"

"Once."

The single word promised a long story. "What happened?"

"I made a fool of myself, embarrassed every vampire in England, and angered Etienne. The latter I don't regret, the others I do." Antonia stood up, obviously unwilling to say any more. "I'm off to do another fly around. I don't believe we have anything to worry about, but the fresh air will do me good."

Totnes. Next morning

"What do you mean 'not here'?" Laran snapped. After an all-night drive across country, he had no time for simpering mortals. "I was told she was staying here." Could that idiot Piet have gotten it wrong yet again? If so, a little discipline was in order on his return to Oregon.

"Sir, we have no Miss Connor here, and according to the register, we haven't for months." To prove the point she flicked back through the heavy book. "We had a Reverend Connor, but that was back last September." And the mortal had the impudence to snap the book closed by way of dismissal. "There's no one here by that name."

"Wait!"

She squared her shoulders as her eyebrows rose. Laran wanted to pluck them out by the roots. "Sir?"

"She sometimes travels under another name: Angela Ryan." He should have thought of that sooner. Fatigue was playing havoc with his brain.

Recognition flashed in her eyes. "We have no one here by that name, sir."

"But you did have."

She smirked. At him! "She left the day before yesterday, sir."

"You have her address."

"I couldn't possibly release that information, sir."

That did it! He was short on time and out of patience. Before he thought to reach for the leather-bound guestbook, the bitch had the effrontery to slide it under the counter. Laran grabbed her by her shoulders and yanked her upwards and toward him. Her scream died as he smashed her face into the oak beam overhead. Her nose broke with a satisfying scrunch, and sweet blood gushed. She let out a gurgle of horror as he tossed her across the hall. She landed in a crooked heap on the bottom steps of the wide stairway, her head hanging at an odd angle.

He didn't have time to properly enjoy her blood. He reached under the counter, pulled up the book, and flipped it open. There it was, on the last page: "Angela Ryan" and the address "The Gables, Havering, North Yorkshire."

Damn! She had been there, left, and come here and now? If only he'd known this other name yesterday. No wonder no one there had heard of Elizabeth Connor! Where the hell was she now? As he scowled at the book, he saw the penciled note beside her address. "Returning Sunday night." All he had to do was wait a few hours.

"What's going on?" Another damn mortal: a pimply youth wearing a white apron walked through the door and noticed the woman lying in a crumpled heap. "Sarah!"

Laran pushed him aside with the flat of his hand. As the youth fell back in a heap, Laran kicked him and grinned at his scream as the bone cracked. With the satisfaction of a productive visit, Laran walked out into the early morning.

He had time to kill. Might was well visit the Marshes and tidy up that loose end while he waited for Elizabeth to walk into his clutches. He started the car and pulled out into the street, turning left by the river. A few hundred yards along, a police car, sirens blaring and lights flashing, passed him going the opposite direction. Drat, he shouldn't have left that boy alive.

Watching in his rearview mirror, Laran saw the the car do a tire-squealing U-turn before it came toward him. Just what he didn't need. In seconds the car was on his tail, lights flashing. Laran waited until they were close, made a racing change into reverse, and slammed into them.

He beat them out into the street.

And waited.

The driver stayed in the car. The other stepped out. No gun in his hand, and nothing in his belt. So it was true. They really didn't carry guns. Not that it made any difference.

"Sir," the policeman said, "may I see your license?"

Laran grabbed him by the neck and squeezed. He'd tossed him into the front yard of the nearest house before the driver caught on. Laran could smell his terror as his puny mortal mind grappled with the impossibility he'd just witnessed. The driver spoke into the small microphone; Laran wrenched off the door and threw him across the other side of the road.

He got back into his own car and drove away abandoning the car soon after on a side street, ripping off the number plates and leaving the key in the engine. He was only a short way from the Marshes. They'd better be in. He needed good, warm blood. All this running around and killing depleted his strength.

They weren't very welcoming, but he took care

of that. The kitchen of the little bungalow soon looked like an abattoir, but he hadn't felt this elated since he'd dealt with Elizabeth and that half sister of hers. And thinking of Elizabeth . . .

Laran dialed Piet's number on the Marshes' phone. Time to make him do some of the work.

"Shit, Laran! Do you know what time it is?"

"I neither know nor care, Piet. Stop jabbering and listen. I need Elizabeth, and you are going to find her for me. Call her friends, that woman you were married to—call the president if it helps, but find her!"

"Laran, I . . ."

"No, Piet. Let us get this abundantly clear. You fail to tell me where she is, I will find her on my own and kill her."

"Laran. No!"

"Make it easy on all of us, Piet. Good luck."

It was late afternoon when the call came. Laran had almost given up. Three fruitless prowls around the town had revealed that the police were out in full force—killing those two cops had perhaps been an error in judgment—but not sight nor sound of Elizabeth. He was close to getting despondent.

"It's not much," Piet began, "but I got this from Heather. I caught her, not her damn mother. Adela is tight-lipped, but Heather was all chatty, going on about someone who'd been robbed and going to lunch with a new friend. Lizzie is going to Totnes sometime today. Seems she's got a new

friend too; she's spending the evening with someone called Meg Merchant."

Just a name, no address. But how many Mer-
chants could there be in this one-eyed town?
Laran had noticed a phone book in the kitchen
earlier. He hoped it wasn't too blood-soaked to
read.

Chapter 19

Tom's house in South Audley Street. Earlier the same day.

"Angela, I'm sorry. Can you wake up?"

She could. But why? Seemed only minutes ago she'd tumbled into bed. "What's the matter?"

Tom waited while she sat up and ran a hand through her hair. "Stella just called. Wants you to call your stepmother. Something's wrong."

That got her alert. Fast. "What's happened? Trouble?"

"Not from what Stella said. Adela just called her ten minutes ago asking to speak to you. Stella was a bit cagey after the trouble last night. Said you were gone. Seems Adela wanted to know if you were safe. Wants you to call her as soon as possible."

Angela looked at the clock. Nine-thirty. "It's the middle of the night in Chicago."

"She's in Columbus, with Jane."

"It's still the middle of the night."

"From what Stella said, it sounded urgent."

She'd planned on talking to Adela anyway . . . but right now? What had happened that couldn't wait? Only one way to find out. Angela punched in the string of numbers and waited while the system clicked her halfway across the globe.

The phone was answered on the second ring.

"Lizzie, thank heavens you called back." Adela sounded frazzled in the extreme.

"What's wrong?"

"I don't know, but I just had the strangest conversation with your father."

"Just now?"

"Ten minutes ago. He woke me up. Half crying, half yelling down the phone at me."

"I'm sorry, Adela." Why was she apologizing for her father? And why was he going off at Adela? "What happened?"

"He was demanding to know where you were. I told him the last time I spoke to you, you were in Devon. He snapped back that you'd left there and he had to find you. Practically accused me of knowing where you were and refusing to tell. Honestly, Lizzie. I finally snapped and told him he'd been unconcerned about you for five months while you were missing and what was setting him off now that you were safe?

"He started crying. Said he had to find you. That everything depended on it. Honestly, Lizzie, if I didn't know he seldom drank, I'd say he'd been tipping the bottle. But after I hung up, I started worrying. I almost woke Heather, but found her list of numbers and called your friends in Yorkshire.

The woman there, Stella, right? Sounded nice but was very cagey. Said you weren't there. She couldn't tell me where you were but insisted you were fine. When I said I had to speak to you she said she'd get you to call. She kept her word, obviously, but . . . Is there some sort of trouble?"

Why lie? "Yes, Adela, there is. But I'm okay. Honestly I am but . . .

"Where are you? With the same friends?"

Adela she trusted completely but . . . "Adela, I'm not telling you where I am. Not because I don't trust you. I do, but this way you can truthfully tell Dad you don't know. I'm going to call him later. I was waiting so as not to wake him in the middle of the night."

"Lizzie, tell me what is going on?"

"I need your help."

"You have it, dear, you know that! What do you want?"

"I'm not certain what I want or need, but this is what's happened . . ."

Adela listened.

Through the distance, Angela pictured her face tilted to one side as she listened, her chin resting on her hand as she propped her elbow on the nearest piece of furniture. If only Adela were right here. With her strength and knowledge, she would have a chance; as it was . . . Doubt would not win. She would. This destroyer would not take her mind or anyone else's again.

"How do you plan to protect yourself?" Adela asked.

"First, I'll find out if this really is Laran. Second,

I'll figure out what to do next. He has to be stopped, and I hope Meg and the rest of the coven can help me."

"Darling, you're counting on an unknown, uncommitted coven?"

"What choice do I have?"

Adela's sigh echoed down the phone. "I wish I were there. It's impossible at this short notice, but I'll add my strength to yours. Heck! I'll get on the phone and call everyone I know. We'll all join with you."

She was no longer alone among skeptics. "Thanks." Just knowing that added hope.

"And darling, what about the vampires?"

"I'm still learning how things are. You never mentioned . . ." She hated that it came out as a reproach.

"Perhaps I should have. But they are so seldom encountered. I wasn't familiar with them, except by hearsay. Didn't know about them at all. I'd never have identified the spoor in Heather's house on my own. Would my telling you have made a difference?"

"No." She'd have loved Tom whatever he was.

"They treat you with respect?"

"Definitely! Other than being a bit leery of my being a witch."

"I found the same. Though, Lizzie, dear, they do have some rather odd notions. While Heather was out yesterday evening, I had long talk with Dixie, this young woman here. Her partner, Kit, was abused by a dark coven, so their prejudices are understandable to a degree. And I owe them all a debt for their care of Heather and you. Not that I told Piet you'd been taken under a vampire's wing. I thought that would have had him calling me crazy!" She paused. "What are they going to do? Leave it all up to you?"

Angela told Adela about the vampire summit held in Tom's seldom-used dining room earlier that morning.

Adela was silent several seconds. "You think this Etienne knows what he's talking about?"

"Everyone who knows him does. He flew over from France in the small hours to help out."

"I see." Again a long pause. "I wish I had ready advice to give you, dear, but for want of anything better. Follow your instincts, keep within your powers, and pray, as I will."

Good advice all, if she was sure of her power and her instincts led her aright. But pray she could, and somehow she would find out what to do. Meg knew about vampires, recognized Tom the first time she saw him. She must know something that might help. "I will, Adela, I promise. Give Jane, I mean Heather, my love. Is she okay after the trouble yesterday?"

"Fine. We have a lot to catch up on. I'm staying here until the court case is over, and then I'm going to convince her to come back, if not to her old house, to Oak Park with me. Not sure I'll succeed. She is happy here."

"Kit and Dixie are good friends."

"Not just them. Heather seems to have been best buddies with this Marie next door—the one who got attacked yesterday. She came by after they released her from hospital and claims Heather saved her life. And then there's the police officer, the one who answered the call for the robbery. She came by after she went off duty. Talked to Heather for ages, and it seems they're going out for lunch and shopping on her next day off."

Glad as Angela was that Jane, no, Heather, was okay and happy, there was a pressing problem weighing them down: the vampire threat that might, or might not, be Laran Radcliffe.

She said good-bye to Adela, gladly accepted a repeated offer of prayer and power from every witch of her acquaintance, and sent her love to Heather.

Angela clicked off the phone and, with it still in her hands, stared out the window into the early morning street beyond. What had she taken on? A one-woman confrontation with a vampire who could overpower three masters? No wonder Tom was opposed and the others skeptical, but what other chance did they have? What was the alternative? To let him wander untrammeled, destroying others as he had her and Heather? If it was Laran, was her father involved? And why her and Heather? There had to be a reason.

Either way, this vampire, if Etienne was right, was susceptible to magic. So magic would defeat him.

With that conviction strong in her mind and soul, Angela got up and treated herself to a long, hot shower.

Tom and Toby were bent over the computers, muttering. Not much had changed since the interruption for the powwow.

"Morning, love." Tom looked up from the computer. "Want to hear what Toby's discovered?"

"Try not telling me!" Tom laughed, Toby grinned, and she pulled up a spare chair and squeezed between them. "What's going on?"

"Well . . ." Toby hesitated. "Sorry to have to say this about your father, but there are some nefarious goings-on here."

"Questionable business practices?"

Tom gave a dry laugh. "The question is how far it goes."

"What did you find?"

"Do the names Horrock Silversmiths, Adana Textiles, Frederick Freeley Tea and Coffee Importers, Kosy Korner Markets, or Parfums Laurelle mean anything to you?" Toby asked.

She shook her head. "Should they?"

"Maybe," Toby replied. "Depends on how much of the setup you were aware of. They're all part of a privately held company: Connor Inc. based in Oregon."

She felt ghosts, or was it vampires, trailing over her shadowy past. "And?"

"We started with Mariposa, since we had their data and you remembered working there. In September, you updated their computers and installed new accounting software. You also . . ." He grinned ". . . got nosy and poked around in a couple of other computers on the network. I think what you found got you into trouble."

"Well, tell!" Another time she'd happily listen to Toby's luscious accent and careful vowels but now . . .

"Impatient, aren't you?" Tom said, reaching out to squeeze her hand.

The caress of his cool fingers almost distracted her. Almost, but not quite . . . "What's so secret, and presumably dangerous, that it could have gotten us ghouled?"

"Money laundering. On a large scale."

Angela stared. Hell! She felt the draught on her tonsils as she gaped at Toby. Doubting him wasn't a part of it. Tom trusted him, so did she, but . . . "Why? I mean how?"

"It's very clever," Toby said. "Ingenious, really. They hold about thirty small companies all over the globe. Lots of importing and exporting between them and outside companies. The ones we hacked into—Mariposa, Horrock, and Freeley— have some very large transactions in the hidden records. Money gets washed around the globe and comes out sparkling clean. Haven't got into all of them yet, and I'm not sure where it starts and ends, but there's enough . . ."

"To put people in jail?" she asked.

"I doubt the slippery chappies who set this up want it known to the law."

Was her father one of those "slippery chappies"? Her head still throbbed, but she tried to focus on the monitor in front of her. Toby moved the mouse, and columns of figures scrolled down, just as when . . . "I found this! But I didn't know what it all meant." She looked from Tom to Toby and back to the shifting columns. "I told Dad, he said . . ." She broke off. "I don't remember what he said." Cold twisted inside. Had her father really had this done to her? Or were the two things utterly un-connected? This tied things closer to Laran. But was he sent by Dad? Or working off his own bat? And why, if it had been over her discovery of money laundering, had they involved Jane?

Her head was aching again, the moment of clarity replaced by a swirling fog of doubts and emotions.

Toby looked so worried. "You're certain about this, aren't you," she said.

He nodded. "Maybe your father never knew. If he left everything to other people . . ."

Kind of Toby to try. "No. Control freak comes more to mind when I think about him. When I came to see him without making an appointment, he made me wait twenty minutes." She remembered now, sitting in the slate-floored hall and Laran there with Dad. Cold twisted in her guts again.

"Perhaps," Tom said quietly, "this racket and your attack are completely unrelated. Purely coinciden-tal."

"Possible, Tom, but improbable. They have to be linked somehow. It makes better sense. I find out something Dad doesn't want known, he sends Laran after me." The thought made her want to puke.

"You don't even know this chap is the vampire we're after," Toby pointed out.

"Playing devil's advocate, Toby?"

"Not necessarily. Just avoiding jumping to con-clusions."

"There's one way to find out. I'll ask Dad!"

"Now?" Tom said. "We're five, six hours ahead."

"Eight. He's in Oregon. Pacific time. All the better. I'll wake him. He'll be groggy. Might get the truth that way."

Tom glanced at his watch. "You really want to wake him up at two in the morning?"

If Dad was responsible for her and Jane's attack, she wasn't sure she ever wanted him to sleep undisturbed again.

She looked up the number Adela had given her earlier. It was as unfamiliar as unknown numbers on ads in the tube. She punched in the overseas code, area code, and number, hoping against hope she was wrong. That Tom was right. That this was all an incredible coincidence. The number rang the other end. She counted, three, four, five, six. Would it go to a machine? Voice mail?

"Connor residence."

"This is Elizabeth Connor. I need to speak to my father."

"Miss Connor," the voice replied, "do you realize what time it is?"

"Yes. If he's asleep, wake him." There was a time and place for being a bitch, and right now it felt good.

The phone was quiet for several minutes. Angela envisioned fumbling for leather slippers, striped pajamas, and a woolen robe and tried to picture her father's face, but . . . "Lizzie?" It was the same voice as last time, but tired and confused. He sounded old. She felt ancient. "Dad, why did you send Laran after me?"

The stunned gasp and silence confirmed her

suspicions. It felt hideous. "Lizzie, he found you then." Thank the Goddess, no.

"Why, Dad?"

"You have to understand, Lizzie. Didn't he explain?"

"I want to hear it from you, Dad."

"Just do as he asks, Lizzie. Please." Desperation came through as clearly as his voice.

"And if I don't?"

"You have to, Lizzie." It was getting closer to panic. "Is it so much to ask? Just forget what you found. Everything depends on it. Please, Lizzie." He was begging. She'd never heard her father beg. He seldom asked. Ordering or demanding were more his style.

"Don't worry, Dad." About as useless as telling herself not to worry, but . . . "Tell me, where did Laran go after he found me?" Might as well keep up the fiction.

"I don't know! The last time he called, he was still looking for you. You weren't in Yorkshire, and you weren't in that place in Devon. Where did he find you?"

"He didn't, Dad. Good-bye."

She hung up, set the phone on the table beside a stack of disks and papers. Without saying a word, uncertain if she could ever speak again for the tightness in her throat and the burning tears behind her eyes, she walked across the room, pulled open the French windows, and stepped out onto the terrace. She leaned her head against the rough stone of the pergola and bawled.

An ironed silk handkerchief appeared in her hand. Through her misery and hurt, she sensed, no, smelled, the comforting presence of Tom. She leaned into him and cried cold tears of rage and hurt into the warmth of Tom's love.

Her feet were icy and her hands tingling with cold by the time her sobs eased into sniffles. "He did it, Tom. He did it!" she said at last. "It was Laran, and Dad sent him." Sent him to turn her and Heather into ghouls, and sent him again to hurt her friends, and do Goddess-alone-knew-what to her. All to protect his nasty, crooked, money-laundering racket.

"It seems that way," Tom said, "but until you're certain, don't condemn. It's easy to accuse the innocent." As if to underscore his words, he stroked the side of her face with his twisted fingers.

"You think he's innocent?"

"I think he's involved, but we don't know how deep."

"He admitted to sending Laran after me."

"Not directly."

She frowned up at him. He'd obviously listened in; Toby probably had too. "Okay, but Laran is here and looking for me, and went up to Yorkshire. Should have asked Dad if Laran was a vampire!"

"I think we can take that as highly probable. What worries me more is what he's done or doing in Totnes. And where he is now."

"Finding him should be easy enough. I just tell my father where I am, and he'll pass it on."

"You are not using yourself as a lure!" Now that he mentioned it, it seemed like a darn good idea.

"Not after what he did to Justin, you don't have a chance."

"I do if I'm wearing silver. I'm going shopping now. Want to come with me?"

Tom did. Toby remained behind, still scrolling screens while the printer spat out sheet after sheet of figures. She'd planned on going to a chain jeweler she'd noticed on Regent Street, but Tom took her to a beautiful little shop on the corner of Half Moon Street and proceeded to buy them out of silver chains and bracelets.

"You bought for the entire colony."

"If Etienne is right, and after Antonia's experience, it seems highly probable we will need them."

And she'd need the colony. She'd never be able to take on a vampire on her own. That much she'd learned, but with the strength of the moon ceremony behind her, she'd have a better chance. "We need to leave soon if we're to get to Totnes. I want to talk to Meg ahead of time and need time to meditate first."

Tom stopped in his stride. "I'm a bit uneasy about going down there. Didn't your father say Laran went to Totnes?"

"And found I wasn't there. He could be anywhere by now. Adela is going to join with me and call on everyone she knows. Of course I'm going. Magic and silver are what we can use against him, right? You provided the silver, I'll provide the magic. And if Laran is still there . . ."

"You'll need the entire colony to defeat him."

"That would ruin any chance I have of joining with Meg and her coven. Seeing you spooked her. What will having the colony descend on her do?"

"We'll find out."

Chapter 20

He wasn't kidding.

While she'd slept, Gwyltha and Justin called every vampire in the south of England. By the time she and Tom returned from their shopping expedition, vampires had descended on South Audley Street. Some she remembered briefly from Columbus. A couple of them she'd met in London earlier with Tom, but most were unknown to her. And it seemed, primed for action, as a dozen of them gathered in Tom's sitting room.

Angela couldn't help reflecting that most of the company predated Tom's elegant antiques by centuries, or millennia. Sobering thought that, or it would be if she wasn't halfway to terrified already, as she repeated all she knew and tried to decide how to tell a dozen vampires they couldn't come to the party.

"The monster," a tall, heavyset vampire muttered. Jude, Angela thought from the hasty intro-

ductions. He frowned, his face set as if to take on
Laran single-handed. "Lady," he nodded to Gwyltha,
"this animal must be stopped."

"He will be," Gwyltha replied.

Toby asked, "What are we doing, Gwyltha?"

"Protecting ourselves with silver and uniting
with a coven in Totnes to use magic."

Not exactly. "Gwyltha," Angela said, "Meg was
ultradubious and suspicious about Tom. Faced with
a dozen of you, she'll most likely refuse flat out."

"I have grave misgivings about this, Gwyltha,"
another vampire, Simon, said. "We have never had
dealings with witches." He gave Angela a short bow.
"With due respect, to present company. Can we
not do this by ourselves?"

"Not if Etienne is to be believed," Gwyltha replied. "Simon, I have serious reservations about
this venture, but what alternative do we have? Sit
by and give this monster freedom to roam our territory and mind-rape any mortal he chooses? Ethics
and protection of mortals aside, as egoistical and
predatory as he is, it's only time before he murders. What if with DNA and modern science his
existence is discovered? We'd risk a return to the
medieval days of stakings, decapitations, and burn-
ings. No. We cannot sit by. Maybe it's time for the
two rifts of the old religion to unite against a common enemy."

"You're assuming the coven will want to work
with you," Angela pointed out. "What if they don't?
Will you insist? You can't all gate crash the ceremony. It's a religious rite."

Shock rippled though the lot of them, a mere ghoul telling off a gathering of vampires, but what the heck? No point in stopping now. "You want to stop Laran. So do I, and I have first dibs, after what he did to me and my stepsister."

"He also attacked us," Justin said.

"Yes, Justin, but you recovered. I haven't. Yet."

"Warn us when you get to full power, please!"

She smiled at him. He was worried too. Scared for Stella and Sam, she knew, but . . . "I will, if I ever get there. Promise." Gwyltha was plainly irritated. Fair enough, levity was a bit out of place here, but on the other hand, what had happened to the famed Brit sense of humor? "Okay." Angela looked around the room. "Just remember, I want to stop Laran ten times more than any of you."

"What should we do?" Gwyltha asked. "In your opinion."

Angela took a deep breath. She'd jumped in and now she had the floor. "Let me speak to Meg and the coven and ask for their help. There are wards and strengthening spells we can work." A ripple of disquiet came from one corner of the room. Simon wasn't the only one uneasy here. "We'll hold the Full Moon ceremony. Tonight. My stepmother and her group are joining with me. We'll work all the magic we can. Then, with that strength in me, I'll call my father and tell him where I am. He'll tell Laran, and when he comes, I'll pour my power against him."

"You will not!" Tom stood up and looked ready to toss her over his shoulder. "You're not using yourself as bait!"

"What other lure is there? He wants me. He made that clear last night."

"No!"

She was heartily tired of coping with big, strong vampires who didn't know diddly-squat about what was involved. If Etienne had been awake, he might have convinced him, but she was on her own here. "Tom, it's the best chance we have. Etienne says magic can defeat him. Magic I can use."

"No!" Tom was repeating himself. "I've never stood behind a woman, and I'm not starting now!"

"Then stand beside me!" Hell, they were rowing in public! Worse than public, in front of a company of vampires.

"Good advice!" Angela turned so fast she almost tripped. Gwyltha spoke calmly, but a sparkle of interest, maybe even amusement, lit her eyes. A suspicion of a smile twitched one corner of her mouth. "I'm sure you did not mean to raise your voice in front of the conclave."

"Sorry." She was.

"We're no nearer deciding what to do," Jude said.

"I think we are," Gwyltha replied. "Tom, despite your misgivings, Angela is right. She has the trust of this coven. We don't. The rest of us will either stay here or wait in Jude's home in Salisbury. But," she added, "I will accompany Angela and Tom to Totnes. Will that cause difficulties?" she asked, looking at Angela.

"I don't know. We can make the point of your Druid origins. That might help. You share the same tradition after all." Maybe they could overlook a two-thousand-year-plus schism.

Tom's unease came off him in cold waves. He might have tacitly agreed, but agreeable he was not. "There has to be a better way," he insisted.

"If there is, Tom, I doubt we have time to debate it," Justin said. "We can't talk forever, and you have a long drive ahead."

"Faster to fly," Simon said. Great for vampires, but she was stuck on the ground. "My plane's at the city airport. I can get to Exeter in half the time that driving will take."

She could fly after all but . . . "That means three vampires. Simon, you have to stay out of sight."

"I'll do what's necessary."

"What about the rest of us?" A tall vampire asked from his seat in a wingback chair. "We could come along and loiter around the town in case we're needed."

Little did he know. "Meg recognized Tom the minute she saw him. She recognized me, come to that, she just didn't know what I was. If she sees a bunch of vampires lurking around, she'll think I lied and most likely call the whole thing off, or hold the ceremony in secret and exclude me. I need them. We need them. I can't do it on my own." She didn't even remember how to, but no point in announcing that to the colony. "There is one other thing: I need silver chains and bracelets for the coven, in case Laran goes after them." No one objected. They were either in total agreement or dumbfounded.

They dispersed. Simon went to call and arrange for his plane to be ready, Toby to call for a car to be waiting in Exeter.

"Angela," Justin said. "I brought this, thinking it might come in handy." He reached into his pocket and brought out a leather-wrapped package. "We know it has power against vampires."

Utterly mystified, Angela unwrapped three layers of stout leather and found a slim, stone knife. An athame.

"Justin, it's just what I need, for the ceremony." The ancient magic in the stone pricked her hand as she tried to read the runes on the blade. "Where did you get it? It's hundreds of years old."

"Thousands," Gwyltha said. "I remember knives like that from my priestess days."

"You've had it all these years?" Imagine owning a treasure like this and never using it.

"No," Justin shook his head. "It's old, yes, but it came into my possession last summer." His voice dropped. "It was used to try to kill Kit."

"Kit? Kit Marlowe? Dixie's Kit?"

"Yes." Tom's voice was sharp. "It nearly did him in."

There had to be a story here. Later. "You think I should use it? It's a sacred ceremonial knife. It's not for killing."

"If you keep it for defense?" Gwyltha suggested.

Not a bad idea. Angela suspected she needed all the help she could get. Maybe she should arrive with a phalanx of vamps. No! She needed magic, and for that she had to have Meg's trust.

"Better get going," Tom said. "Toby, will you drive us to meet Simon?"

Angela grabbed her coat. She placed the athame in her pocket and made a detour to raid the fridge. She'd need all the sustenance she could get for the next few hours.

"Angela," Toby said, following her to the kitchen. "The stuff we found on the computer. Interpol and your FBI would have a field day with it. What do you want me to do with it, if you don't come back?"

Angela stared at him. No point in asking what he meant. She wasn't that thick, but making a decision like that with her brain whirling wasn't easy. "Okay, if I'm hurt, or Tom, or Meg, or anyone else is hurt, sell it to the papers! Tell Interpol, the FBI, the CIA, the Special Branch, anyone who'll listen. Throw them to the wolves!"

"Right you are." He smiled. "Just for the record, you'll be back. I have a bet on it."

"You're wagering on my succeeding?"

He grinned, "Of course. Had a bet with Jude. Two bets actually. I bet you'd be running the show, he lost that one, and that you'd prevail. I had the advantage, admittedly as he hadn't met you. He wanted to renege after he lost the first one. I wouldn't let him."

Torn between irritation at their betting over something so desperate and encouragement at the implied vote of confidence, she hugged him.

"Get your hands off my ghoul!" Tom growled from the doorway.

Toby laughed. "If you insist." He stood back. "I suppose I'd better find a ghoul of my own."

Angela groaned. "Stop! It wasn't that funny the first time."

But the fooling lightened the mood. Just a tad.

An hour later they were in the air, Simon at the controls, and heading west.

Visibility was perfect; a car waited for them in Exeter. Simon stayed behind with the plane, and Tom drove Angela and Gwyltha over the Exe bridge and through the Devon countryside toward Totnes. Angela's uneasiness grew. Being confident in the safety of Tom's drawing room was one thing. Down here was another matter entirely.

The afternoon light was fading. Soon Etienne would wake. She pictured him and Toby waiting together by the phone. Justin would be back with Stella by now and reassuring Sam that everything was fine, while she was about to use herself as live bait, ghoulish bait to be precise.

Her confidence faded with the miles. One major disadvantage of insisting everyone did things her way was having to lead. What now? At what point should she call Dad and lay the trap? Immediately after the Full Moon rite? Or just before? A lot depended on where Laran was. Given he could move fast, even if he couldn't transmogrify or fly, and that was assuming Etienne had guessed right, how long would it take him to get from where he was to where she'd be after the ceremony? And given she had no idea how strong Laran really was, other than able to overpower Justin and Gwyltha, how strong did she need to be?

Quit! This was approaching panic, and what she needed, above all else, was calm and concentration.

As if sensing her unease, Tom reached out and grabbed her hand and squeezed. "You're not alone, remember that."

Right. She was traveling with vampires.

She stifled a nervous giggle. Instinct had gotten her this far. She'd stick with it.

Laran was sick of Devon weather, furious at Elizabeth, and generally pissed off. He wished damn well he'd not had to abandon his car. He considered stealing another but on reflection decided against it. The town seemed to be crawling with police. After appropriating clean clothes from John Marsh's grossly inadequate wardrobe, Laran found the phone book, spotted with Mavis Marsh's blood but nonetheless quite legible, found this Merchant woman's address, and set off.

He'd avoid the Royal Oak until the activity of police and repairs died down. A street map and an eager-to-be-helpful fool of a woman showed him the way to Merchant's house. A careful reconnoiter found a mean little house in a street of other mean little houses, but quite adequate for a mortal who would soon be dead.

He shouldn't gripe too much. Mariposa was taken care of. The Marshes were silenced. All he had to do now was take care of Miss Elizabeth Connor and they were home and dry.

Which was a lot more than he was right now!

But could be patient. Elizabeth was coming back here. If he didn't get her at the Royal Oak, he'd snag her tonight at the Merchant woman's. With a backup like that, how could he fail? Piet might cut up rough, but he'd overcome that with a couple of feedings. Piet Connor had the most malleable of minds.

They drove most of the way from Exeter through Devon drizzle. By the time Tom pulled into the parking lot in front of the Royal Oak, the afternoon was fading and an air of dejection hung over the town. Even the Royal Oak looked different. Almost sad. Nonsense! How could a building look sad? It had been perfectly fine yesterday, and for the past few hundred years.

But there was a change. Despite obvious cleaning-up efforts, it looked as if someone had taken a sledge-hammer to the area around the check-in desk, and the dining room no longer had oak double doors. It had one, with a hastily repaired plywood panel, and the dark red Turkish carpet from the first flight of stairs was missing.

"What happened?" Angela asked the clerk. Not Sarah but a thin girl she'd noticed in the back office.

"We had an unfortunate incident this morning," she replied. "Hasn't affected anything, I assure you. Will you be in for dinner?"

It was on the tip of her tongue to say no, but Tom said, "We may want room service. Will that be a problem?"

The girl thought for a minute. "Not really, I suppose. We don't usually do it, but if you get your order in early, I expect they can manage."

"Lizzie! At last!"

Angela wasn't sure if she heard it aloud or in her mind, but she knew the voice. She spun around while Tom was still negotiating room service terms. "Laran!"

If she'd had any doubts, they dissipated the instant she saw him blocking the entrance: nasty eyes, almost red, and his smile as venomous as a cobra's. "At last!"

Laran lunged forward and grabbed her but recoiled. "Silver! Again! Damn you!"

Score one for Etienne! If only Laran had waited until after the ceremony tonight. Tom and Gwyltha moved beside her.

"Is this the one?" Tom asked.

"Yes." As she spoke, her hand closed around the stone knife in her pocket. It needed blessing, reconsecrating, but she had no time for such niceties.

Laran grabbed the clerk; her scream was cut off as he clamped his hand over her mouth and bent her head sideways. "Take off the chain, Lizzie, or I rip her throat out." The girl mewled with terror. Laran appeared to enjoy that. "In fact, all of you take off that silver and toss it away."

Fingers tight on the knife, Angela leaped forward, driving the blade into the side of his chest.

Laran screamed an echoing cry of pain and frustration. The poor girl hit the floor with a thud. She'd mercifully fainted. As Laran flailed at Angela, she pulled out the knife and stabbed again. He snarled, and for a few, hideous seconds, she met his eyes. A rush of memories engulfed her—the night in Heather's house, the terrified run after, and their fearful cowering in the park. She pulled the knife back, ready to strike a third time, but Laran disappeared.

She heard Tom cry, "Angela!", as a black mist swallowed her.

Chapter 21

She was too terrified to open her eyes. What if Laran had carried her off? And could the hideous memories bouncing in her brain be true? If every one was, she couldn't do much about it. Not now. Eyes closed, Angela concentrated on her surroundings. She was lying on a bed. She smelled freshly laundered linens but barely felt them. She was still clothed. Dressed and alive. Or at least as alive as a ghoul could be. And aware she was ghoul. It was a start. She caught the scent of lavender—Tom's gift from yesterday. She was in her hotel room!

Angela sat up with a jerk and had the satisfaction of seeing ever-composed Gwyltha astounded. And relieved. "Tom, she's fine!"

Tom appeared at the other side of the bed, and Angela sagged into his arms.

"Praise Abel, you're safe," he said. She barely heard him. She wanted to lose herself in his arms and blot out the world. But she wasn't so uninhibited to follow her inclinations further than to kiss him. For one thing, she'd probably never stop, and for another, Gwyltha might be smiling halfway indulgently, but they were still, presumably, in a the middle of a grade A predicament.

"Of course I'm safe. I'm with you." She stayed snuggled against him, head on his shoulder. "Did I get Laran?"

"You got him, twice," Tom replied, "but unfortunately not permanently."

"Ah! Scotch'd the snake not killed him."

Tom winced. "If you're going to misquote, you might at least pick one of *my* plays."

Now was not the time to admit she'd never read one, and only done *Macbeth* because she'd had her eye on the teaching assistant who taught English Lit 101. Heather had been right, the man was an opinionated snerd, but easy on the eye. That was long before she met Tom of course, and . . .

"Spare me," Tom said. "If you must indulge in reminiscences of your past conquests, could you please veil your thoughts?"

"Forget it, Tom! Don't you see? I remember! I'm Elizabeth Connor. I grew up in Oregon. I went to University of Chicago. Graduated in History and then took grad classes in IT at De Paul so I'd be employable. Dad gave me the temporary job at Mariposa, installing a new system. And when I looked into Laran's eyes . . . Oh, help us! I have to stop him! He's using Dad's mind!"

"You're certain of this?" Gwyltha asked.

"Yes. When he tried to probe my mind, I saw

into his." She shuddered. "That's why I passed out. It wasn't pretty."

Gwyltha chuckled, something Angela seldom heard. "I suspect his aim was to pull you back under his thrall, not reveal himself."

"I'm damn glad he failed, but I could have done without the look into his brain." She gulped. "The creature really is disgusting. He and my father . . ." She refused to think about it. Okay, her father was a grown man, and unmarried, but the thought of him and Laran was too gross to dwell on. "We need to go talk to Meg."

Tom nodded. "I tried to call the shop but got a message saying they were closed for the day. But I have her directions to her house."

"And I have a map of Totnes."

Was she really doing this, taking Tom and Gwyltha with her? What if Meg shut the door on them? Without Meg's help, and the support of her coyen, they were back to square one. Meanwhile, what about the trouble here? "Did anyone else see what happened with Laran?" Explaining that to the management would be a trip.

"Fortunately, no," Tom replied. "Other than the poor little receptionist he knocked out. Gwyltha took that memory from her while I carried you up here. The girl went home thinking she'd fainted. They're getting short staffed here. I discovered, by asking some very nosy questions, that the usual day receptionist was killed this morning, and a young lad who works in the kitchen was badly injured. They were both found, mid-morning, in the front hall. The police are mystified as to what happened."

Angela could make a darn good guess. "Laran arrived early?"

"So it seems," Gwyltha said. "And was waiting for us."

"That's not all," Tom went on. "In a small town where crime supposedly seldom happens, the first police car to answer the call was, for want of a better word, ambushed, and both officers were killed. Hence all the 'panda' cars we saw on the way down."

"Pity they can't catch him and haul him off to jail." Angela could only wish. This got worse by the hour. "Where do you think he is now?"

A knock on the door precluded either of them replying.

In walked the bar man from downstairs, obviously doing double duty as room service waiter. "You ordered dinner, sir," he said, carrying in a vast tray stacked with three plates with covers and a bottle of port and glasses. The most wonderful aroma wafted from under the metal covers. Tom's idea of room service was verging on brilliant.

"For you, my love," Tom said. "Three large rump steaks, very, very rare; I stipulated they had to be cold and bloody in the middle."

They were, and delicious and luscious, and gone in next to no time. The French fries, tomatoes, and peas she left. Veggies didn't have the appeal of fresh meat. As the nourishment flowed through her body, she felt ready for anything, even, Goddess help her, a further encounter with Laran.

"You look better," Gwyltha said. "Incredible, the difference solid food makes. Knowing you and Jane has certainly broadened my experience."

Getting to know vampires had changed her life too! But this wasn't the time to ponder the good and the bad outcomes of that. She had her work cut out for her, and she still didn't know how she was going to eliminate Laran and rescue herself, her father, and Heather from his clutches.

Start small. "I'm off to the shower," she announced. "I need to scrub Laran's touch off me." She could still feel the cold of his body on her fingers when she'd stabbed him and . . . "What about Justin's knife?" Had she dropped it when she passed out?

"It's here." Gwyltha indicated the bedside table. "I grabbed it."

Angel saw the knife lying on the bedside table and remembered hideous screams, and the poor girl's terror. "Didn't the noise get any attention?" Even being short staffed.

"It was really all too fast," Gwyltha replied. "The receptionist collapsed, and Laran disappeared. Eventually a young man did emerge from the kitchen, but I took care of him too. No one will remember anything, except the poor girl fainting from delayed shock after the morning's horrible events."

Angela wished she could forget as easily. Unlikely, but she could, at least, wash her hair.

After the unlikely-to-ever-be-forgotten interlude in there with Tom, just showering was a bit of an anticlimax. She chuckled at the choice of words. Given the threat hanging over them, she'd best set her mind to serious concerns, but it was impossible to forget Tom's lovemaking, the way he'd held her high and sucked her nipples, and then . . . Right! She grabbed the soap and scrubbed. She hadn't been kidding about wanting to leach Laran's presence from her skin.

Warm water and scented soap did the trick. By the time she'd dried her hair and put on clean underwear, she felt a new woman. New woman, yes. New ghoul, certainly. New witch, maybe. Was she really up to magic? Would it help?

One way to find out. She tugged on black slacks and a gray sweater, wishing she had ceremonial robes. Maybe she could borrow from Meg. She definitely needed to talk to Adela.

To be alone, she walked into the sitting room of the suite and dialed Heather's number. Adela answered.

"Lizzie. Something's happened to Heather!"

"Oh no! What?" Not another robbery.

"It's good, darling, really it is. Marvelous. Just a little while ago. A couple of hours if that, she was leafing through the photo albums. We've looked at them heaps of times. She always took my word for the people in the pictures, but she never really recognized any, except you. But as she was looking pictures of the trip to DC we took for your thirteenth birthday, she started talking about how the airlines had lost your luggage and we had to go to Garfinkles and buy you new clothes, and you charged far more than you needed and then shared them with her. And one was a cropped black T-shirt I wouldn't let either of you wear as it was too revealing."

She remembered it too. "And the taxi driver was obviously drunk, and you insisted we get out, and it was in the middle of nowhere, and freaky, until a police car came by and gave us a ride to a metro station." She hadn't remembered that either, until just now.

"Oh, Lizzie! Heather remembers so much. Not everything by any means, but certainly she's getting better."

Heather's memories returned after the confrontation with Laran. Was it too much to hope he was dead? Did she want the responsibility of killing a living creature? Okay, an undead creature. Could she not take it on? "Tell Heather how thrilled I am, and please, Adela, be with me tonight."

"Didn't I promise? I've been on the phone ever since you rang. I have a phone tree all set up. Tell me what time and we'll join with you."

"Moonrise is nine-thirty here. Can't be the same time with you."

"We'll go by your time, dear. We'll meld our prayers and power."

"Thank you, Adela, from the bottom of my heart."

"May we succeed."

Did Adela have any notion how crucial it was? Yes! Adela understood. Angela—she still could not think of herself as Elizabeth—sat in the silence for several minutes. Tom and Gwyltha stayed in the bedroom, giving her the solitude she needed. Outside, it was already dark. Etienne would be roused by now. She pictured him and Toby seated in the sitting room and wished she were safe on South Audley Street instead of venturing out into the dark.

Tom was ready to snarl. Angela had the flea-brained notion of going alone to the old witch's house. "Gwyltha and I came down for the specific purpose of going with you," Tom insisted, trying to keep the exasperation from his voice.

"I know that, but I think two of you is pushing our luck."

"If difficulties arise," Gwyltha said, "I'll leave, Angela, but I share Tom's misgivings. We are walking into danger."

Or driving into it. Meg's directions were straightforward enough. What awaited them wasn't. Under Angela's calm demeanor, Tom caught her self-doubt and anxiety. She had that much sense. A street thug with a knife he could handle. A machine gun he could face without much more than a ruined shirt. But a coven of witches! Tom glanced at Gwyltha in the rearview mirror. She looked as serene as if strolling in a spring meadow, or across her beloved moors, not into a cabal of witchcraft, but she had to be worried. This was ludicrous! And their only hope it seemed.

Meg's house turned out to be a small, semi-detached bungalow. Aside from the orange door, it was a clone of a dozen others on both sides of the street. Inside, he heard three mortal heartbeats.

Even numbers if it came to trouble. Tom rapped
the lion's head knocker, a miniature version of the
one that had decorated his own front door for a
couple of centuries. The old witch had good taste
in door knockers.

"You!" It was acknowledgment, not welcome.

"Meg." Angela came forward. "You invited me
to share the Full Moon ceremony with you."

Meg nodded, peering through the four-inch
gap the chain lock allowed. "I invited you, and perhaps your friend here, but who's that?" Her eyes
flickered left toward Gwyltha.

Had anyone, ever, addressed the colony leader
as "that"?

"Let me in, Meg, and I'll explain. We really,
really need your help."

Meg let Angela in but left the others standing
on the front step. Not at all what he cared for. It
was only Gwyltha's "Patience, Tom" that kept him
from barging in.

"They could be doing anything to her," he muttered.

"They're not. They are talking, as you'd hear if
you stopped mumbling to yourself and listened."

Talking! Angela was telling her life story. Didn't
she realize these were mortals? Fifteen more minutes and he'd be rescuing her from an unmarked
gray van headed for the nearest insane asylum.
Three minutes later, she opened the door.

"Come in," she said, smiling, as Meg, another
woman, and a white-haired man looked on, un-
smiling. "They'll let you stay, if you both promise
not to interfere and not to spread negative energy."

"You have my word," Gwyltha said to the peering group.

"And mine," he added, wondering what in Hades he was agreeing to.

Meg led them into a small, overfurnished and cluttered room. No, on a second look, one end was cluttered. The room reached from front to back of the house, and all the furniture was pushed to the front end. Standing clustered in the crowded end of the room, Angela introduced the man as John and the other woman, a thin-faced spinster sort with red-rimmed eyes and straggly dark hair, as Pat.

"How do you do"s and cautious handshakes exchanged all around, the witches and vampires eyed each other cautiously. Only Angela appeared unperturbed, but her anxiety was clear as birdsong to Tom.

"Pat's best friend was Sarah, the receptionist killed this morning," Angela said.

"I nearly didn't come tonight," Pat said. "I was so shocked at her death but needed the company of my friends. Now I see it was providential. It was a vampire who killed Sarah."

"A monster, a perverted vampire," Gwyltha said. "We do not consider him as one of us. We have our tenets, as do you: ours is to never harm mortals, yours is to do no harm. We stand for the same but on different bridges of life."

"You think you can get him?" Pat asked. "The police have no idea."

"I don't know if I can," Angela replied, "but I do know he'll come back after me and that I have it on the best authority he is susceptible to magic. This is our best hope. This and wearing silver."

Yes, silver. All three witches now sported the silver chains he'd bought that morning in Half Moon Street. Angela had been busy in her ten minutes. And successful. Three silver chains was a small price for Wiccan neutrality.

"They can't join in the ceremony." John said. "They're unbelievers."

"They are my friends and protected me when I was helpless," Angela said. "They stay."

"He's also your lover," Meg said, a suspicion of a smile on her old lips.

"Yes," Angela grinned and looked his way. "Tom is. And he's asked me to marry him, but right now that's beside the point."

So, Tom decided, was the searching look Gwyltha gave him.

"He's the one restored your aura?" Meg asked. He'd forgotten all her blathering about auras and lights.

"I don't know?" Angela said. "Has it changed?"

Meg nodded. "Oh yes. It's strong and bright, with the same pink flashes when you look his way or he comes near you. Yes, I'd say something's changed."

Something had better get going or he was giving up. All this talk about auras, and pink lights, and Abel alone knew what! The things he did for Angela.

"Your aura is golden," Pat said. "There's some gaps, and it's strong, as Meg said, but those two," she nodded toward Tom and Gwyltha, "have none."

"That's because they're not alive," John said. "Angela explained all that!"

"Oh!" Pat put her hand to her mouth. "She did. It just didn't sink in."

Given the woman had just lost her best friend, John was being a bit sharp with her. "Once we had them, I'm sure," Tom said, smiling at Pat. "But walking dead lack living aura."

"Of course." The poor woman swallowed. "Angela did explain, but actually seeing you, in the flesh so to speak, well . . ."

"After all you've suffered today, I'm not surprised you're a bit confused. I thank you from the bottom of my heart for your courage and willingness to help us."

Pat smiled at Tom. "If this will stop the monster who killed Sarah, I'm glad to be here, and all my powers are at your disposal." She straightened her spine and pulled her shoulders back. "We should prepare. It's less than an hour until moonrise."

"First," Angela said, "we have to reconsecrate this." She put the athame, now wrapped in the silk scarf from her pack of cards, on the table.

Meg carefully unwrapped it. All three witches stared.

"It looks like a knife you see in old books," Meg said.

John reached and picked it up. "Where did you get it? It's truly old, isn't it?"

"Dates from about the coming of the Romans, I believe," Gwyltha said. "Maybe a little older."

"You know these things?" Meg asked.

Gwyltha nodded.

"It's been used for harm," Angela said, "and this afternoon, I took it against Laran. It needs consecrating for its proper use."

"Its proper use may be to repel evil," Meg said.

"Its proper use is to draw the sacred circle," Pat said.

"After it's reconsecrated," Angela insisted, and placed the knife on the small table in the middle of the cleared end of the room.

No one argued. John sprinkled it with water, and Meg lit a pair of candles while she and Pat muttered in unison.

Gwyltha took a seat on the end of the sofa, picking the only clear spot. Tom perched on the arm of an easy chair stacked with cushions and a magazine rack and watched Angela, and the other three, don long, pale blue robes that looked remarkably like bedsheets. Tom stopped himself. This was important to Angela—Angela who'd just announced to everyone he wanted to marry her. She hadn't actually said she'd accepted, but he took the announcement as such and now should try to regard this ritual in the same way she did. It was darn difficult, but he managed not to stare when John strapped a pair of stag's horns on his head.

"Cernunnos," Gwyltha said, "the God of the Underworld, the Master of the Animals, and the Lord of Fertility."

"Madam, you recognize these things?" John asked.

"I do," Gwyltha replied. "Maybe Angela didn't mention how old I was, but I remember these from my girlhood, long before they went underground."

That left everyone speechless for a several seconds. Pat looked ready to ask questions. Meg looked at Gwyltha in pure amazement. "When were you a girl?"

"The first century BC."

Silence as three mortals grasped this.

"So, you remember the ceremonies we only know by tradition," Meg said.

"I was a Druid priestess, yes," Gwyltha replied.

"Then you should lead the ritual," Meg said.

Gwyltha shook her head. "No, our ways have been too long parted."

"At least join with us," John asked.

Tom had wanted to be involved, but not quite this much. But when Gwyltha accepted the invitation, he stood by her and watched while Angela, at John's invitation, took the newly reconsecrated athame and traced a large circle on the floor. Meg produced a large wine glass, filled with what looked like sherry, and a shallow dish that she placed between the candles on the altar. Pat placed four lighted candles on the floor around the circle Angela traced.

At a signal from John, Gwyltha stepped forward. Tom followed to stand with Meg, Angela, and John inside the circle.

When Pat drew back the curtains, he saw why they'd picked this end of the room. The full moon was clearly visible through the French windows.

Meg dropped a lighted match in the shallow bowl. Pale smoke and the sweet scent of incense filled the room, as chanting began. Their voices were light and soft and invoked thoughts of green woods, and running water, and wind in the trees.

Angela was part of it, her face calm and her eyes bright. After a while they paused to pass the chalice. It was sherry, but a good one, and the scenario reminded Tom of boyhood tales of clandestine papist masses. But the chanting that resumed was unlike any heard in any church. Soon he was caught in the cadence of the song, the warmth and the sweetness in the air, and the presence of Angela by his side. As the chants continued, the hair on his neck prickled—something he hadn't felt in centuries—the sensation spread down his arms, back, and legs as if his skin were springing to life. Without thinking, he reached out to clasp Angela's hand. The sensations multiplied and then eased. He glanced sideways; her eyes beamed with life.

Pat took his other hand. They were joined in a human circle, power flowing between them. Angela seemed lost in the music, her face gleaming in the moonlight. There was rush, like a sharp breeze; more and more energy poured into the circle. Angela stood tall—not just her face now, but a radiance glowed from her entire body.

It was magic, but to what end? As he watched, the light faded, and she slowly turned to smile at him, her eyes still sparked with energy.

What happened now?

The French windows fell inward with a crash, scattering glass and wood fragments. Meg shouted, poor Pat screamed, and John yelled. Tom grabbed Angela as Laran Radcliffe filled the doorway.

"Playing games with your puny mortal friends?" he asked.

"No," Angela replied, stepping forward. Try as

he would, Tom couldn't hold her, the power in her blazed in his hands, tingling up his arms. "No games, Laran. You injured me and Heather." Angela took another step forward. "You killed Sarah at the Royal Oak, injured the lad who worked in the bar, killed two cops, and hurt the clerk at the front desk. To say nothing of using my father. You've done enough."

"And you'll stop me?" His laugh came like breaking glass on a frosty morning.

"With the Goddess's help, yes."

In a second of crystalline understanding, Tom recognized truth. Angela was the vessel of all that power. She alone could stop this monster. Staying put and letting her was the hardest thing he'd ever do.

"Come in, Laran," Angela said, "and meet your fate."

With a triumphant leer, he stepped forward, grabbed for Pat who was nearest, and recoiled. "Protected your little friends with silver, did you? They can't wear it forever, you know."

"They don't need to, only until you are rendered harmless." As she spoke, Angela reached for the altar. Tom expected her to take the athame, but instead she barely touched it. He moved with her. "Let me, Tom," she said. "I have enough power. Adela sent hers." Maybe she had. Angela still glowed. It was more than a trick of the moonlight. She took another step toward Laran, and Tom made himself let her go. This was her moment. "Leave and make amends while you still can, Laran, or the harm you've done will recoil tenfold."

As Laran laughed again, she stepped out of the circle. The light of the moon incandesced around her. She stood there, shining with primal power. As she reached toward Laran, the light around her flickered and leaped like tongues of silver fire. Laran stared, mesmerized. With a twist of her wrists, the light surged and engulfed Laran. His scream was cut short as he staggered backward through the doorway and collapsed, a glowing heap on the winter lawn. Pat's scream was long and piercing. John passed out. Tom hoped to heaven it wasn't a heart attack. Meg stood and watched as the cold flames of magic consumed the destroyer.

Gwyltha closed the French windows. The wood was splintered around the frame, but at least they managed to shut out the night, and Laran's pyre. Angela just stood, but as Tom touched her she wobbled into his arms. "What happened to him?" she asked, grasping his sleeves for support.

"I was hoping you'd tell me."

"Must have been magic." She was almost too weak to smile. She needed feeding. Fast.

And if that wasn't enough, they had a dying or dead vampire on Meg's lawn, an unconscious man in her house, and a hysterical woman. Poor Pat had had a rotten day. But Gwyltha had her arms around her, soothing, maybe taking care of a few stray memories.

Meg went out and came back with a glass of water, which she tossed in John's face. He opened his eyes and swore. Not a heart attack after all. Good.

"She's all right?" Meg asked, nodding at Angela.

"She needs meat."

Meg frowned a minute. "All I've got, my love, is a packet of beefburgers in the freezer."

Angela didn't complain. She devoured them, frozen made no difference. Meg stared, and Tom let her. A ghoul chomping on frozen beefburgers was the least of the events of the evening.

"Does make a difference," Meg said, staring in amazement, as Angela restored. "Incredible. I've got some nice back bacon if it would help."

It did, along with a can of corned-beef Meg unearthed from the back of a cabinet.

"I'm fine, now," Angela insisted, as Meg stared offering tinned sausages. "I'll last. Thank you for letting this happen. I'd never have done it alone. I need to call Adela and let her know we were successful." She paused. "But what about your house?"

"It can be repaired," she said with a chuckle. "What's a few broken windows after what I just witnessed? I'd heard talk of harnessing moon power, but thought it just an old tale. Doubt many living witches have ever witnessed that."

"We can't leave you with broken windows," Angela insisted. "Or a charred corpse in your backyard."

"Wait here a minute," Tom said to Angela. "Let me check on things outside."

Outside was a heap of half-incinerated fabric and brittle bones.

"Good grief!" Angela said, coming up beside him. "I did that?"

"Seems so. And in the circumstances, we should be glad. He can do no more harm."

"We can't leave him here."

They couldn't. But Meg had a roll of black bin liners, and one held the last immortal remains of Laran Radcliffe.

Pat and Angela straightened the room while Gwyltha helped Meg clear away the altar. There was no talk of mistrust now.

"You'll want this back, won't you?" Meg said, wrapping the athame in a length of silk.

"Yes," Gwyltha replied, "It was lent to us and must return to its guardian."

"Fair enough." Meg's fingers lingered over the stone handle. "Just seeing one is more than I ever dreamed of, and to hold it . . ." She handed it to Gwyltha. "That was Moon Magic, wasn't it?" Meg asked as she snuffed out the candles and put them away.

Gwyltha hesitated. "Angela harnessed all the power she could. Her stepmother, and others beside us, were praying together."

Meg gave a sly smile. "Keep your secrets then, vampire. But I know only the ancients could direct that sort of power."

Gwyltha picked up the linen cloth and started folding. "Where shall I put this?" she asked. "I thank you for you help, but we must be leaving soon."

Tom and the now-recovered John found a sheet of plywood in Meg's toolshed. John helped cut it to fit the missing panes, impressed by the speed Tom wielded a saw, until he watched him press in nails with his thumb, and then looked in danger of passing out again.

It was well into the small hours by the time they

sat down in Meg's kitchen, drinking tea. Tom wanted to just take Angela away. She needed real meat, and Meg was at the point of offering meat paste or tinned luncheon meat, but refusal would have been churlish after they'd half-ruined the woman's house and left a charred patch on her lawn. Spring and Devon rain would take care of the lawn, but what about the three witches?

Don't worry, Gwyltha thought to him. *When will they ever see us again?*

Never, he hoped, but he knew Angela would miss old Meg.

"I don't rightly know what I saw," Pat said, stirring three spoons of sugar into her tea. "That creature was destroyed, but . . ." She shook her head.

"Does it matter?" Gwyltha replied, with a sideways glance at Meg. "It was what we needed. That monster can harm and destroy no more." She turned to Pat. "My sympathies for your friend, and remember, that animal was not what we vampires stand for."

Pat nodded. "I know that now, and I'll miss Sarah, more than I can say. But she'd be glad to know that creature was stopped."

Tom tossed the rubbish bag that held all that remained of Laran into the boot. There were hugs, farewells, and thanks all around, a parting everyone knew was permanent. Seemed unfair to disrupt these lives and then leave, but mortal lives took different paths from immortals.

Angela stretched out on the back seat and was

asleep before they'd gone five miles. At the airport, she woke long enough to eat two cut-up chickens Simon found in a late night shop, and slept all the way back to London.

While Tom and Gwyltha caught Toby and Etienne up with the events of the night, Angela called Adela to thank her for her help.

"Lizzie," Adela said, as she heard her voice, "I was about to call you. I just spoke to that young man who works for your father. Seems your father had a severe stroke a couple of hours ago."

Chapter 22

Twenty-two hours later, jet lagged and worried, Elizabeth walked into her father's hospital room. Alan, the panty counter, hovered in the ICU waiting room.

"Miss Connor," he said, grasping her hands with his clammy ones. "So glad you arrived. This has been the most terrible thing, and with Mr. Radcliffe away as well . . ."

Permanently away, she amended to herself. The last immortal remains of Laran Radcliffe now lay at the bottom of the Thames, the Serpentine, and the Regents Canal. Toby and Etienne had taken care of that. "I'm more concerned about Dad than Laran!" Snippy, yes, but under the circumstances . . .

Her father lay, unmoving, on the white sheets. He looked at her with vacant eyes, his hand limp in hers. He was cold despite the overheated ICU unit. How much had he really known about her horror? And how much had her father been Laran's tool? Would she ever know? Did it matter?

A long talk with the doctors explained nothing. Her father hadn't had a stroke or a cerebral hemorrhage, or an aneurysm. His mind had stopped functioning, but he wasn't brain-dead. He responded quite clearly to stimuli but seemed unable to think or reason. They were utterly mystified. Elizabeth wasn't. Laran had overpowered and controlled his mind, and now that Laran was destroyed, there was nothing left but the shell that had once been her father.

Two weeks later, at her insistence, she checked him out of hospital and took him home to Devil's Elbow. She'd have done it a week or more earlier, but proving her identity with Angela Ryan's papers had been a stumbling block. After calls across the Atlantic, computer activities she wasn't sure she wanted to understand, and the expenditure of vast sums of money, Elizabeth Connor had a set of IDs. Fake ones maybe, but for a real person this time.

"Thanks, Tom," she said as she looked at her future spread out on the kitchen table.

"Don't mention it. They're yours. I just greased the wheels. Getting duplicates of real ones was much easier than manufacturing them."

"You made it possible for me to get on with my life. Hell, you gave me my life back!"

"I think you did that yourself."

"With a lot of help."

He nodded. "You're staying on here then?" He sounded desolate.

"I have to, for a while. I'll need help with sorting out the business. Getting powers of attorney will take some doing. A lot was under Laran's control, and guess what? He appears to have vanished in the UK. The police are looking but so far no luck . . ." she grinned. "Makes this very complicated and will take ages to sort out."

He was quiet several seconds. "I'll miss you."

"Don't leave! Tom, you can't! Please stay!"

"You mean that."

Darn the man! "Of course I mean it! How could I do without you?"

"Angela needed me. I wasn't sure Elizabeth did."

She almost thumped him for that. "I need you! I love you! Angela was just a mask until I found myself. I haven't changed. How could you even . . ."

He never let her finish, just pulled her into his arms and mashed her body against his. Vampire hugs left little space to wiggle, but she wasn't complaining. "Want me, do you, after all this?"

He didn't deign to answer that, at least not with words. His lips spoke for his heart, opening hers and sending sweet need coursing through every fiber of her body. She responded with a heat and need that all but overwhelmed her. He was hers. Her Tom. Her own. Her love. The immediate future was complicated in the extreme, but what was a few years of legal tangles when they had eternity ahead of them?

As his hand eased up to her breasts, wild longing rushed her mind. "Let's go upstairs," she whispered into his mouth.

"Brilliant suggestion," he replied, pressing his mouth closer to hers,

"Ahem, excuse me, Miss Connor," Alan said.

Elizabeth turned, but she couldn't pull away. Tom had her all but plastered to him and wasn't about to ease his hold.

Tom got his words together first. "It had better be important, lad. What is it?"

Alan coughed, his face an highly embarrassed pink. "The night shift nurse has arrived, and I'm about to leave. I'll see you in the morning, Miss Connor. Just wanted to remind you we have an appointment with the lawyer in Eugene." He took an awkward step back. "Good night. Miss Connor, sir."

"Irritating twerp," Tom muttered as the door closed behind Alan.

"Agreed, but he does know where Dad kept all his papers and is helping sort things out."

"But he's gone. Thank Abel. And now." He cupped the back of her head with his hand. "Where were we when he so rudely interrupted?"

Three months later.

"Heather says she's staying in Ohio," Elizabeth said as she and Adela walked along the beach.

"Yes. She insists she likes the job at the Vampire Emporium and plans to keep working there, at least over the summer. Dixie and Kit have found a small studio in German Village, and Heather plans on setting up her pottery. She was in Chicago a month or so back to pack up her kilns and equipment and have it shipped. She's selling the house and using that as a down payment on the studio. She'll pot and work in the shop while she looks for another teaching job. I'll miss her, but she's happy there and has made a good friend in that young police officer."

"I hope she makes a wild success with her pottery. There's a shop in Florence that sells it now, and she's joining a traveling craft show that is part of Dad's odd accumulation of sidelines. She mustn't let her talents go to waste."

"Talking of talents, you can't let your powers go fallow again."

"I won't. I've found two other practitioners, and we're establishing a small coven of our own here."

"You're staying?"

"Part time. A friend of Tom's, Toby Wise, is coming over to help with the business side. He's an American and has agreed to sort things out. Tom and I will split our time between London and Oregon. I've an army of attendants to take care of Dad. I'm not moving him from here. It is his home after all, and he loves the ocean. We've converted his old office suite to living quarters, to save the stairs with his wheelchair."

"Will he ever recover?"

"Who knows? He recognizes me, and Tom. It's as if he knows places and people but can't think much. He seldom talks, but when he does, he mentions people and events from way back. He mentioned you the other day."

"What did he say?"

"Just that you were right."

"I wonder which of our many arguments that referred to."

"Doesn't matter really, does it? He's safe, if not exactly well." Elizabeth paused. "Tom and I are leaving in couple of days."

"Don't you go and get married without us!"

"I wouldn't dare. It's a shame Dad can't be there, but we have to get married in England. As Tom pointed out, blood tests here would cause no end of consternation."

Adela laughed.

"I can see that. I'm still astounded at all this. Incredible really."

"But you set it in motion. Without your persistence with Vlad, Heather and I would still be living in our created identities."

"But you destroyed Laran and freed yourself and Heather."

"With a lot of help. Without you and Meg, I'd never have succeeded."

They were quiet after that. Even talking about that evening still gave her cold prickles and a tight chest. But as they walked back toward the house across the damp sand, Elizabeth looked up toward the house. Tom was waiting on the porch overlooking the ocean. He waved as they made their way up the cliff path, and her heart leaped.

Yes, her future was now, and forever, with Tom Kyd.

Try these other great titles in Rosemary's vampire series!

KISS ME FOREVER

He's Hot. He's Sexy. He's Romantic. He's Immortal . . .

If there is one thing Dixie LePage does not need in her life, it's complications. And the man sitting across the table from her in a crowded English pub, the one offering to buy the library of her inherited estate in a small English village, is a major complication. For starters, there's the broad shoulders. The slightly amused smirk. That smoldering look that makes it impossible to concentrate. And that infuriating, old-fashioned, and well, okay, incredibly appealing sense of chivalry. No doubt about it, the guy is hot and sexy. Of copurse, there is one wee little problem: He claims to be a vampire named Christopher Marlowe, as in THE Christopher Marlowe, famous playwright, contemporary of Will Shakespeare. Right. Amend that to hot, sexy, and totally insane. Please see "no more complications." So why can't Dixie seem to resist the warmth of Christopher's charm, the protective feel of his strong hands, or the tempting pull of his full mouth when the sun goes down . . . ?

KEEP ME FOREVER

Some Guys Are Real Animals . . .

Antonia Stonewright isn't about to change her views on love. A sexy mortal companion is fine every now and then, but a soul mate? A partner for life? Please. She was burned once, and hundreds of years haven't healed the wounds. But reclusive potter Michael Langton is . . . different. His gorgeous wares are perfect for her new art gallery—and his gorgeous body is perfect for her. She can't get enough of his toned muscles or his amazing, dark eyes. Their nights together make them both purr with pleasure—except in Michael's case, purring comes naturally. So much for finding a regular boyfriend. Antonia has a truly sexy beast on her hands . . .

MIDNIGHT LOVER

There Are Beings Worse Than Vampires . . .

Vampire Toby Wise knows there is a spy in his organization. He thinks Laura Fox, the beautiful nurse who looks after the invalid founder of Connor Corp., is one. But Laura is no mere spy—she's a reporter out for a hot story. So when Toby receives a call for aid from a witch, Toby reluctantly involves Laura. There are sinister goings-on in Dark Falls, Oregon. A bloodthirsty beast of the night has been plaguing the town. As Toby struggles with his feelings for the irresistible Laura, she struggles to except the alluring yet perilous world of the vampires. And as their attraction grows, so does the danger. For the prey they are hunting will prove to be a more deadly predator than either can imagine . . .